Lights, Cameras, Witches

A WICKED WITCHES OF THE MIDWEST MYSTERY
BOOK 21

AMANDA M. LEE

WINCHESTERSHAW PUBLICATIONS

Prologue

TWENTY YEARS AGO

"What did I say?"

Aunt Tillie, her face streaked with green, black, and brown camouflage paint, fixed us with a dark look. We were crouched behind a bush in the alley behind Mrs. Little's new business venture. Aunt Tillie had promised mayhem and hot chocolate, luring us out of the house despite the cold descending upon Walkerville in the run-up to Thanksgiving.

I, Bay Winchester, could not be bought. I also didn't want to be left behind and called a kvetch, so apparently, I could be bullied, as long as it was my great-aunt doing the bullying.

"You said that we should be quiet and wait for your signal," my cousin Clove replied. Her smile was serene as she fixed it on Aunt Tillie. "You said you would spit in our hot chocolate if we ruined things for you, but I don't believe you would do that. You're too wonderful."

"Thank you, little suck up," Aunt Tillie replied, rolling her eyes.

"You wanted to bring her," my cousin Thistle reminded her. "I told you it was a bad idea. If you want a good soldier, you don't bring Clove."

"That's the meanest thing you've ever said to me." Clove's lower lip jutted out and trembled. "You're making my eyes leak."

1

"Knock that off." Aunt Tillie jabbed a warning finger in Clove's direction. "What did I say about that eye-leaking thing?"

Clove turned off the waterworks in an instant. "That I'm only supposed to use my superpower for evil and never on you."

"That's right." Aunt Tillie's eyes flashed with annoyance. "So shut it."

"You're going to make my eyes leak for real if you're not careful," Clove warned. She was only ten but wily beyond her years thanks to Aunt Tillie's years of serving as our babysitter.

"You're fine," Aunt Tillie insisted. When her gaze landed on me, I did my best not to cringe. I could tell things were about to take a turn. "Now, are you ready to hear the plan?"

I was in no mood for a plan, whatever it was. It was already dark, and my mind was drifting to the book I'd just checked out of the library and the warm bed I could be reading it in. Aunt Tillie wouldn't let us leave until we'd completed our mission, however, so there was no sense fighting it. "Sure." I folded my arms over my chest. "What's the plan?"

"Margaret just opened that store." She pointed to the rear door of the Main Street building.

"I know. You've been complaining about it for three weeks."

"That's because it's a stupid store. Anybody with a brain would complain about it."

"I think it's kind of nice," Clove said. "It has fake flowers and stuff. And baskets. Oh, and I saw a pretty doll through the window earlier today. Who doesn't like that stuff?"

Thistle's hand shot in the air.

"You don't count," Clove fired back. "You're a little monster, and you don't like anything. Your opinion doesn't matter." She turned to me. "Tell her she's a monster, Bay."

I had no intention of doing that. "What do you want us to do?" I demanded of Aunt Tillie. "Mrs. Little will know you put us up to it if we go in there and cause a scene."

"Did I say I wanted you to cause a scene?" Aunt Tillie looked more annoyed than usual.

"No, but you don't often tell us to make a scene. You just think we'll automatically do it because that's who we are. I'm not an idiot."

"No, you're far from an idiot." Aunt Tillie patted my head as if I were a two-year-old. "That's one of my least favorite things about you. I was praying you would be stupid—I had hope when you were three and you ate bugs off the ground—but it didn't turn out that way."

"You ate bugs?" Thistle said with a derogatory laugh. "That's so stupid."

"What are you laughing at?" Aunt Tillie challenged as I glared. "You used to eat paste. You'd put it above your lip like it was a mustache and then lick it for an hour. You weren't any smarter at that age."

Thistle's eyes narrowed. "You take that back."

"I don't think so." Aunt Tillie flicked her eyes to Clove. "And since you whine whenever you're left out, I don't remember you eating weird things, but you used to wear your mother's bra like it was a hat and claim you were a nun."

Clove's glare could've set ice on fire. "I don't want to play this game any longer."

"Well, you don't have a choice." Aunt Tillie was matter-of-fact. "We've only got one shot at this. I need you three to get it together."

"We've only got one shot at what?" I demanded.

"Do you see that store?" Aunt Tillie pointed again.

"Good grief. It's not going to start doing tricks," Thistle complained. "We know you hate the store."

"She hates Mrs. Little more than the store," I offered.

"Shut up." Aunt Tillie hissed "I have a plan."

"For the store?" I was intrigued. "What's the plan?"

"Ooh, are we going to rob it?" Clove rubbed her hands together. "I really like that doll."

The look Aunt Tillie shot her was withering. "We're not thieves, little whiner."

"Then what are we doing?" I whined.

"We're giving Margaret a reality check."

That made no sense. "How?"

"Well, it just so happens that she knows somebody who knows somebody at Channel 7. That somebody has agreed to do a story on her new store for the news."

"She's going to be on television?" I was impressed.

3

"Yes, unless we stop her."

"Why do we want to stop her?" Clove asked. "Wouldn't being on television be good for her?"

"I think you just answered your own question," Thistle replied blithely. "Aunt Tillie wants to ruin the story."

"Not ruin it," Aunt Tillie corrected. "I simply want to change the narrative."

She was being awfully fancy with her words. That never worked out well for us. "Just tell us what you want."

"I was thinking that you could interrupt the interview and let it slip that Margaret is a dipsomaniac."

"What's a dipsomaniac?" Clove asked me.

"How should I know?" Now I was irritated.

"I thought you knew everything." Clove started pouting again. "What's a dipsomaniac?" she asked Aunt Tillie.

"An alcoholic," Thistle replied.

Aunt Tillie's eyebrows practically flew off her forehead. "How do you know that?"

"I know things." Thistle made a face. "I'm smart."

"Or you heard someone else talking about it," Aunt Tillie countered. "Where did you hear that word?"

"Maybe Mrs. Little told her friends that you're a dipsomaniac," Thistle replied. "Maybe she was in the bakery the other day when we were getting doughnuts with Mom, and she said that you're a dipsomaniac because you make your own wine."

"I knew it." Aunt Tillie clutched her hand close to her chest. "I heard that rumor was spreading. People claimed they didn't know where it was coming from, but I knew. I'll make that old bat pay."

"Isn't that why we're here?" I asked.

Aunt Tillie flashed a feral smile. "Do you know what you need to do?"

"Not even close." I was so over this excursion. "Can't we just go home? Or, even better, call Mom to get us, and you can stay here? She'll take us for hot chocolate."

"Yes. Let's do that." Clove bobbed her head.

"No," Aunt Tillie hissed again. "I need you."

"How much do you need us?" Thistle suddenly looked shrewd. "Like, do you need us enough to get us out of our chores this week?"

Aunt Tillie's hands landed on her hips. "Are you seriously going to stand there and try to shake me down?"

"Yup."

"That's why you're the smartest one of them all," she growled. "I'll get you out of your chores for a week if you do what I ask."

Amusement flooded Thistle's face as Aunt Tillie laid it out for us. "Huh," she said after Aunt Tillie explained the plan. "We can work with that."

Aunt Tillie's smile was very Saturday-morning cartoonish. "Awesome. Can you work with it right now?"

"Absolutely." Thistle grabbed my arm and started dragging me down the alley, away from the back of the store and toward Main Street. She barked at Clove to keep up and then lowered her voice so only I could hear. "I've got this," she assured me.

"You've got what?" I still wasn't sure what the plan was.

"I know exactly what Aunt Tillie wants."

"Just because you know what she wants doesn't mean you should give it to her." I opted to be rational, rare in a family that reveled in theatrics. "She could get us in trouble if we're not careful."

"Oh, you know as well as I do that we won't get in trouble if Aunt Tillie put us up to it. Our mothers think we can't figure stuff out on our own. They'll blame her, and we'll get two mugs of hot chocolate."

She had a point, but I remained leery. "What are you going to do?"

"Just trust me."

"Thistle..."

"I've got it." Her voice was cold. "Just let me handle this. I know what we're supposed to do."

THE TELEVISION CREW WAS IN FRONT of Mrs. Little's new store when we rounded the corner to Main Street. I was still in the dark about what we were supposed to do. Thistle, however, seemed intent.

"Wait here." She went to the garbage receptacle on the corner and peered inside, coming out with a crinkled brown paper bag and an empty beer bottle.

"What are you doing?" I hissed as she slid the bottle in the paper bag and then cinched the bag around the bottle's neck.

"I watch television," Thistle replied. "I know how to make it look like someone is a drunk."

My mouth hung open as Thistle headed for Mrs. Little. The store owner—a woman who had been horrible to us for as long as I could remember—had remained focused on the camera crew as she rattled on about her new business. I glanced over my shoulder and saw Aunt Tillie watching us from beneath the streetlight.

She made shooing motions with her hands, indicating that I should follow Thistle, and because I didn't know what else to do, I stuck out my tongue and skulked along in Thistle's wake. Clove, much more eager to be a part of the show, ran her hand through her hair as we got closer.

"Mrs. Little, I think these young girls would like to visit your store," the perky blond reporter holding the microphone said when she caught sight of us.

"What do you mean?" Mrs. Little looked confused ... right up to the point she realized who was approaching. "What do you want?" she demanded.

The reporter looked taken aback but didn't stop her cameraman from recording the scene.

"We just brought your ... drink ... like you asked," Thistle replied. She held up the bottle in the bag. "I'm sorry we're late. Please don't take it out on Bay and Clove. It was my fault."

"What are you talking about?" Mrs. Little barked.

"We did as you asked," Thistle insisted. She looked like a terrified urchin, shaking in the shadow of Mrs. Little's annoyance, a deliberate choice on her part because Thistle had never shown fear in front of Mrs. Little. She wouldn't lower herself to do anything of the sort.

"Just tell me what you want," Mrs. Little growled.

"I told you she would be mad," Clove said, her voice breaking as tears sprang to her eyes. Clove could cry at will. It was a skill Aunt Tillie had used to her advantage more than once, deeming it her superpower. "Please don't be mad. We didn't mean to make you mad. We're so sorry." The back of Clove's hand moved to her forehead as she preened for the camera. "We did the best we could."

I pressed my lips together, uncertain. I knew what Aunt Tillie expected of me, but this felt wrong. Of course, because we were dealing with Mrs. Little, I couldn't work up the sort of guilt that would've propelled me to drag my cousins away. Instead, I watched.

"Listen up, you little monsters," Mrs. Little growled. "I don't know what you're doing—or why you're out this late without supervision—but I know you're up to no good. You need to scram."

Thistle managed to maintain an air of innocence. "We're so sorry, ma'am. We know you needed this for your dipsomania before the camera crew arrived, but we did the best we could." She shook the bottle for emphasis. "Just take it, and we'll go."

"And we'll try not to upset you ever again," Clove added in earnest fashion.

Mrs. Little's expression told me she was about to go nuclear. I realized that's what Aunt Tillie had wanted from the start. She wanted Mrs. Little to make a fool of herself on television ... and that's exactly how things were playing out.

"We're doing our best," Clove said to the camera. "She has a disease. We're trying to help her, so she doesn't get upset again. She's so mean when she's upset."

Mrs. Little didn't realize she was no longer in control of her destiny. "Listen here, you little brat." She grabbed the shoulder of Clove's hoodie and tugged.

Clove cried out as if she'd lost a limb, and the reporter stepped between the two of them.

"Ma'am, these are little girls." The reporter looked horrified.

"Don't be ridiculous." Mrs. Little wrinkled her nose. "They're heathens, and they're being raised by the biggest heathen of them all. Where is your aunt?"

"We're so sorry," Clove said with an exaggerated sniffle. "Please don't use the flyswatter again. We didn't mean to upset you."

The reporter shifted into hero mode.

"Flyswatter? Does she hit you with a flyswatter?" The reporter wrestled Clove from Mrs. Little and started stroking her hair. "You poor thing."

Clove shot me an evil smile when the reporter started fussing over her. I remained quiet, mostly because that guilt I didn't think I could muster was starting to manifest after all.

"What is happening here?" Mrs. Little screeched. "You're supposed to be focused on me, not them. They're just here to cause trouble."

"We try so hard," Thistle said mournfully. "We don't mean to be bad girls. We do our best."

I darted my gaze to the corner and found Aunt Tillie bent at the waist, laughing. Part of me wanted to admonish her, unveil her as the villain. The problem was, Mrs. Little was so often the villain that I couldn't overcome my dislike of her to do the right thing.

"Come on." The reporter slid her arm around Clove's shoulders and motioned for Thistle and me to follow. "We'll get you some hot chocolate. Here, throw that nasty thing away." She took the bottle from Thistle without even looking inside the paper bag. Anger pulsed across her face—all reserved for Mrs. Little, of course—when she tossed it in the nearest trash receptacle.

"Can we have doughnuts, too?" Clove asked through her fake tears. "She never lets us have doughnuts."

"You can have ten doughnuts," the reporter promised. "As for her, don't worry. I can guarantee she won't ever hurt you again."

I held Aunt Tillie's gaze as I crossed the street. She looked amused for the most part, but there was a thoughtfulness to her expression. She waved and then shuffled down the sidewalk in Mrs. Little's direction. She was going to make things worse, because that's what she did.

"What are you doing?" Thistle hissed when she saw me focusing on the police station. "We're getting doughnuts."

"We're going to need a ride home," I replied simply. "Mrs. Little and Aunt Tillie will be going at it for hours."

"Doughnuts first. Then you can call Officer Terry to take us home. Don't ruin our fun."

"Fine, but you know this is going to come back to bite us."

"No, I don't know that."

"Aunt Tillie's games always come back to bite us."

"Well, maybe we'll get away with it this time. There's a first time for everything."

We both knew that wasn't going to happen. Still, I glanced over my shoulder one last time. Mrs. Little launched herself at Aunt Tillie, her hands aimed at our great-aunt's throat.

"Do you think they'll ever stop?" I asked.

"Not until one of them is in the ground. Besides, I kind of like it when they fight. They're never boring."

"I guess." I blew out a sigh. "Mom is going to be mad when she hears what happened."

"Not at us. She'll blame Aunt Tillie."

We did have that to look forward to. "I'm going to have two dough-nuts," I said.

"That's the spirit." She clapped my shoulder. "Let Aunt Tillie deal with the aftermath. We'll focus on the doughnuts."

One

PRESENT DAY

"Flex."

I narrowed my eyes and glared at Aunt Tillie. She sat in a wooden chair on the patio of The Overlook, the inn my mother and aunts run, an electric blanket settled over her legs and a mug of coffee in her hand. Fall had taken hold in Hemlock Cove, a small hamlet in northern Lower Michigan, and even though the days could still be comfortable, the mornings were brisk. Why Aunt Tillie was covered in a blanket, while I was freezing in my yoga pants and hoodie, was a mystery.

"What did she say?" Stormy Morgan, a witchy friend from one town over, had her blond hair pulled back in a ponytail and her hands planted on her hips. Her face was red, her breath coming in small puffs, and she looked as if she was ready to roll over and die.

"She said she's a pain," I growled as I glared at my great-aunt. "She doesn't really have to announce that, though, because we already know it."

"Yes, that memo has been sent," my cousin Clove readily agreed. She was also in a chair, her infant son wrapped in a blanket as she cuddled him. Her presence during what was supposed to be a training session was an added layer of crap I really didn't want to deal with.

"Nobody asked you," Aunt Tillie said, though her expression softened when she looked at baby Calvin's round features. She wasn't a fan of babies—something she told us over and over—but this baby was named after her late husband, the only man in the world who had truly claimed Aunt Tillie's heart during the course of a long life, so she made an exception... Still, she preferred not doing so in front of witnesses.

"I'm still confused," Stormy said, rolling her neck. She was lithe, and she filled out the yoga pants better than I ever could ... not that I was keeping score or anything. "I get that we're supposed to be training. After everything that's happened, training is good. What I don't get is why we're approaching it like a gym class."

"Your bodies need to be as strong as your minds if you want to be good witches," Aunt Tillie replied. "Physical fitness is as important as mental fitness. Also, do you want your butt to sag before you lock in that boyfriend of yours? If you follow my lead, that won't happen. Really, you should be thanking me."

Stormy made a face but glanced over her shoulder in an attempt to look at her butt.

"Ignore her," I said on a hand wave. "Your butt is fine."

"Your butt is great," Clove agreed. "I wish my butt looked that good."

"Your butt is like a pancake because all you do is sit around on it," Aunt Tillie snapped at Clove. "If you want a better butt, you should be working out."

"I just had a baby," Clove reminded her. "I'm still recovering."

There was no missing Aunt Tillie's eye roll. "It's not like you gave birth last week," she said. "That baby has been here for months."

"Only two months," Clove protested. "I'm still getting my mojo back."

"Oh, that's cute." Aunt Tillie looked suddenly pensive. "Is that the story you use on Sam?"

Sam Cornell was Clove's husband. As far as I could tell, he didn't care in the least if Clove had a pancake butt. He was so thrilled with his wife and son he didn't notice anything but how happy they made him.

"Do you think Sam hates my butt?" Clove asked me, her eyes wide.

"Ignore her," I repeated. "She's just looking for attention."

"Shouldn't you be flexing?" Aunt Tillie said to me. "You wanted extra training, if I remember correctly."

I frowned. If denial had been an option, I would've done it in a heartbeat, but nobody would believe me. She'd caught me in a weak moment. Her life had been on the line, and my magic was the only chance we had to save her. I'd pulled it out—she was free and clear of the bad luck curse—but I'd been left feeling vulnerable in the wake of the fallout. That's why I'd asked for the training. In hindsight, it had been a terrible idea.

"We're supposed to be working on magic," I reminded her. "Flexing was not part of the deal."

"I'm in charge. What I say goes." Aunt Tillie's haughty expression told me she was enjoying herself a bit too much. "If I say you need to fix your butt, you need to fix your butt."

I darted a look to Stormy, who had returned to stretching. She was new to the witch game and was more open to Aunt Tillie's methods. She would learn. "I'm going to focus on you right now," I said. "How are things going in your life?"

"They're pretty much the same," Stormy replied as she leaned to the side. "Hunter is packing his stuff and slowly moving it to my grandfather's extra garage."

"Is he living with you at the apartment?" I asked. Stormy and her boyfriend, Hunter Ryan, were about to start cohabitating in the apartment above her grandfather's restaurant. The goal was to buy their dream house in the spring. Until then, their living arrangements had a temporary feeling.

"We spend every night together," she replied. "Sometimes I'm over there with him to help him pack. On nights when I have to get up early to work with Grandpa, we stay at the apartment."

"That sounds fun." Before I could say anything else, Clove cleared her throat to get my attention. "Yes?" I asked.

"It's time to focus on me." She showed no signs of embarrassment for redirecting the conversation. "I need the truth about my butt. How bad is it?"

I shifted my glare to Aunt Tillie. "Are you happy? You've got her all worked up."

"I'm not unhappy." Aunt Tillie leaned back in her chair. "She needs to practice too. She's the weakest of your entire group."

"Hey!" Clove's eyes flashed with annoyance. "Did you just say what I think you said?"

"That you're the weakest witch in your age group?" Aunt Tillie challenged. "That's exactly what I said."

"That's the meanest thing you've ever said to me."

"And yet it's true." Aunt Tillie was back to focusing on me. "If you want to be the power you were born to be, you need to get your sidekicks in order ... starting with this one." She jerked her thumb in Clove's direction.

"Did she just call me a sidekick?" Clove demanded in a heated whisper.

"I believe so," I replied. "Stop letting her get to you. She gets off on it, and you keep feeding the beast."

"I have a question." Stormy's hand shot in the air, and she smirked when Aunt Tillie gave her a perfunctory head bob to proceed. "Am I considered a sidekick in this little scenario here?"

"I was talking about Clove and Thistle, but that's an interesting question." Aunt Tillie cocked her head as she thought about her answer. "As of now, you'd probably be considered a sidekick. You're still learning, but you've taken the lead several times and did just fine. Even if you're still a sidekick—which is debatable—you won't be for much longer. You'll be a leading lady before you know it."

"Huh." Stormy didn't look as if she knew how to react.

"This conversation is stupid," I complained as I rolled my hips. "We're not even doing regular yoga. These are just stretches you made up."

"You'll live." Aunt Tillie flicked her eyes to Calvin. "Should that baby be outside? It's cold."

"It's not that cold," Clove replied. "He's fine. Besides, I'm here to talk to Bay. I only get two mornings out a week because of the baby, and I need adult conversation."

"Hit me," I said as I leaned forward and pressed my palms to the ground to stretch my calves.

"Did you hear about the television show?" Clove asked. She almost sounded giddy.

"Are you watching *Bridgerton* again because you like the history, or have you finally admitted the sex gets you off?"

Clove's eyes narrowed. "First off, smarty pants, I happen to love learning about history. You're just jealous because I'm such a diligent learner."

"That must be it," I agreed dryly.

"Second, that's not the television show I was talking about," she continued, barely taking a breath. "I'm talking about the one coming to town to film over the next few weeks."

I cringed at the mention of the show. I wanted to pretend it wasn't yet another problem about to upend our world. That was naive and ridiculous on my part because the camera crew was scheduled to arrive tomorrow.

"Wait ... you guys have a television show coming to town to film?" Stormy gave up all pretense of stretching and stared at me.

I nodded. "Yeah, and nobody is happy about it."

"Speak for yourself," Clove said. "Everyone is excited. Well, except for Bay and Thistle. They've been whining, but they're no fun anyway."

"I'll have you know I'm tons of fun," I shot back. "I'm lost." Stormy glanced between us. "What sort of show is it? It's not a Lifetime movie or anything, is it?" She frowned at the prospect. "That would be disappointing. But *Stranger Things* could film here. That would be awesome."

I made a face. "*Stranger Things* I could deal with. I wouldn't be happy about it, but I could deal with it. This is something else entirely."

Stormy waited for me to expand. When I didn't, she waved her hands in impatient fashion. "Don't just leave me hanging," she complained. "Give me the skinny."

"See, even when she speaks, she wants the skinny," Aunt Tillie said to Clove. "She's a trooper. You don't care about the skinny."

"You're going to make my eyes leak," Clove warned. "When that happens, Calvin starts crying because he can't stop himself. Is that what you want?"

Aunt Tillie didn't look bothered in the least. "I can ignore a crying baby."

"Yes, but my mother and aunts can't, and if they figure out you made Calvin cry, you'll face Aunt Winnie's wrath."

I froze in place, my lips curving, and watched Aunt Tillie for her response. She would never own up to it, but my mother was the only person who could strike fear in her heart. It wasn't often, but it did happen, and Clove was right. The second my mother and aunts found out Aunt Tillie had made the baby cry, she would be in a world of trouble.

"About that television show," Aunt Tillie prodded.

I had to bite the inside of my cheek to keep from laughing.

"What sort of show is it?" Stormy asked. "If it's not a scripted show, what does that leave?"

"It's a reality show," Clove replied. "It's called *Haunted Traditions,* and it's really popular. We're going to be the first episode of the new season. At least that's what I read online."

"Not that you've been stalking the production pages or anything," I muttered.

"I think I've seen that show," Stormy said. "They go to what they claim are the most magical places in the world and look for ghosts and stuff, right?"

Clove bobbed her head. "Yup. They've been on zombie hunts in New Orleans, ghost hunts in Savannah, Chupacabra hunts in Texas, and even witch hunts in Salem."

Slowly, Stormy tracked her eyes to me. I didn't have to guess what she was thinking. "Why are they coming to Hemlock Cove?"

"One guess," I replied grimly.

Stormy didn't need more than that because her eyes were already going wide. "It's a witch town. They're going to be hunting witches."

"Yes." Clove clapped her hands together and squealed like a teenager.

"Isn't that bad for us?" Stormy asked. "I mean ... wouldn't it be better if they were looking for Bigfoot or something?"

"Oh, why did you say that?" Clove whined. "You know how I feel about Bigfoot."

In her arms, Calvin stirred and let loose a yelp. All eyes drifted toward him until he settled again.

"Watch it," Aunt Tillie warned as she jabbed a finger at Clove. "The one thing this morning doesn't need is a screaming baby."

"I'm not the one who brought up Bigfoot," Clove growled.

"We were branded as a witch town years ago," I explained to Stormy. "That's what we're famous for. I'm sure they wouldn't turn up their noses at a Bigfoot sighting, but they're here for witches ... and they've made no bones about their aim. They've been trying to set up an interview with me for two weeks."

Clove's eyes widened. "Why didn't you mention that?"

"Because I'm not doing it." I was firm. "I have no interest in being on a television show." *Especially one that could ruin my life if the truth comes out*, I silently added.

"Why not?" Clove was either oblivious to my feelings or didn't care. "You could be the face of Hemlock Cove."

"That's exactly what I don't want," I fired back.

"If it's not you, it's going to be Mrs. Little," Clove warned. "You know darned well she agreed to their interview request."

That hadn't occurred to me. I still didn't care enough to try to usurp her throne. "She can be the face of Hemlock Cove all she wants," I replied.

"Well, let's not be hasty." Aunt Tillie squirmed in her chair.

"Oh, don't even," I warned. "You were on my side when we talked about this yesterday. We both agreed the television show was a bad idea when Twila said she was going to try to get on."

Twila, Thistle's mother, was a bit of a scatterbrained loon. I loved her, but she wasn't the sharpest knife in the butcher block.

"I don't care about being on the show," Aunt Tillie said. "I just don't want Margaret to be the face of Hemlock Cove."

I sensed trouble. "This isn't going to be like when she opened the store with the antiques and dolls, is it?" I whined. The memory still haunted me. "She had to close that one down in less than three months because of what we did when that reporter showed up."

"What did you do?" Stormy asked.

"Nothing I want to own up to," I said. "Can't you just lay low for the next few weeks?" Whenever I thought about what could go wrong with a film crew in town, my stomach threatened to shred. And this wasn't just any film crew. This was a crew looking for paranormal activity.

We were real witches pretending to be normal humans pretending to be fake witches. That made for an uncomfortable existence. As it was, too many people in town had witnessed some of our paranormal shenanigans. There was no way we would get out of the filming unscathed if we weren't very, very careful.

"Why don't you take a chill pill and let me worry about the film crew?" Aunt Tillie suggested. "You said yourself that you don't want anything to do with this *Haunted Tapestries* show."

"*Haunted Traditions*," Clove corrected. "If you expect to schmooze with the bigwigs, you'd better get the title right."

Aunt Tillie, keeping her eyes on me, waved off the comment. "You're too much of a worrier," she said. "These people are idiots. They'll spend all their time hanging around the cemetery trying to get people to dance naked under the full moon."

Naked dancing was a regular occurrence at The Overlook, so that didn't make me feel any better. "Maybe we can come up with a spell to make them want to leave," I mused.

"I said I have everything under control," Aunt Tillie barked. "Have a little faith. Not everything revolves around you. I bet they won't even approach you after you shot them down for an interview."

I hoped that was true. The odds of me getting that lucky seemed slim, however.

Rather than drag out the conversation, I shook my head. "Let's finish up. I have actual work waiting for me in town."

"Fine, as long as you stop kvetching." Aunt Tillie's gaze was dark. "I've got this. You have nothing to worry about."

If only I could believe her.

Two

Whe were getting nothing of substance done, so I called time on our training session and headed to the guesthouse I shared with my husband to shower and change. Then I headed into town.

As owner of The Whistler, Hemlock Cove's only newspaper, I had a lot on my plate. I handled the bulk of the planning duties, covered stories, and other than a part-time page layout person, photographer, and ad sales representative, I was the entire show. I figured it was best to get ahead before the film crew arrived.

My attention was drawn to the police station when I parked in front of the newspaper office. Three people stood outside, all looking very intense. I recognized two of them.

Chief Terry Davenport and my husband, Landon Michaels, were talking with a younger man. I was curious enough to head in their direction rather than immediately going inside and getting to work. I was a busybody, so if something was up, I wanted to know about it.

Chief Terry saw me first and broke into a wide grin. He'd been dating my mother for months now, essentially living at the inn with us, but he still acted as if I was the greatest person he'd ever met whenever we crossed paths.

I liked that about him.

"There's my girl." He leaned in and gave me a side hug. "How are you today? I only got to see you for a few minutes at breakfast."

"I'm good." I couldn't very well tell him about my training session with Aunt Tillie in front of someone who wasn't in on the big magical secret. "What's going on here?"

Landon addressed Chief Terry's comment before answering my question. "How is she your girl?" he demanded. His relationship with Chief Terry was almost like father and son. Sometimes it bordered on siblings, however, given the way they liked to poke at one another. "I married her. That makes her my girl."

"I've known her longer," Chief Terry replied. "She's always been my sweetheart. That makes her my girl."

"No, her mother is your girl. Bay is my girl." As if to prove it, Landon slung an arm around my shoulders. "Tell him."

There was no way I was getting involved in this argument. "What's up with you guys?" I asked in an effort to redirect the conversation. My gaze was on the young man standing between them. He was handsome in a rough-and-tumble way, dark brown hair almost hitting his shoulders and about two days' worth of beard growth giving him a dangerous look. His smile was warm and friendly, but there was a leeriness in his eyes.

"I can't believe you left me hanging like that," Landon groused. "And here I thought I was your favorite person in the world."

"Get in line," Chief Terry challenged.

Clearly, there was some weird testosterone thing going on that was beyond my comprehension. Because I didn't want to deal with it, I focused on the outsider. "I'm Bay. Landon is my husband, and Chief Terry is my protector. That makes them rude sometimes."

The man flashed a dimple when he grinned. "Kevin Gallagher." He shook my hand. "I'm working with your husband and father on a case."

"I'm not her father," Chief Terry said, shifting from one foot to the other in obvious discomfort.

"He's one of them," I countered with a soft smile. "Are you from this area, Kevin?"

"I'm from Shadow Hills originally," he replied. "I was there until I was ten, and then we moved to Bellaire. Now I live in Traverse City."

"Do you still have family in the area?" I wondered what else I should ask him, but Landon swooped in.

"Kevin is going undercover," he explained. "The meth trade is picking up, and we need eyes and ears on the ground. Because it's easier for him to check in here than to keep driving back to Traverse City, we've gotten involved. We're going to be his primary partners."

I was taken aback. Given the expression on Kevin's face, he obviously was too.

"It's okay," Landon assured the younger man. "Bay's familiar with how this works. We met when I was undercover doing almost the exact same thing you are."

"Really?" Kevin didn't look convinced. "Um ... don't you work for the newspaper?" He pointed to where I'd parked my car.

"I do," I replied.

"She *owns* the newspaper," Landon corrected. "She's an entrepreneur." He grinned at me. "She understands about keeping a secret. I was going to tell her anyway."

"You were?" Kevin's eyes filled with worry.

"You can't check in at the police station once you're established with the gang." Landon was matter-of-fact now. "They could have eyes in town, and we figure it's best for your check-ins to happen elsewhere."

"Like where?" Kevin looked confused.

"Like an inn where one of the owners has a certain reputation," Chief Terry replied, his eyes on me.

That's when realization washed over me. "Aunt Tillie's pot field," I surmised.

"What now?" Kevin was clearly having trouble keeping up with the conversation.

"I already talked to your mother about it, Bay, and she's fine with it," Chief Terry said. "Everybody knows that I'm with Winnie and Landon is with you, but Tillie's reputation, when it comes to that pot field, is notorious. We think it will work."

"Plus, the woods are thick surrounding the inn and guesthouse,"

Landon added. "We're going to alternate between buildings for check-ins."

I wasn't certain how I felt about their plan. Having a new agent—was he a police officer or with the FBI?—loitering around the guest-house when magical things kept popping up didn't strike me as a good idea, but I could hardly lodge my concerns now.

"Where is this gang operating?" I asked.

"Between here and Shadow Hills." Landon was grim. "They've taken over a former motel on the river. It's about a dozen bungalows."

I could picture the location. "Tommy Dornan's old place," I said. "The Sand Lake Motor Inn."

Chief Terry nodded. "It's been closed ever since he died. Nobody has wanted to take on the property, mostly because it needs so much work. Apparently, the leaders of the gang swooped in and got the property for a song."

It made sense ... in an odd sort of way. "It's isolated. They can control the road going in."

"It's easy to defend," Landon agreed. "Nobody can get close enough to spy on them without being seen. That's why we have to send somebody in."

"And that's you?" I flicked my eyes to Kevin. "That must be terrifying."

"Oh, no." Kevin was solemn as he shook his head. "This is why I became an agent. It's exciting."

"Kevin graduated from the academy about six months ago," Landon explained. "He's gung-ho to go undercover. I don't think he realizes how much work it is."

"Oh, I know it's work." Kevin's eyes sparkled. "That's why I got into this career. I've never been the sort of guy who wants to sit behind a desk doing paperwork or go home to the same place every night. Under-cover is my dream. I never want to be one of those guys who's comfort-able watching television at night. This is what I want."

A muscle worked in Landon's jaw, and his expression went momen-tarily hard before he recovered.

"Well, it sounds like you're in for a fun ride," I said. "Stop by the guesthouse whenever you want if you need to slide some information through. Also, if you're ever in a pinch, you can hit up Hypnotic downtown. You can leave a message for Landon or Chief Terry there and be assured that it gets to them."

"Awesome." Kevin's smile was so wide it almost swallowed the lower half of his face. "I can't tell you how much I'm looking forward to this."

"Let's go inside and go over protocols one more time," Chief Terry suggested. "Your motorcycle is being delivered to The Overlook in a few hours. Until then, we've got some time to burn."

Kevin tipped an invisible hat in my direction. "It was great meeting you. These two talk about you constantly." His finger zigzagged between Landon and Chief Terry. "I almost thought they had to be making it up because nobody could be that cool, but I get it." His grin bordered on flirty.

"Hey!" Landon tugged me to his side while glaring at the new agent. "Don't be cute."

"I can't help it," Kevin offered, his dimple coming out to play again. "She's hot, and you just told me she likes guys who go undercover. But maybe she used to like that." His smile disappeared, and he looked as if he was giving it real thought. "You don't go undercover anymore. You stay home, right?"

If looks could kill, Kevin would be dead. "I approach my work differently now," Landon replied stiffly.

Perhaps sensing trouble, Chief Terry clapped Kevin's shoulder and directed him toward the police station. "Come on. We shouldn't be standing out in the open like this. Let's go inside, go over protocols, and get you set up." He shot me a worried look, and I didn't have to ask what fueled it. I waited for the duo to go inside and then slipped my hand into Landon's.

"You still love me?" I was going for levity, but the annoyance in his eyes was obvious.

"What are you even asking?" he groused after several seconds of staring.

"I saw your reaction. You're upset."

"I'm not upset." His denial lacked teeth, so he tried again. "I'm a happy guy."

"Uh-huh." I chose my words carefully. "Do you want to go back undercover?"

"No."

His response was a little too quick for my comfort level. "If you do—"

"Bay, even if I wanted to go undercover, that wouldn't be an option." He was calm, but there was an edge to his tone. "I'm the face of the FBI in this area now. I've been interviewed on camera. I've made the newspapers. Going back undercover is out."

I wasn't quite certain how to respond. "You miss it," I surmised.

"Actually, I don't. I'm happiest when I'm curled up on the couch with my wife at night." He poked my side and managed a smile.

"Are you?" I couldn't help worrying, at least a little. I knew he loved me and enjoyed our life, but his reaction to Kevin was enough to tip me into unease.

"Don't be ridiculous," he insisted. "I wouldn't trade our life for anything. It's just … he's the new kid on the block. All the women in the office are talking about how hot he is and how they want to hop on the back of his motorcycle. I used to be the hot guy on the motorcycle."

"You're still hot," I offered. "I find you very hot."

"Of course I'm hot. Who said I'm not?"

This was a sticky conversation. "I happen to know you're the hottest man in the state."

"The world," he corrected.

"Let's not go crazy. I love you, but you're no Jason Momoa."

His eyes narrowed.

"Landon, I don't know what to say to you." I gripped his hands in mine. "Are you angry because he's the new hot FBI agent on the block, or because he thinks that sitting in front of the television at night is boring?"

"He's not hotter than me," Landon insisted. "I'm hot … and I'll be hot forever. Nobody can steal my crown."

This conversation was getting us nowhere. I knew him well enough to recognize he needed to calm down before we could hash this out. "I'm going to let you go back inside," I started. "I just want to ask how sure you are about having him swing by the guesthouse to share information. I'm guessing that will be at odd hours of the night—when we're often fighting evil."

"I know." His expression changed in an instant. "I considered that. It's safer for him to stop there than in town, though. We need to be careful. This is the first time I've been an undercover handler."

And there it is. He wasn't just upset about no longer being the young stud. He was getting more responsibility placed on those wide shoulders, something he both craved and shied away from. "Listen." I squeezed his hands and forced him to stare directly into my eyes. "I'll make you feel like my undercover hero tonight. I promise, it's going to be just as good as the real deal."

"You're going to play undercover games with me, are you?" His eyes gleamed with delight. "How? And be specific."

"I'll do whatever you want." I meant it. "I just don't want you to be sad." I brushed my fingers over his cheek. "I'm sorry that you don't get to be the young buck this go-round."

Landon's scowl returned. "I don't want to be the young buck. I'm happy the way things are. I just don't want anybody saying he's hotter than me. I'm way hotter."

"I agree. He's ... blech. There's nothing hot about him. I mean, who would even think that? Crazy people, that's who."

He narrowed his eyes, telling me I'd gone too far. Ultimately, he grinned. "I'm totally going to make you play a very specific game tonight." He lightly swatted my rear end. "Now, go finish your work. I don't want you distracted when we're supposed to be focusing on each other. You're mine tonight."

I smiled all the way back to the newspaper. I was hoping for quiet to get my work done when I let myself inside. That apparently wasn't in the cards, because Viola, the office ghost, started buzzing around the second she saw me.

"Did you hear the news?"

I eyed her speculatively before moving to the desk to look at the mail. "I'm not sure I want to hear the news." I opted for the truth. "This isn't about Bigfoot again, is it?"

Not too long ago, she'd claimed to have seen Bigfoot in the woods. I hadn't believed her—for obvious reasons—and that had come back to bite me. She hadn't really seen Bigfoot, but that didn't mean there wasn't a monster in the woods causing problems. I'd learned a hard lesson that day. No matter how crazy Viola seemed, she sometimes came in handy.

"Bigfoot is dead." She stopped fluttering around the lobby. "I heard he's living in a garden gnome in Tillie's greenhouse these days. Is that true?"

"Not quite. Bigfoot was never really the bad guy. The being trapped in Aunt Tillie's gnome is somebody else."

"Somebody evil?"

"Yup."

"What's she going to do with the gnome?"

It was a fair question, but I didn't have an answer. "I think she plans to torture him with bad country music, but I haven't asked." I fixed Viola with a pointed look. "If it's not Bigfoot that has you excited, what is it?"

"Just the best news to ever hit this town," Viola enthused as she stopped directly in front of me. "There's a television show being filmed here."

I told myself I should've seen it coming. Viola was a gossip fiend, collecting news at every turn while flitting to and fro around Hemlock Cove. "I heard about the television show. I believe they're coming tomorrow."

Viola's gaze turned dark. "And you didn't tell me? Why would you keep that from me?" Her tone was accusatory.

"I didn't realize it was important to you. You're a ghost. You can't be on television. You understand my confusion as to why you're so excited?"

"Not in the least. I'm a ghost, and they're ghost hunters. I'm destined to be a star."

I had to hold back a sigh. "They're here searching for witches."

Viola waved off the comment as if I'd just told her the sky was red rather than green. "I'm going to be famous. Just you watch. It's going to be glorious."

"Okay, well ... good for you." I didn't have the heart to tell her these people likely couldn't see ghosts. She was too excited for me to burst that particular bubble. Instead, I focused on the important news for the day. "Have you heard anybody else talking about this? What about Mrs. Little? How does she feel?"

"Oh, she's excited for the coverage. She said it will make Hemlock Cove famous. And she's plotting ways to keep your family from taking over the spotlight."

I shrugged. For once, Mrs. Little and I were on the same page. "I don't think you have to worry about that. We don't want to be in the spotlight. In fact—"

An earsplitting scream rocked me back on my heels. It wasn't the sort of scream that could be mistaken for kids having fun. This scream signified trouble, and it was the last thing I wanted with a television crew due to descend tomorrow.

"Son of a witch!" I didn't hesitate before bolting through the front door. Whatever this was, I had to put an end to it ... and fast.

Three

T he scream had come from somewhere. I just had to figure out where. I was about to call Landon to see if he'd found the source when another scream shredded what was left of my nerves. It was easier to track the sound this time, and I headed toward the alley behind the Unicorn Emporium.

I registered three things in quick succession as I started down the narrow alley. Two people stood directly behind the Unicorn Emporium. Cady Falls and Carla Becker owned the hat shop about three doors down.

Then I noticed something on the ground. I'd been around enough crime scenes to recognize they were standing over a body.

The third thing I noticed—and this bothered me most—was that the body was glowing. A creamy yellow haze surrounded the body.

"What happened?" I asked when I reached Cady and Carla. They were not on my list of favorite Hemlock Cove residents. They both had platinum-blond hair, bad haircuts with way too much bang, and were dressed in black dresses that showed off their assets, both top and bottom.

Cady jerked her eyes to me. She was pale, to the point I worried she might pass out, and her finger trembled as she pointed to the body.

I had to bite back a snarky comment. "I see him," I said. "Where did he come from?" The man appeared to be in his twenties. His eyes were wide open and staring.

"How should I know?" Cady shot back. Then, to my utter surprise, she opened her mouth and let loose another scream. It was bone-chilling and earsplitting, and I desperately needed her to stop.

"What are you doing?" I didn't hold back my disdain this time. She was a complete and total moron on her best day. This was clearly not one of her best days.

"I'm calling for help," Cady said.

I narrowed my eyes and pulled my phone out of my pocket with exaggerated slowness. Landon was at the top of my contact list, and I called him, all the while my glare freezing Cady in place.

"Hey," he answered after the second ring. "Miss me already?"

"I need you," I blurted, still organizing my thoughts.

"Ooh, is it nap time?" Landon sounded a little too excited at the prospect. "Be naked and on your couch in five minutes. Oh, don't look at me that way, Terry. It's not my fault she needs some Landon in her day."

Under different circumstances, I would've laughed. My head buzzed because of the glowing body, however, and I couldn't focus on anything but that. "Come to the alley behind the Unicorn Emporium," I instructed. "Bring Chief Terry."

I could practically see Landon's frown. "You want me to bring Terry? That's not how I roll, Bay."

He was trying to be funny, but I had no time for his games. "Landon, there's a body behind the Unicorn Emporium. I need you right now."

All traces of mirth fled as my words registered. "I'm on my way. Sit tight."

True to his word, he reached me in record time. His gaze was keen as he glanced between faces before ultimately focusing on me. "What happened?"

"I don't know." I looked over his shoulder and met Chief Terry's wide-eyed stare. "I heard screaming and came to check it out."

"You heard screaming?" Chief Terry stepped carefully as he moved closer to the body. "He was screaming?"

"I'm pretty sure it was Cady," I replied, pointing.

Cady took offense at my accusatory finger. "What else would you have me do, Bay? There's a freaking body on the ground. When you stumble across a body, you scream."

"Or call 911 for help," Chief Terry replied.

"Well, I didn't make it that far." Cady pinned him with a glare before turning her attention to Landon. "I was shocked."

"I don't blame you." Landon unleashed his most devastating smile. "This is a shocking situation." He circled the body. He didn't mention the glow, but I could tell he was curious.

I shrugged at his unasked question. I had no idea what was causing the glow, and I couldn't very well get a closer look when Cady and Carla were watching me. They were already difficult. I didn't want to give them a reason to be more difficult ... or overly chatty with the other town gossips.

"Okay." Landon huffed out a heavy exhale. "Okay." He squared his shoulders. "Ladies, I'm going to have questions."

"We're at your disposal, officer," Carla drawled as she batted her eyelashes at him.

"I'm an agent, but okay." Landon shot me a quick glance, perhaps to see if I was jealous, and then took control. "I assume you work in this area."

"They own the hat store," I volunteered. I needed to move this conversation along because if Carla and Cady had their way, they would drape themselves against Landon and drag things out until I wanted to pop their heads like zits. "It's three doors down from Mrs. Little's store."

Landon nodded. "Okay, why don't you go back to your store," he said to the women. "Chief Terry and I need to secure the scene and get the medical examiner out here. We'll talk later."

"We can do that," Cady confirmed. Her eyes were on me instead of Landon. "Bay has to leave too, right?"

Landon's smile didn't diminish. "Bay has to answer some questions first, and then I'll cut her loose as well."

"If only you hadn't saddled yourself with the Winchester baggage in the first place," Carla sighed.

I narrowed my eyes, but a quick shoulder squeeze from Chief Terry had me keeping my mouth shut—with considerable effort.

"We need to close off the alley," Chief Terry said. "Go inside, and we'll join you as soon as we can manage."

Cady shot me one more dubious look and then nodded. She almost looked to be tortured at the prospect of being separated from my husband.

"Go ahead," Landon prodded. He was doing his best to keep his expression neutral, but I could feel the agitation wafting off him. "We won't be long. Just out of curiosity, though," he called out as they moved toward their store. "Do you recognize him?"

"Sorry," Carla replied. "I've never seen him before. I don't think he's a local."

"He might be a delivery guy," Cady offered. "That would explain why he's back here."

"Okay. Thank you." Landon winked at them. "We'll question you just as soon as we have the scene secured."

"We're looking forward to it," Carla purred.

I waited until they'd left the alley. "Way to flirt with them in front of me."

Landon's smile was replaced by a scowl in an instant. "Oh, don't even. We needed them out of here. I got them out of here. I'm not sorry."

"You should divorce him," Chief Terry suggested as he dropped to one knee next to the body. He was fixated on the dead man. "I never thought he was good enough for you anyway. This just proves that."

"Don't you start," Landon growled. "You're just angry because you overheard the couch thing." He looked exasperated when he rested his hands on my shoulders. "You can't seriously be jealous."

I thought about it. I might've been jealous two years ago, but we were way beyond that now. "I just don't like them. I mean ... who hits on someone's husband right in front of them like that?"

"Desperate women who are clearly intimidated by you," Landon replied. "What can you tell me about this?" He waved his hand over the body.

"The glow? I have no idea. I've never seen anything like this."

"Well, it has to be magical," Chief Terry said. He extended a finger as if to poke the body, but I caught his wrist before he made contact.

"Don't do that." I flashed a smile I didn't feel and leaned over the body.

"Is it dangerous?" Landon grabbed my belt loop and started to haul me back before he'd finished asking the question.

"Knock that off." I slapped at his hand. "I'm trying to ... feel ... something."

"Feel?" Chief Terry arched a questioning eyebrow.

"It's got to be magical. Nothing natural could cause that glow."

"Not that I know of," Chief Terry conceded. "We can't completely rule it out until the medical examiner does."

I balked. "You can't let other people see this."

Chief Terry made an incredulous face. "How do you suggest we get around that? We can't just throw a body in the back of Landon's Explorer and hide it in the woods. We have to call this in, Bay."

I felt like a bit of an idiot when he was forced to say it out loud. "I know," I said after a beat. "I just ... have no idea how to explain this." I extended my hand until it was about a foot over the body and tried to scan the magic being used. Rather than bouncing against something, I found a black hole of sorts. "It's almost like this is happening in a vacuum."

"Meaning what?" Landon asked. When we first got together, he was leery about the magic. He didn't like to talk about it and often lived in fear of exposure.

"It's not like the magic isn't there," I explained. "It's like the magic is blocking out other magic. I don't know how to explain it."

Landon glanced between the body and me. "What do we do?" he asked.

"Your guess is as good as mine." I pressed my lips together and glanced up and down the alley. It had been quiet on Main Street when Cady started screaming. Nobody but me had followed the sound to the alley. "I don't know what to do, Landon. My initial instinct is to cover it up because this glow is going to cause issues. I don't know how to do that without causing other issues."

Landon nodded in understanding. "Can you hide the glow?"

"Like with a blanket or something?"

"With magic. Like, can you do that glamour thing to hide the glow?"

It was an interesting possibility that I hadn't considered. "Wow. Sometimes you think more like a witch than I do," I said with a half-hearted laugh. "I might be able to manage that."

"Really?" Chief Terry looked relieved at the prospect. "If we don't have to explain the glow, that'll help more than you know."

"Just let me think." I tapped my bottom lip as I slowly turned in a circle. Glamouring a living human was different, but the principle should be the same. "How long do you want the glamour to last?" I asked.

"How long can you make it last?"

"It depends on the spell and how much magic I funnel into it."

"Just get us through the next forty-eight hours or so," Chief Terry said. "That should give us time to get a foothold into this investigation."

"Okay." I raised my hands in front of me, but before I could unleash the magic, Landon slid between my arms and pressed my body tightly against his for an awkward hug.

"There, there," he said, patting the back of my head.

Confused, I looked up at him. "Are you trying to cop a feel when we're dealing with a murder?"

"May we help you?" Chief Terry called out, causing my shoulders to hop.

When I turned, I saw he was moving to the far end of the alley. "What's going on?" I whispered.

"We are no longer alone." Landon kissed my forehead and then pulled back. "Do not wave those fingers."

"I wasn't going to wave my fingers."

"Well, just don't do anything." He moved away from me and leaned to the side to get a better look down the alley. "This isn't good."

I was shorter, so I had a harder time seeing around Chief Terry.

When I finally made out what we were looking at, a sense of dread washed over me. "Landon…"

"I see it." Landon's hand landed on the back of my neck, and he lightly squeezed. He was trying to ease my anxiety, and yet I could feel agitation coursing through him.

I chewed my bottom lip as Chief Terry approached the individuals staring at us. The redheaded woman appeared to use a dye that could come from Twila's stash, it was so bright. With her was a younger man with brown hair and what looked to be a very expensive camera.

"They're with the television show," I realized, jolting when I heard footsteps behind us. I swiveled, prepared to fight, and my heart skipped ten beats when I saw another man with a camera moving in our direction from the opposite end of the alley. "Oh, crap."

Landon looked in both directions. I knew his face well enough to recognize that he'd already come to the same conclusion: whatever was about to happen, it wasn't good, and there was nothing we could do to stop it.

"Are you Chief Terry Davenport?" the redhead asked as she moved to intercept Chief Terry. "One of the uniformed officers in your office said you were out here … somewhere."

"I am," Chief Terry replied. "Who might you be?"

"My name is Debbie Bateman. I'm the producer of *Haunted Traditions*. You were expecting me, correct?"

I couldn't see Chief Terry's face, but I could almost hear his heavy swallow. "I heard that you were coming to town," he replied. "I didn't expect you until tomorrow."

"Well, we were all so excited to get here." Debbie sounded thrilled to be in Hemlock Cove, which made me leery. "It looks like we got here just in time too."

"What do you mean by that?" Chief Terry asked in a measured tone.

"It appears you have a body. That's what the women in front are saying."

"Cady and Carla," I muttered. "You should've warned them not to tell anybody what they saw."

"Well, it's too late for that," Landon said. "Sir, please step back." He moved away from me and toward the cameraman approaching from the south end of the alley. "This is a crime scene."

"I see it." The blond man looked dumbstruck as he focused his camera on the body. "Do all bodies in Hemlock Cove glow?"

I pressed my eyes shut. Whether the glamour would've worked, I couldn't say, but it was no longer an option.

"Just stay back," Landon barked. "You can't film a dead body."

"Sure I can." The cameraman didn't sound bothered in the least. "We'll blur the face. We do it all the time."

Landon threw his hands in the air and locked eyes with me. "What now?"

I had no idea how to answer that question.

Four

"You can't be back here." Chief Terry used his most authoritative voice. "This is a crime scene."

"There's no tape," Debbie pointed out.

"There will be soon." Chief Terry pulled his phone from his pocket. "I need you to leave the area."

"Sure." Debbie bobbed her head agreeably. "I understand. This is a fluid situation." Her eyes landed on me. "Perhaps we could interview the witness on Main Street while you're getting a handle on things."

Oh, well, crap on a cracker. "I'm not a witness," I said. "I just ... stumbled across the situation and placed a call."

Landon shot me a quelling look, basically ordering me—wordlessly —to watch myself. I understood, but he didn't seem to understand that we'd already lost control.

"Let's move this to Main Street." He pulled his badge out of his pocket and flashed it to add some authority to the order. "Chief, I'll leave you to secure the scene and get the medical examiner on site."

Chief Terry hesitated a split second before nodding.

Landon lightly gripped my elbow and directed me toward the blond cameraman. "Everybody needs to get out of here right now. I won't ask again."

I pressed my lips together and glanced over my shoulder to make sure Debbie and the second cameraman were following his instructions. Thankfully, they were, but we weren't out of the woods.

Once we were clear of the alley, I could breathe a little easier. We still had a massive problem on our hands, and it didn't have an easy solution.

"What's going on?" Thistle asked as she appeared on the street corner in front of Hypnotic, the store she owned with Clove. Concern lined her face—her hair was a bright orange these days to mark fall—and she didn't even fake a welcoming smile for the cameraman.

"Go ahead," Landon said when I shot him a questioning look. "I'll wrangle the television crew and ... start figuring this out."

I wanted to ask how he was going to do that. Instead, I merely nodded and headed to Thistle. "Come on." I dragged her toward Hypnotic, not stopping until we were inside. "We're in big trouble," I announced.

"What else is new?" Thistle didn't look all that worried. Of course, she wasn't privy to the facts from the alley. Well, at least I hoped she wasn't. That would mean word had spread even faster than normal.

"There's a dead guy in the back of the Unicorn Emporium."

"Seriously?" Thistle's eyebrows moved toward her hairline. "Who is it?"

"I have no idea, but that's not our biggest problem."

"There's a bigger problem than a dead guy? Oh, this must be good." She folded her arms across her chest and waited.

"The body is glowing," I supplied.

She waited and scrunched up her nose. "Glowing? How does a body glow?"

"I have no idea, but I guarantee it's not naturally occurring."

"And the television crew saw it?"

"They did."

"Well ... crap." Thistle turned away from the store window. "What are you going to do?"

"I have no idea. It's a mess."

"You could lie."

Was she kidding? "What do you expect me to lie about?"

"Well, was the dead guy murdered?"

"I don't know. I didn't see any marks on his body. I wasn't really looking past the glow." I felt a bit stupid because I hadn't bothered to use my observational skills. That might come back to bite me too.

"Well, if you didn't notice how the victim died, the camera crew probably didn't either." Thistle sounded too pragmatic. I was usually the calm one. Well, for my family, which wasn't exactly saying much. "Just say that the killer made the body glow, and you have no idea how."

I worked my jaw. "Like a calling card of sorts," I mused.

"Yeah."

I considered the suggestion and then started for the door. "You know, people say you're a menace, but you're smarter than they give you credit for."

"Thank you so much for that," she drawled. "What are you going to do?"

"I'm going to get a handle on this situation."

For some reason, that struck Thistle as funny. "You know you're not in charge?"

"No, but I can help Landon."

"Well, good luck with that." Thistle moved to follow, slowing when I narrowed my eyes. "What?"

"Where do you think you're going?" I asked.

"There's no way I'm missing this. I don't want the camera crew here any more than you do, but it will be entertaining to watch you and Landon try to juggle them."

"You could try to help."

"I could, but what fun is that?" Her grin was impish. "It's going to be a mess, from start to finish. You know I love a good mess."

"Just don't add to the mayhem," I warned. "We have enough on our plates, what with a potential murder and a glowing body."

"Yeah, yeah, yeah." Thistle waved her hand in dismissive fashion. "I've got this. You worry about yourself."

I was definitely worried about myself.

When I caught up with Landon, he had the entire camera crew—plus Cady and Carla—grouped around him.

"What makes the body glow?" the blond cameraman asked.

"Why was he killed in the alley like that?" a young woman with waist-length blond hair queried. She barely looked old enough to drink, and her pants were painted on. Her attention was glued to Landon in such a way it made me frown.

"We don't have any answers to those questions yet," Landon replied. His patience was dangling, and when his eyes flicked to me, there was a silent plea.

There was only one thing I could think to do. "I bet the killer did something to the body," I said. "Like, it could be some weird concoction he made to cause the glow. This is a witch town. He's probably trying to point the finger at witches."

Landon blinked several times and then slowly nodded. "The medical examiner will test for outside compounds. There was a smell in the alley."

I hadn't remembered a smell—well, other than the overwhelming smell of death—but I nodded. "I'm sure it will take time to run all the tests."

"Definitely." Landon shot me a grateful look and then dragged a hand through his shoulder-length hair. "Let's get to introductions. I'm Landon Michaels."

"You're the FBI agent who lives in town?" Debbie seemed to be reading notes from her tablet. "I was given a rundown of all the players in town." Her eyes were considering when she lifted her chin. "What's an FBI agent doing in a town this size?"

Landon had answered the question before and didn't look ruffled when pressed again. "My wife runs a business here. I'm stationed out of the Traverse City office but do most of my work remotely. I have to go into the office once a week for meetings and such, but otherwise I run investigations without direct supervision. I use the Hemlock Cove Police Station as my home base."

"Your wife?" The young blonde looked sad at the news. "You're married?"

Landon shot her an amused look. "Happily so. And you are?"

"Maya Goodings." She shot out her hand for Landon to shake. "I'm the assistant to the producer for *Haunted Traditions*."

"She means me," Debbie offered.

Landon shook Maya's hand and then shifted his gaze to the others who had gathered around him. "And everybody else?"

The blond cameraman was Greg Porter. The dark-haired cameraman was Reid Prentiss, and he had a "been there, done that" air about him I found grating. The on-air talent came in the form of Elle Nixon, another blonde, and Falcon Bridger, a guy I was convinced was using a stage name because he was wearing so much makeup it looked like I could run a fingernail down his cheek and leave a visible line.

"We're the whole crew," Debbie offered. "We've been doing this show for almost a year now. We know what we're doing when arriving in a new place."

"Does that include breaking the law?" Landon demanded. "Because that's what happens when you film a dead body."

"That's not against the law," Reid replied, combative. "There was no tape signifying we were crossing into a crime scene. Also, we haven't aired anything yet. We know not to air the face of a dead man."

Landon momentarily narrowed his eyes and then forced a smile. "I think we might've gotten off on the wrong foot."

"We didn't mean to cause problems," Debbie reassured him quickly. She was friendly, but she carried herself like a woman used to getting what she wanted. Something told me that she was ready to go toe to toe with Landon if need be. "We were excited when we saw the hoopla. It's rare that we show up on a scene and have a ready-made murder mystery waiting for us."

"This is going to be the best episode ever because of that," Maya enthused. Her eyes were still on Landon, and I wanted to punch her in her lady bits to wipe that stupid look off her face. "Like, the absolute best episode ever. Right?" She looked to Debbie for confirmation.

"As much as I don't like saying things like that before we've even started editing, I can't disagree." Debbie beamed at her. "I knew when we got the application for this place that we'd hit pure gold. I had no idea it was going to pay off so quickly."

One word jumped out at me, and I focused on Debbie. "Application?"

She took a moment to look me up and down. "People nominate their towns. This town was nominated almost three months ago. Our team took a few weeks to research it, but it was glaringly obvious that we were going to love this place ... and so far, it's proving to be the best decision ever."

"Who nominated Hemlock Cove?" I demanded. There was a sharp edge to my voice that probably wasn't necessary.

"I'm afraid we're not at liberty to say," Debbie replied. "I didn't get your name."

"My name doesn't matter."

Landon shot me a sidelong look. There was worry there, but he didn't prod me to play nice with the television crew. "I understand that you've already procured the proper permits to film here," he started. "The information was passed on to us when the permits were issued. That does not, however, mean you have free rein in the town. You have to follow privacy laws."

"Yeah, dude, we know how it goes," Greg said. He had a laid-back air about him that I would've found comforting under different circumstances. I was predisposed to hate all of them, however, and that included him. "We're not going to break the law. That's not how this works."

"How does it work?" I asked.

Debbie was back to looking at her tablet. When she finally lifted her eyes, there was a smug smile on her face. "You're Bay Winchester, correct?"

How could she possibly know that? "I don't ... who told you that?" I knew I sounded accusatory, but I couldn't seem to get a handle on my emotions.

"That would be me," a familiar voice said from behind me. I didn't have to turn to see who was talking. I would recognize that voice anywhere.

"Mrs. Little." My shoulders were squared when I turned. "I'm guessing you submitted the application for Hemlock Cove."

She didn't look ashamed in the least when she bobbed her head. In fact, she looked a little too proud of herself. "As one of the town's leading representatives, it's my job to help promote Hemlock Cove. We are a tourism town, after all, and with winter coming, we need all the attention we can get until spring."

I could think of a few other ways to get attention. None of them were the sort of things Mrs. Little would embrace. "Can I talk to you?" I gritted out. I didn't wait for her answer, grabbing her elbow and dragging her back into her store.

"Bay," Landon called after me. He sounded worried.

"I've got it," I snapped before letting the Unicorn Emporium's heavy door fall shut. "What were you even thinking?" I demanded as I glared at her.

Mrs. Little looked smug. "Whatever do you mean, dear? I'm just trying to do what's right for Hemlock Cove."

She was full of it. We both knew it. Worse, I knew darned well she wasn't done. "What did you tell them?" I growled.

"Just the truth. We're a town of witches. Ghosts roam our streets regularly. Magic is all around." Anybody who wasn't familiar with her special brand of mayhem would think her smile was sweet and genuine.

"You pointed them to us, didn't you?" I didn't need her answer.

"I told them all about the town," Mrs. Little replied. "The application was quite thorough. I could hardly leave your family out. You are the premier inn in Hemlock Cove, after all. They want the full experience."

"They're booked at The Overlook." It made sense. "Did you bother to tell my mother and aunts a film crew was booking the reservations?"

"Why would I do that?" Mrs. Little was the picture of innocence. "Money is money, right? I helped your mother's little inn. You should thank me."

My stomach constricted. I'd thought it was weird when my mother explained that every room had been rented out after the fall leaf tours had ended. The Overlook was the most popular inn Hemlock Cove had to offer. It hadn't even occurred to me that the television crew was taking over the rooms.

"What do you hope to accomplish?" I asked as I crossed my arms. "What do you think is going to happen?"

"I think *Haunted Traditions* is going to film an outstanding episode, and we're going to be inundated with visitors. That's good for all of us, isn't it?"

I hated her. Like, truly hated her. She was an evil woman, one Aunt

Tillie had gone out of her way to save weeks earlier. It was so Mrs. Little to come at us like this after we'd saved her life.

"I'm not just going to sit back and let you do this," I warned, darting a look out the window and finding Landon watching me with overt worry. "I won't let you win."

"Win?" Mrs. Little chuckled. "I have no idea what you're even getting at. It's not a competition. Their presence means we all win."

I was furious. "We've been keeping Aunt Tillie on a leash the past few weeks. You know, after you had that horrible string of bad luck. We didn't want to add to your woes." The way Mrs. Little's eyes narrowed indicated she understood. "Perhaps it's time to let her off that leash."

"Is that a threat?" Mrs. Little demanded.

I used to play nice with her for the sake of the newspaper and the town. I was beyond that now. "Take it however you want. Just remember, you've never won a single game when we were your opponent. You won't win this time either."

"That definitely sounds like a threat," Mrs. Little growled. "Perhaps I'll file a police report."

"You're more than welcome to do that." I reached for the glass door. "Just remember, we've always exerted a modicum of control over Aunt Tillie when she comes for you. What do you think will happen without that restraint?"

Fear momentarily flashed in Mrs. Little's eyes, but she recovered quickly. "You want to be very careful, Bay," she warned. "I'm in the position of power this time. You need to recognize that."

"Uh-huh." I pushed open the door. "I guess I'll be seeing you soon."

"I guess you will."

Five

"Please tell me you didn't curse her." Landon pulled me away from the group. The television crew was excitedly talking about the establishment shots of the town they needed. They didn't seem interested in us in the slightest. Well, except for Maya. She tracked Landon with her eyes, and it was obvious she liked what she saw.

"Not yet," I replied, dragging a hand through my hair. This day had gone off the rails in spectacular fashion.

"What did she say?"

I filled him in.

"Well, you can't be surprised, Bay." He used his most reasonable tone. "It was only a matter of time until she pulled something like this."

How could he be so calm? "Do you want to know where they're staying?" I gritted out.

He stilled. "Please tell me it's the Dragonfly."

My father and uncles—Clove and Thistle's fathers—owned The Dragonfly, located a few miles from The Overlook. "We're not that lucky," I replied. "Mrs. Little told the crew The Overlook was the premier inn in the area."

"I'll bet that's not all she told them." Landon slid a dark gaze in the direction of Mrs. Little's store. She was watching us and offered a happy wave in response. "I'm so glad we went out of our way to save her life two weeks ago. That doesn't feel like a mistake in hindsight or anything."

I blew out a sigh. "I'm not sorry for saving her life." That was mostly true. "I just wish she wasn't such a horrible person."

Landon brushed my hair from my face with gentle fingers. "What do you want to do?"

"What can we do?"

"We can fake a gas leak and force them to move to another inn."

Now that was an idea. Unfortunately, I couldn't get behind it. "I don't think my mother will go for that. They booked the entire inn. That's big money, and right before the dead season."

"I get it, but there are more important things."

"Yeah." I rolled my neck and slid my attention to Thistle as she joined us. "We have a problem," I announced.

"Aunt Tillie has always been a problem," Thistle replied dryly. "I can't believe you're just now noticing it."

"Don't start." I wasn't in the mood for Thistle's brand of sarcastic wit. "They're staying at the inn."

"Oh." Realization dawned on Thistle, and she nodded. "That makes sense. We wondered who would book the entire inn when the color season is dead. I guess that answers that."

"Mrs. Little encouraged them. She actually brought them here."

"You can't be surprised." Thistle let loose a short bark of laughter. "I can't believe we didn't figure out it was her before today."

"That doesn't change the fact that we're in trouble," I insisted. "It's not just the magic, although that's a concern. We have Aunt Tillie's pot —she has way more plants than allowed by law—and her still. We can't allow any of that to be filmed."

"Huh. I hadn't considered that." Thistle rolled her shoulders. "What do you want to do?"

"I'm going to start by talking to my mother." I was grim at the prospect. "Maybe we can convince her to forego the money and send them off to another inn."

Thistle's snort was full of doubt. "And when that doesn't work?"

"I thought we could ward the greenhouse and search the inn for contraband."

"Who is this 'we' you're speaking of?"

I merely waited.

"Ugh. Fine." Thistle threw her hands in the air. "I'll close the store and call Clove. She might still be out there with the baby. If we have to run around like crazy people to protect the family, then she has to help. That baby is no longer a get-out-of-jail card."

"I don't care who helps; it has to be done," I said. I turned back to Landon. "Will you keep me in the loop as to what's going on with the dead guy?"

Landon nodded as he leaned forward to kiss my forehead. It wasn't lost on me that Maya was watching ... and seemed downright depressed about the situation. "I'll be in touch regardless. Focus on what you have to do for right now. I'll handle the other stuff."

I nodded. "Okay. Good luck."

"Funny, I was just going to say the same to you."

I HIT THE FRONT LOBBY OF THE OVERLOOK on a dead run from the parking lot. I practically skidded to a stop in front of the check-in desk when I realized my mother was already there.

"Did you know the television crew was staying with us?" I demanded.

My mother wasn't the sort to melt down over trivial things, and there was no doubt she considered the crew's lodging precisely that when she started laughing. "Are you about to get dramatic?" she complained.

I stilled. "Did you know?"

"Not until this morning when they checked in," Mom replied. Her tone told me she wasn't going to put up with what she considered "emotional nonsense" and served as a warning that I should tread lightly. "They showed up about ten minutes after you left for town. They seem like lovely people."

Of course she would think that. "Mother, they'll have cameras on the property."

"I know. I signed the release."

My heart skipped. "You signed a release?" Despite my best efforts, my voice was dripping with accusatory disgust.

"Do you have a problem with that?"

There was warning in her tone, but that didn't stop me. "So very many problems." The sound of footsteps behind me served as a warning that we were no longer alone. Thistle had joined us. "Mother, do you have any idea what could happen to us if they film the wrong moment?"

"What are they going to film, Bay?" Mom crossed her arms over her chest. "Also, I hate when you call me Mother. It's as if you want to tack on another word after it, and I don't appreciate that."

"I don't appreciate you signing a release for a television crew to film on the property without talking to me."

"Last time I checked, it was my property. We allow you to live in the guesthouse—for less than half the rent we could get from a stranger. On top of that, we feed your husband. He doesn't eat like a normal person."

I refused to acknowledge that she had a point. "Mom." I used my most reasonable tone. "Have you considered what's in the greenhouse?"

"Plants?" Mom's forehead wrinkled.

"I think she means the pot and still," Thistle replied, speaking for the first time. "Aunt Tillie has more plants than are legal, and the still is totally against the law."

"And yet weirdly a police chief and an FBI agent are aware of both and have never done a thing about it," Mom mused. "How very weird."

I wanted to hurt someone. Mrs. Little was tops on my list. "You'll be putting them in a terrible position," I argued. "It's one thing for them to look the other way when it's just us. It's quite another for the information to be broadcast on national television. They could get in trouble for letting it go. Do you really think Landon's boss is aware that he's been ignoring Aunt Tillie's extracurricular activities?"

Mom barely took a breath before responding. "I've met that man. Something tells me he's well aware that Aunt Tillie doesn't follow the rules."

She was killing me. I balled my hands into fists and rested them on the counter. "Were you aware that Mrs. Little brought them to town?

She nominated Hemlock Cove and directed them to us as the premier inn."

Mom stilled. Hope coursed through me. Would it be enough to change her mind? Apparently not, because after a few seconds of contemplation, Mom started shaking her head.

"That doesn't matter," she said. "They're paying good money to stay here. Besides, everybody in town pretends to be witches. It's a good thing."

"Not everybody in town is a real witch," I reminded her.

"Well, you could always limit your time visiting the inn," she suggested primly. "You could cook for your own husband for a week or something. You know, do something wild."

I wanted to laugh ... and then maybe cry. "Mom—"

"It's done." The way her eyes narrowed told me she wasn't going to listen to a word I said. "They're staying here, Bay. I understand if you feel the need to adjust your visits this week. I can't make decisions for you, just like you can't make decisions for me."

I glanced at Thistle to gauge her response. She didn't look surprised. "I guess that means we need to commit to Plan B."

"Yup." Thistle was grim as she nodded. "I'll hit the family living quarters."

"I'll hit the greenhouse." I scuffed my shoes against the floor as I headed for the door. "Is Clove here?"

"She is," Mom confirmed. "She's taking a nap in the library though. Marnie is watching the baby."

"I guess we should let her sleep."

"I should think so. She's a new mother. She needs to get her rest wherever she can."

"Great. I'll handle the greenhouse on my own."

"Do whatever you want." Mom's tone was deceptively breezy. I recognized a warning was coming my way. "Just remember, this is my inn. You don't have a vote in how we operate."

"I'm well aware, Mother."

"Keep it up, and I really will make you cook for Landon. You'll be crying by the time I'm done."

"Whatever you say, Mother."

. . .

I WAS UNBELIEVABLY CRABBY AS I STOMPED out to the greenhouse. My phone dinged with an incoming call right after I escaped the inn, and I put Landon on speaker as I began tackling protection wards on the greenhouse.

"My mother is impossible," I said by way of greeting. "Absolutely impossible."

"You're on speakerphone, Bay," Landon warned in a tired voice.

"So are you."

"I'm with Chief Terry."

"I'm alone, but I'm in the mood for a good rant."

"It had better not be about your mother," Chief Terry warned. "That woman is a saint."

"You're just saying that because she's giving you regular sex," I said with a frown. "Also, I don't ever want you to confirm the sex thing. I'm fine throwing out snarky comments, but you should never acknowledge that fact."

"Hey, if I have to listen to Landon plan nooners in your office, then you can suck it up." Chief Terry sounded like he was having a rough day. It was rare for him to snap at me. As much as he loved my mother, I'd carved out a special place in his heart as a child. He doted on me, though the tide was beginning to turn in my mother's favor.

"Way to go, Landon," I muttered. "I'm getting punished, and it's all your fault."

"Somebody's in a foul mood," Landon noted. "I take it things didn't go well with your mother."

"Not even a little." I threw down the first ward line, an anchoring green line of magic that raced around the perimeter of the greenhouse flaring to life. "She said she didn't know our guests were the film crew until they showed up this morning, which was apparently ten minutes after I left—not that I think that would've mattered. When I explained that this was all part of some master plan on Mrs. Little's part, do you know what she said?"

"I have a feeling I know," Chief Terry replied. "I don't think we need it spelled out."

I barreled forward as if I hadn't heard him. "She said that she didn't care, and if I was truly upset about it, I could stay away from the inn for the week and feed my husband myself."

"Hey, I didn't do anything," Landon complained.

I stilled, the purple ward line I'd thrown on top of the green pulsing hot. "Is that a dig?"

"Oh, baby, you know that I love you beyond reason," Landon whined. "You're a talented individual, on almost every front."

"But?" I prodded.

"But you missed out on the kitchen gene."

The sound of a hand smacking against a head on the other end of the call was obvious. Chief Terry had obviously delivered the cuff.

"She's a beautiful girl, and you should thank your lucky stars she lowered herself to marry you," Chief Terry barked.

"That's what I said," Landon complained.

This conversation was getting us nowhere. "Thistle is checking the house for anything that needs to be hidden. I'm hoping that includes Aunt Tillie's gun and any other weird stuff she might have."

"And what are you doing, light of my life?" Landon drawled. He was clearly trying to get me to forget he'd called my kitchen abilities into question.

"I'm handling the greenhouse." I tugged on a purple ward line and snapped it into place. "I don't know what else to do besides keep the film crew out of the greenhouse. It's cold out, and there's no reason for them to be out on the property, but that might not stop them, so I'm adding some extra layers of protection." I started drawing the final ward line.

"Smart," Chief Terry said. "You're a genius. I've always thought so."

"Stop cozying up to my wife," Landon growled. "Your girlfriend is the reason my wife is so upset right now."

"No, Margaret Little is the reason Bay's upset," Chief Terry countered. "Unfortunately, there's very little we can do about that because Margaret is ... well, Margaret. She looked positively giddy when I saw her talking to the television crew ten minutes ago."

"She thinks she's won," I said. "In a way, she has. This is a decisive victory for her, and it's totally going to screw us before it's all said and done."

"That's the spirit, baby," Landon offered. "Way to look at the bright side of things."

I ignored him. "I'll have to unleash Aunt Tillie on her," I said. "It's the only thing that will distract her. Plus, if the action is happening at Mrs. Little's store, the television crew won't be focused on the inn."

"Are you sure that's a good idea?" Landon asked. "If you do that, won't Mrs. Little melt down and accuse you guys of whatever happens?"

"Maybe, but it's better than them seeing what's really happening out here."

Landon was quiet a moment, then let out a breath. "We called for a reason. The medical examiner has the body. We still don't have an ID. The medical examiner has no idea what caused the glow, but he sounds excited at the prospect of running tests."

I felt sick to my stomach. "He's going to run a million tests, none of which will turn up positive." I cast one more look around the greenhouse and then moved to the door. I'd done what I could do. I could only hope the wards would be strong enough to keep the television crew away from the structure.

"There's nothing we can do about that now, Bay," Landon said. "If it goes down as a medical mystery, so be it."

"I guess." I pressed the heel of my hand to my forehead as the blast of cold hit my face. "Man, this really sucks. All I want to do is climb under a blanket in front of the fireplace and hide until they go away."

Landon said, "We can still cuddle in front of the fireplace. We'll get takeout. There's no need for you to cook."

"I've got it, Landon." Irritation bubbled up. I rarely wanted to fight with him, but I was in the mood today. "You don't have to keep hammering it home. I'm a terrible cook. I get it."

"Bay, that's not what I was saying." He sounded petulant. "Don't turn this into a thing."

"Whatever. I... " A shadow appeared on the ground in front of me. It took the shape of a man—a big man—but there was a problem: there was no sun in the sky to cast a shadow. "What in the hell?"

The shadow moved toward me, a weird feral growl emanating from it. I took a step back all the same.

"What is that?" Chief Terry demanded. "Did you guys get a dog or something?"

When I saw the shadow separate from the ground and become corporeal, I scrambled back to the greenhouse. I figured I would be safe on the other side of the wards, but a black hand grabbed my shoulder and spun me around before that same hand wrapped around my throat.

I gasped when my air supply was cut off and dropped my phone as I put all my effort into fighting the shadow.

Landon's voice was full of panic as he called my name.

"You need to stay away," the creature rasped as it shook me. "You need to die."

With more force than should've been possible, the creature slammed my head into the greenhouse frame. Darkness encroached on my vision as I sank to the ground. A voice inside my head warned me not to pass out, because I would likely never wake up.

It was too late, though. I had no control when the light disappeared, and the darkness overwhelmed me.

Six

I wasn't completely out. My mind kept firing, and I could make out movement around the dim edges of consciousness. The shadow paced in front of me, and after several minutes filled with dread that seemed to drag out, the sound of voices near the inn forced it to flee.

I floated a bit. I heard talking—they were close and yet far away at the same time—and I knew I should call out.

Thistle ultimately found me. She yelled for help from the inn. Twila was the first to join her, and their conversation was almost enough to overcome the cloudiness threatening to drag me under.

Almost.

"I think she's putting on an act for the television crew," Twila offered as Thistle tried to pull me to a sitting position.

"Why would she do that?" Thistle barked.

"Because it's a surefire way to get attention. It's on my list too. I can't believe Bay went this route. I could see Clove doing it, because she's so emotionally needy and adept at faking tears, but not Bay. Wait ... you don't think she saw my list, do you? I don't want her stealing all my ideas."

"I guarantee Bay isn't stealing your ideas for attracting the film crew's attention," Thistle snapped.

More footsteps had me trying to will myself to full consciousness, but I couldn't open my eyes or mind.

"What happened?" I recognized my mother's voice. "Did she fall?"

"I don't think so," Thistle replied. "Landon called. He said he thought something happened to her in the greenhouse. He was on the phone with her when it happened. I figured she was just melting down because that's what she does, but I headed out to check and found her like this."

"On the ground?" Mom's hand landed on my forehead. "She's hot."

"She has a fever?" Thistle sounded frustrated. "I don't understand. She must have been leaving the greenhouse when something went down. The wards have been set to keep the film crew out. So ... what happened?"

"I don't know." Mom sounded only mildly worried. "We need to get her inside, so we can treat her."

"I suppose you want me to somehow get her into the inn," Thistle drawled.

"That would be great."

Thistle grumbled as she grabbed me under my arms and began dragging me to the inn.

"You need to lay off the bacon with your stupid husband," she complained. "You guys are ridiculous with the food. There's a reason Aunt Winnie isn't worried about you following through on your threat to stay away from the inn while those TV people are here. She knows you're incapable of feeding yourself."

Thistle got me to the back door before pausing for a breath.

"It would be great if you woke up now, Bay." Her voice threatened to crack. "I need you to start bossing me around like you usually do. I mean ... that's your favorite thing to do. How about you give it a shot?" She waited and then sighed. "This is so freaking weird. I'm totally going to melt down and start yelling at you. You've been warned."

I floated again, partially aware of what was happening. Once she got me in the family living quarters, Twila helped her put me on the couch. The familiar scents of home surrounded me, and I became more alert.

And then I heard him. Landon. He'd arrived ... and he didn't sound happy.

"Where is she?"

"She's on the couch." Mom intercepted him from the sound of it, which was to be expected. He could steamroll just about anybody but her. "We found her on the ground by the greenhouse. We're still trying to figure out what happened."

"She can't tell you?" Landon sounded as if he was going through a forced twenty-four-hour marathon of the Kardashians, and it was about to take over his life. "Let me see her."

His hands were warm when they brushed over my face. "Baby, can you open your eyes for me?" he asked after several seconds of stroking my hair. "Come on, Bay. It's time to wake up." More silence. "What happened to her?" he demanded.

"I just told you we're not sure," Mom said. "She was in the greenhouse because ... well, because she was whining like a little kid. I told her if she didn't want to be around the film crew, she could stay away from the inn for the week and feed you herself."

Landon growled. "She saw something right before it happened. I was on the phone with her. It wasn't your decision to choose the film crew over her that caused this."

"It could've been the film crew," I said, finding my voice. "That would serve her right."

I felt Landon's surprise, and then suddenly there was warm breath on my face. "Bay?"

Slowly, I opened my eyes. I was no longer lost in my own body. I was alert and aware ... and like a zoo animal on display as almost everybody in my family leaned over me staring.

"She looks like she's alive," Clove announced. She had Calvin in her arms, lightly patting his back. "That's good, right?"

"No, Clove, we would prefer she be dead," Thistle shot back. "Are you stupid?"

"I was just asking." Clove's tone was shrill. "Why do you always have to be so mean?"

"Because I'm forced to shepherd you through life. Of course I'm mean, you moron."

"Shut up!" Mom snapped. "Both of you." When she regarded me, there was an ingratiating smile on her face. "Would you like a cookie?"

In any other house, the question might've seemed strange. We were a food-oriented family, however. "Um..."

"The cookie can wait," Landon said. "I want to know what happened." He lifted my arm to study it. "Did you hit your head?"

The image of the shadow popped to the forefront of my brain. "There was something out there."

"Was it Bigfoot?" Clove demanded. "What?" She shrank in the face of my mother's fury. "It's only a matter of time."

"It wasn't Bigfoot," I replied, struggling to prop myself up on the couch.

Landon lifted me forward and slid in behind me, his chest warm against my back as he rubbed my arms. "First, tell me you're okay and that I don't need to get you to the hospital," he instructed.

"I'm fine."

"Are you just saying that because you don't want to go to the hospital?"

"I'm saying it because it's true. I'm good. A little confused, but mostly good."

"Okay." He patiently moved my hair away from my neck so he could rest his chin on my shoulder and press his cheek against mine. "Tell me what happened."

"I was on the phone with you."

"I know."

"I was mad ... and ranting ... and then I saw a shadow when I left the greenhouse. It belonged to a man except ... there was no sun."

It took a moment for everybody in the room to understand.

"Why is that important?" Twila asked Thistle in a stage whisper.

Okay, clearly *everybody* in the room didn't get it.

"Aunt Marnie will explain later," Thistle muttered.

"No, I won't," Marnie said.

Landon ignored them. "Did the shadow attack you?"

"It was two-dimensional at first," I said. "It was flat on the ground. Then it wasn't. It was three dimensional, and it was already coming at me. I tried to retreat inside the greenhouse because I figured the wards would protect me."

Landon's lips pressed against my temple. "Did it hit you?"

"That part's a little fuzzy. I think it grabbed me around the neck. I didn't have time to react."

Landon studied my neck. "She's going to have bruises." His tone was accusatory.

"We've got mugwort," Mom reassured him.

"We don't want the film crew to see strangulation marks on her neck," Thistle agreed. "They'll assume Landon is an abuser ... or into some really freaky stuff in the bedroom."

"It's not funny!" Landon barked.

"Landon..." I groped for his hand.

"Shh." He rubbed his cheek against mine. "It's okay. I'm going to take care of you."

I wasn't certain what to say to make him feel better. I knew him well enough to recognize the only thing that was going to placate him was good food and eight hours wrapped around me in our bed, the rest of the world locked out.

"Did it say anything?" Thistle asked, directing the conversation back to something constructive. "The shadow, I mean."

"It warned me that I shouldn't be here and said that I had to die."

"Oh, well, that's great," Clove drawled. "Who doesn't love a shadow that makes threats?"

"Stop being a kvetch," Mom warned, channeling her inner Aunt Tillie. "Not that I'm not happy that you're alive, but if you were already down, Bay, why didn't the shadow finish you?"

"Don't put that thought in my head," Landon hissed. "I'm already freaking out."

"Will rosemary chicken make you feel better?" Mom asked. "That's on the menu for dinner."

Landon hesitated and then shook his head. "Food will not fix this."

Everyone snorted in unison.

"I'm serious," he insisted. "Some things are more important than food."

"Bay is fine," Mom reminded him. "She's a little dazed, but she can rest on the couch here until dinner. She won't even have to risk the film crew seeing her. It will be fine."

"You know what would be better than fine?" Landon challenged. "You could send the film crew somewhere else. That would be better for all of us, especially Bay."

"I'm not doing that." Mom's tone practically dared Landon to keep pushing. "They're staying here. If you don't like it, you don't have to visit."

"Right." Landon sounded genuinely disgruntled. "This family is way too codependent to go that long without seeing each other, and you know it."

"Sounds like you've already come to grips with what's to come." Mom was all smiles as she sat in the chair and met my gaze. "Why do you think the shadow didn't kill you?"

"I don't..." I broke off when I thought about what had happened with a clearer head. "Where exactly did you find me?"

"In the greenhouse doorway," Thistle replied. "I didn't immediately see you because you were in a shadow. You weren't moving, and I thought maybe you were dead."

"Do you have to say things like that?" Landon complained. "I'm already going to have nightmares."

I patted his hand. "I'm okay. I also think I know why it couldn't hurt me."

"Because you're a superwitch, and your magic is far superior to his magic?" Landon asked hopefully.

"Kind of. Well, in theory." I gave him a reassuring smile. "I think I fell back into the area the wards covered. He couldn't reach me and wasn't strong enough to break them. My magic did protect me ... at least for the most part."

"It was a fluke," Mom mused.

I nodded. "But I'm still alive."

Mom smiled. "What should we do about the shadow?"

"I don't know. I don't think it's a coincidence that it showed up in the aftermath of a glowing dead body."

"That would be difficult to imagine," Landon agreed. "We still don't have a name on the dead guy."

"And there's very little we can do until we know who died," I said. "We're stuck."

"It's hardly the first time," Thistle said. "We'll figure it out."

She sounded more certain than I felt. Still, I didn't say anything. Instead, I closed my eyes. "I think I'll take that cookie now."

"Of course." Mom was already on her feet. "You'll rest in here until dinner. Landon, you can go back to work. We'll keep an eye on her."

Landon balked. "Um ... I'm not leaving her."

"Do what you want, but if your dead guy has something to do with Bay's attack, the faster you find out who he is, the faster we can knock out any threat."

Landon cursed under his breath, but he ultimately gave in. After kissing my temple again, he got to his feet. "You'd better keep a firm eye on her. If something happens, I'll hold it against you forever."

"I love it when you threaten me," Mom drawled. "It makes me feel all warm and fuzzy inside." She lightly rapped her knuckles against the side of his head. "Do you really think we'd let anything happen to her?"

"I just ... feel the need to make sure she's covered." Landon squared his shoulders. "She's my wife. It's my job to protect her."

Multiple groans reverberated through the room.

"Fine, she usually has to protect me," Landon conceded. "I love her. I was already freaked out because of the glowing body. A shadow that can attack on this property doesn't fill me with happy thoughts."

"He has a point," Thistle noted. "If the shadow is responsible for the dead guy, how did it know to come out here so fast?"

"That's just another question to consider," Mom said. "For now, Landon, you need to give it a rest. We'll take care of Bay. You're free to return to work."

"You're still having chicken?" Landon pressed. "I don't want to tell you your business, but chicken is the ideal food when you've been attacked by a shadow."

Mom's smile was soft. "I'm still making rosemary chicken. It will be ready when you return from work, as will Bay, who will be napping here the rest of the afternoon."

I thought about arguing but saw no point. I was tired, and there were no angles to chase until we had more information.

"Keep her safe," Landon instructed. His eyes were full of concern as he leaned over me. "Do what your mother says, okay? I want you to rest."

"I plan on resting." I meant it. "See if you can get an identity on that body. As soon as I'm done resting, I want to start chasing that story."

"I'm on it." He gave me a kiss and then left me with the rest of my family.

"Are you really going to nap?" Thistle asked. She seemed surprised when I nodded. "That thing must've taken more out of you than you let on in front of Landon."

"I'm just going to take a nap. I'll be fine in a few hours."

Thistle hesitated and then nodded. "I'll handle the rest of Aunt Tillie's contraband. It shouldn't take long."

"Good. I don't want to hand the film crew ammunition on a platter."

I closed my eyes as my family drifted away. I thought I might doze a bit, but I fell into a deep dreamless sleep, to the point I felt like a slug when I woke several hours later and found Aunt Tillie watching me from the end of the couch.

"Where have you been?" I demanded, frowning at my rusty voice. I almost sounded sick.

"I've been around," she replied. "Your mother told me what happened in the greenhouse. I went out there but couldn't find anything. Nice wards, though. You're getting better. Not as good as me, mind you, but better."

I pinned her with a dark look. "Do you have to go there? I'm not quite up to a competition."

"I guess it can wait." She looked thoughtful. "I followed the film crew most of the day. They're poking their noses into every corner of town."

"Mrs. Little is responsible for bringing them here." I was still angry about that. "She's such a psycho."

"Under different circumstances, I would remind you that she's only here because we saved her. We could've been rid of her."

I glared at her. "I'm not in the mood."

"I'm just saying." Aunt Tillie rubbed her hands over the knees of her leggings. They were the faux leather Spanx she'd been wearing on and off the past two weeks. She claimed they gave her the butt of a supermodel. I was convinced they gave her the butt of a supermodel's grandmother, but I didn't tell her that.

"Is something wrong?" I propped myself on one elbow. "Has something happened?"

"No, I'm just thinking." Aunt Tillie shook her head. "I've never heard of a two-dimensional shadow turning into a three-dimensional attacker. It's weird."

"I concur."

"I'm going to have to do some research."

"Okay. Is anything else wrong?"

"I'm thinking of infiltrating the film crew."

"What does that mean?"

"They're looking for a star, and I think it should be me."

My heart skipped. "You should stay as far away from the film crew as possible."

"We're going to have to agree to disagree."

"Aunt Tillie." I frowned as she headed to the door that led to the kitchen. "Don't do whatever you're planning. The smart move is to lay low while they're here."

"Since when have I ever done the smart thing?"

I hated that she had a point. "This could blow up in our faces."

"It could, or we could totally thwart Margaret's attempt to ruin us and make her look like an idiot."

Tempting as it was, I didn't embrace the possibility. "Let's just be quiet, huh? It's best for all of us."

"I'll do what I want to do."

"Of course you will." I flopped back on the couch and pinched the bridge of my nose. "I knew this was going to be a disaster as soon as I heard they were coming to town."

"I've got this," Aunt Tillie promised. "You don't have to worry about me. I've got everything under control."

That was ludicrous, and yet there was nothing I could do to stop her. "My life is about to suck," I complained to nobody in particular.

"On that we can agree." Aunt Tillie's smile was impish. "This is going to be a busy week. You should start drinking protein shakes now."

"Yeah, I'll get right on that."

Seven

I splashed some water on my face and ran a brush through my hair before joining the group in the dining room. Landon and Chief Terry hadn't arrived, so I stuck to the outskirts and did my best not to frown as the film crew excitedly talked about the footage they'd collected during the day.

"The footage we've already shot is unbelievably cool," Maya enthused. She had a glass of wine in her hand and kept bobbing her head as Debbie praised the cameramen. "This is going to be an amazing week."

"It is," Elle agreed. She sat in one of the chairs and kicked out her feet. "Plus, there are quite a few hot guys in this town. Did you see the guy at the stable? Wowza."

Wowza? Who said that? Since the "guy at the stable" could only be Thistle's live-in boyfriend, Marcus, I couldn't see this conversation going anywhere good. When I flicked my eyes to Aunt Tillie, who had taken up position at the head of the table, she looked amused.

"Don't worry," she said, not bothering to lower her voice. "Thistle won't be here for dinner. Neither will Clove. They figured it was best to avoid all of ... *this* ... tonight."

At least that was something. I was about to ask if I could avoid it all when the film crew turned in unison to stare at the dining room door as Landon and Chief Terry entered the room.

"Well, isn't this fortuitous," Debbie purred. "Are you here for us? We can delay dinner to set up those interviews we talked about earlier."

"Nobody is doing interviews tonight," Landon replied as he crossed to me. His eyes searched my face. "How are you feeling?" Apparently, he didn't care that all eyes in the room were on us.

"It was a nice nap," I replied. I couldn't very well talk to him about anything important with so many witnesses around. "I'm fine."

He didn't look convinced, but he graced me with a quick kiss anyway. "You're getting a full night's sleep tonight, okay? You still look tired."

I just knew there was an insult buried in there, but he was right. I did feel draggy. "After the chicken."

"Oh, we're OD'ing on chicken," he agreed. "And the garlic mashed potatoes that come with the chicken ... and even those crispy brussels sprouts your mom makes. Come on." He nudged me toward the table. "You could use some juice."

"Is this your wife?" Debbie looked more curious than anything else, but Maya's stare was darker.

"My one and only," Landon confirmed as he left me in my regular chair and headed for the drink cart. "She's not feeling well."

"Do you live here?" Maya looked excited at the prospect.

"We live on the grounds," Landon replied.

"And what about you?" Debbie asked Chief Terry.

"I'm ... here quite often," he replied, looking uneasy. "I don't expect that to change despite your presence."

"He's dedicated to the cook," Landon offered as he slid a glass of orange juice in front of me.

I didn't like the concerned look on his face, so I acquiesced. It also gave me something to focus on.

"Do you have more information on the dead guy?" Falcon asked. He had a conceited air about him, and I knew from minimal interaction that he was going to be one of my least favorite members of the crew.

"Not yet," Chief Terry replied. "Once we've identified him, we'll have to make notification. We won't be releasing his name to the public until after notification has been made. That's standard operating procedure."

"And when do you think that will be?" Debbie asked. "We need to figure out how to plot this one."

I narrowed my eyes. "I thought it was a reality show. Isn't it supposed to be real?"

Everybody at the table who wasn't related to me laughed.

"So adorable," Elle crooned. "I can see why you fell for her," she said to Landon. "She's utterly adorable."

Landon blinked twice and smiled. "She's my favorite person in the world," he said. "I'm with her on this one. How can you plot a reality show?"

"'Plot' probably isn't the right word," Debbie conceded. "It's more that we need to think about editing the episode ahead of time. There's more that goes into a reality show than just filming. It's probably above your head."

I slid my eyes to Landon and found a muscle working in his jaw. "I think she just said you're stupid," I noted.

"I picked up on that," he agreed, stroking the back of my head. "We'll leave as soon as dinner is over. We'll take dessert home and eat it in bed."

It was the best offer I'd had all day.

"I wasn't calling you stupid," Debbie replied quickly, concern lining her eyes. "Far from it. I just ... um ... it's difficult to explain."

"I think Agent Michaels is trying to be difficult," Greg said. He also had a glass of wine, though he hadn't yet touched it. "He knows you weren't trying to insult him, but he wants to be insulted, so he'll find a reason to pick you apart."

"Yes, that sounds just like me," Landon agreed.

Chief Terry sat on the other side of me, serving as a protective wall of sorts. It was his normal spot, but he was somehow making himself bigger and there was only one reason he would bother. "I think you guys are going to be disappointed. We're not working on your schedule."

"Don't worry about us," Elle said. I didn't know her, but I had to wonder if she was already tipsy. She was drinking Aunt Tillie's wine, so it was a definite possibility. "We always get our story."

"Awesome," Landon drawled. His hand moved to my back. He and Chief Terry had essentially built an electrified fence around me, and they looked keen to protect their territory. "What's your plan for the rest of the week?"

"Well, we only got the downtown area today," Debbie replied. "We have a list of places we want to visit. There's a lighthouse."

Clove's lighthouse, I said to myself.

"There's a bluff out here that's supposed to be fantastical," she continued.

Our bluff.

"Oh, and something called Hollow Creek. Apparently, that place is crawling with ghosts and magic."

How could she possibly know that? I locked gazes with Landon. He was clearly wondering the same thing.

"I'm assuming Margaret Little gave you all these locations," Chief Terry said. "You might want to be careful following her tips. She's been known to exaggerate."

"She's been very helpful." Either Debbie didn't pick up on the thread of irritation weaving throughout the room, or she didn't care. I had a feeling it was the former. Some of the others, however, were definitely reading the room better. "She also pointed us toward some old camp near a lake that's supposed to be haunted. We're going there tomorrow I think."

My stomach constricted until it was nothing more than a ball of fury.

"You're not going to that camp," Landon said.

"We're not?" Now Debbie looked amused. "We have permits signed by Mrs. Little herself. We can visit all public areas in town."

"Well, that might clear you for Hollow Creek, but the other areas aren't covered in your little agreement. The Dandridge—that would be the lighthouse—is privately owned. The bluff is as well. In fact, the family that owns this inn owns the bluff. As for the camp, Bay and I own that, and nobody is going out there."

"Do you have something to hide?" Elle asked. Her demeanor had changed, and even though she wasn't aggressive, there was something forceful about the slope of her shoulders.

"It sure sounds like it," Falcon said. For the first time since I'd sat down, he looked interested in the conversation.

"Do we have something to hide at the old summer camp we bought because we want the land for our eventual home? No," Landon replied. "There are old buildings on that property. They're falling down. They're death traps. I don't want anybody getting hurt on my property."

"We promise not to sue," Greg offered on a predatory smile. He seemed to be the smartest in the group, though that might not be saying much.

"I can't take your word for it," Landon replied. "That's our land, and nobody is allowed out there. That includes you."

"Well, that's disheartening." Debbie sniffed. "I guess we'll have to talk to Mrs. Little again. She suggested we could visit these areas. We thought it was a done deal."

"She doesn't own any of those properties and has no say in it," Landon replied. "The campground is off limits. Consider this your official notification."

"I guess we have to follow your rules then."

"Yup. That's how it goes in Hemlock Cove."

DINNER WAS TENSE mostly from our end. Debbie and her merry band of busybodies had a great time. After three sharp glares from my mother, I stopped being difficult and retreated into myself. As soon as dinner was over, Landon took that as a sign to head out. He took two huge pieces of red velvet cake when we left.

We drove when we otherwise might've walked because he didn't want to risk being in the frigid darkness with a rogue shadow on the loose, and even though I'd been looking forward to the cake, I passed out almost the second my head hit the pillow. If Landon had complaints, I didn't hear them.

The next morning, he was up long before me. He was still in bed, his phone clutched in his hand.

"What are you doing?" I asked as I rubbed the sleep from my eyes.

His gaze was on me the second he realized I was awake. "How do you feel?"

"As if I'm being treated like a child."

He didn't respond.

"I'm fine," I said when it became apparent he was going to make a thing out of it if I didn't appease him. "I was exhausted last night—which explains why I missed out on cake—but I'm feeling a hundred percent this morning."

"Good." He kissed my forehead. "The cake is in the refrigerator. We can have it for breakfast if you want."

"Both pieces?"

The question—and the tone in which I delivered it—made him smile. "Believe it or not, all I wanted to do last night was hold my wife. You were down before I even stowed the cake in the refrigerator, so you might not remember, but I valiantly clung to my beloved all night despite the temptation of cake."

Laughter bubbled up. "Wow. That was a bit dramatic."

"Totally," he agreed. "It's still the truth. I didn't want to eat the cake without you."

"I'm sorry I passed out like that. I was tired."

"Don't be sorry. I want you to rest if you need rest."

"Yeah." I scrubbed my cheek and then glanced at his phone. "Anything?"

"Not yet. I've been thinking, though, is it possible that the increase in meth trade in the area could have something to do with the body glowing like that? I ask because the initial coroner's report said our dead guy had three tattoos on his chest. One was a skull and crossbones."

I blinked several times. "Isn't a skull and crossbones a fairly common tattoo?"

"This one was specific." He held up his phone so I could see the photo he'd been looking at. "See the three lines in the skull's hat? That's a gang tattoo. It's a way for members to recognize each other."

"Huh." That was the sort of thing I would never be able to figure out without him. "How would meth heads make a body glow?"

"That I can't answer. I haven't been near any of those guys for obvious reasons. The only reason we know they've been setting up shop is because you can't keep a secret in Hemlock Cove. Everybody knows everybody else's business. Even though they're technically outside the township limits, they're close enough for people to know what they're up to."

I rested my head against his shoulder. "The timing is convenient, especially if you think this guy was a member of their gang."

"I think that's the reason we haven't been able to ID him yet. He was likely the sort of guy who wanted to stay off the radar."

"Which would explain why he didn't have a wallet on him."

"Pretty much."

"Did you find an unclaimed vehicle in any of the parking spots downtown?"

Landon's grin was lazy. "One of my favorite things about you is how smart you are. I don't have to explain things to you. Ever. You just know how investigations work."

"Is that a no?"

"We haven't found a vehicle ... yet. It's possible, if he was on a motorcycle, somebody else rode it away."

"Right." I pursed my lips, debating. "Are you going out there to question them?" I asked.

"That's not my first choice. I don't want them to know we're aware of their existence."

"It might come across as suspicious if you ignore them," I pointed out. "If they expect you to come but you don't, that might make them suspicious of any newcomers."

"Like Kevin."

"Yeah, like Kevin ... the guy nowhere near as hot as you."

Landon chuckled before digging his fingers into my side to tickle me. "You know the way to my heart, don't you?"

"Through your ego. I won't ever make the mistake of not feeding your ego."

"Ha, ha." His smile faded as we got comfortable again. "Are you sure you're okay, Bay? That shadow thing was freaky. I don't even know how to combat something like that."

"I'm fine," I reassured him. "I'm also prepared should it happen again. I won't be caught off guard a second time."

"I hope that's true. I want you to be careful."

"I plan to be. But I have a question."

He stiffened beside me. "Oh, you're using that tone."

"What tone?"

"The 'Bay is going to do something I hate' tone."

"I don't have a tone."

"You're a Winchester. You totally have a tone. More than one, in fact. It must be genetic."

"So is that whining thing you do."

"I don't whine."

"Uh-huh." I traced my fingers over his bare chest. "So, I do have an idea."

"Here we go." He didn't pull away but there was a stern look in his eyes.

"I was thinking, since you can't check out the meth dealers that maybe I should."

He was already shaking his head. "Absolutely not."

"Just consider it." I used my softest tone, the one he had no defense against. "At the very least I can get the lay of the land. I might even be able to pick up on any magic roiling around out there."

"What if they realize what you're doing?"

I shrugged. "They'll realize regardless. Why not put it out there?"

"Because it will give me an ulcer."

"I can take care of myself."

"I know." His sigh was heavy as he rubbed his forehead. "You're actually pretty good at it. But meth heads, Bay, are wily animals. You'd think they'd be stupid because of all the brain cells they've fried, but they're paranoid and come across as geniuses sometimes."

"You're worried." It wasn't a question.

"I am."

"Does that mean you don't want me to go?"

"What will happen if I ask you not to go?"

I hesitated. "Um ... I honestly don't know. I haven't gotten that far yet. Tell me if you want me to go, and I'll give you a response."

"I don't want you to go, but I think you'll go anyway." He took a long moment to think. "You're strong," he said. "Heck, you're the strongest person I know and then some. I have faith that you'll do what needs to be done, and that includes protecting yourself."

"Then you're okay with me going?"

He held his hands palms out. "You're the witch of my dreams, Bay. I'm not here to dictate to you. If you could call me when you're done, that would be great. I'll worry less when I know you're no longer around those guys."

"I can do that." I was quiet for several seconds "Is this us compromising again?" I asked when his grin expanded.

"I think it is."

"I like when we compromise."

"I do too." He leaned his cheek against my forehead. "Let's get in the shower and then head to the inn. I want to check on the film crew to make sure they won't get into trouble today."

"You want your bacon."

"That too."

"I could do with a shower ... and maybe a little romance. I mean, if you're feeling up to it."

He shot me a dirty look. "When don't I feel up to it?"

"I was just asking. I mean, you're not the hot stud these days. That mantle has been claimed by another. I just wanted to be sure."

"Keep it up. I'll tie you to the bed all day and prove I'm still the hot stud I always was."

"Is that a threat?"

"It's a promise."

"Well, something to look forward to for tomorrow."

"For the rest of our lives."

Eight

The film crew was already at the dining room table, elbow deep in juice and coffee. Several curious looks flitted our way when we entered the room from the kitchen.

"Do you eat here often?" Debbie asked.

"My wife doesn't cook," Landon replied as he drew out my chair for me. "My mother-in-law loves to cook for me. I'm glad they came as a package deal."

I shot him a dirty look.

"Your wife is too cute to cook," Chief Terry said. He seemed to realize what he'd said when it was too late to take it back. "Wait ... that came out wrong."

"Don't worry." I patted his arm. "I'm not talking to my mother right now anyway. Your secret is safe with me."

"I, on the other hand, might use it to my advantage," Landon mused as he poured me a glass of tomato juice. "Do you think she'll make those maple bacon doughnuts again if I tattle on Terry?"

"Ignore him," I instructed Chief Terry when he started bristling. "He's just trying to get a rise out of you."

"It seems to be working," Debbie noted. Her gaze was solely for me even though Maya and Elle were more interested in Landon. "So, he's not your father?" She gestured to Chief Terry. "That's what you said, if I'm not mistaken. Or perhaps someone else mentioned it last evening. I can't quite recall."

"He's my second father," I countered. "He was there for my entire childhood, and I love him dearly."

"Yes, Terry is definitely lovable," Aunt Tillie drawled from her spot at the head of the table. I knew her well enough to know that trouble was brewing.

"You're up to something," Chief Terry complained as he regarded Aunt Tillie with overt suspicion. "I know you. You're only nice when you want me to look the other way."

"The love comes and goes," Aunt Tillie said. "Right now, it's going, going, gone."

"What are your plans for the day?" Landon asked Debbie. "Have you landed on new locations to film?"

"Not exactly. Turns out, it wasn't necessary after all." Debbie looked smug. "Winnie gave us permission to film on the bluff, and she also got the owner of the Dandridge on the phone after you left last evening. Seems they're building up business and are keen for the free publicity."

I froze with my glass halfway to my mouth. Part of me was surprised that Clove had folded so easily. The other part recognized I should've realized that was the route she would ultimately take.

"So, you're going out to the Dandridge?" Landon said.

"It's on our list. We also want to go to Hollow Creek. It sounds like an interesting place."

Two months earlier, I would've panicked at the news. We'd cleaned up the mess out there in recent weeks, however, and now it served as a desolate spot in the middle of the woods. Nothing there could get us into trouble.

"Well, that sounds fun," I said. "I hope you get everything you're looking for." I didn't mean it, but since I was reasonably assured they would find nothing but bitter winds and cold water at Hollow Creek, I opted to play nice.

"What we'd really like is to follow you," Falcon volunteered, ignoring the dark look Debbie sent his way. "You're the most famous person in the town, right? You should be the star of our show. Well, after me that is."

"And me," Elle said sharply. It was clear she and Falcon didn't have the best of relationships. I was guessing the time they spent jockeying for coverage was part of the explanation for the way they interacted when the cameras weren't rolling.

"If you say so." Falcon's smile was purely for show, but I had no doubt it had brought more than a handful of women to their knees. "We want you to star in the episode, Bay. What do you say?"

What did I say? There was no way that was happening. "I've never really fancied myself a television star," I replied over the rim of my coffee mug.

"I can be a television star," Aunt Tillie offered.

Thankfully, nobody took her up on the offer. They were too focused on me.

"How can you not want to be on television?" Maya asked. "That's the dream for most people."

"Well, I'm not most people," I said. "I'm happy with my life."

"Well, yeah, because you've got him." Maya gestured to Landon. "Don't you want something for yourself?"

I frowned.

"Bay is her own person," Landon replied before I could. "I happen to love her the way she is. As for television, I think perhaps your view on the subject is warped. Not everyone wants to be a star."

"I do." Aunt Tillie's hand shot in the air again.

I murdered her with a dirty look.

"What?" Aunt Tillie made a face. "I didn't say anything."

"You just said you want to be a television star," I pointed out.

"That's because this face was born for television," Aunt Tillie replied. "So was my ass when you think about it." As if to prove it, she climbed up on her chair and showed off her faux-leather Spanx in case the film crew had somehow missed her outfit. When she'd originally modeled the leggings for me, she'd paired them with a corset. Thankfully, the straps on the corset had broken the first day, and she'd decided to pair the leggings with flowy shirts since then.

"What do you think of my bottom half?" Aunt Tillie asked Falcon when nobody initially responded. "Nice, huh?"

Falcon's cheeks flooded with color, and he showed a genuine emotion for the first time since I'd met him. "Um..." His eyes were wild when they flew to Landon, seeking guidance.

"Oh, don't look at me." Landon slid his arm around the back of my chair when he leaned back. "It would be inappropriate for me to answer." He was looking a little too pleased with himself, right up to the moment when Aunt Tillie's pet pig, Peg, made a sudden appearance.

Snort. Snort.

Landon was out of his chair and on the floor like a rocket. "There she is," he crooned to the pig, dressed in a purple tutu today and looking just as excited to see him as he was to see her. "Did you miss me?"

Snort. Snort.

"It's very odd to have a pig as an indoor pet," Reid noted. He was the quietest of the bunch so far, which made me like him the best. "Is she housebroken?"

"Are you?" Aunt Tillie shot back.

Reid was obviously taken aback. "I meant no disrespect."

"Ignore her," I said. "Everybody is protective of Peg. She's the real star of the family. If you want someone to film, you should focus on her."

"Oh, don't worry," Debbie offered. "Peg will definitely be included in the footage. The audience will love her. They'll also love you." Her gaze, as well as the statement, was pointed.

"Listen, I don't want to be difficult," I hedged.

"Don't listen to her. She idles at difficult." Aunt Tillie was seemingly in her element, arguing with all sides, and more than happy to continue needling anybody who opened their mouth. "I tried to tell her she was never going to snag a good man if she kept up with the attitude. Did she listen? No."

Landon jerked up his head. "What did you just say?"

"You heard me." Aunt Tillie's lips curved. "I stand by what I said."

I knew what she was up to. "You just want to prove that you're entertaining, so they'll follow you with the cameras all day," I deduced.

"That's an ugly thing to say about your great-aunt."

"But it's not wrong." I thought about it for a moment and then bobbed my head. "You know what? It's actually a good idea."

"What is?" Debbie asked, confusion lining her forehead.

"You need a star for your show." I gestured to Aunt Tillie, who was still standing on her chair. "She was born to be a star."

Landon's lips quirked as he continued to stroke Peg's head. "You know, I think that's a fabulous idea. Aunt Tillie was definitely born to be a star."

Mom exited the kitchen with a huge platter of pancakes just as Landon said it. She paused next to the table, her gaze bouncing between faces. "What's that?"

"Aunt Tillie wants to be a star," I replied.

"I was born to be a star," Aunt Tillie corrected. "Get it right."

"I'm sorry. She was born to be a star."

"I think there's been some sort of misunderstanding," Debbie said, her hands fluttering toward her throat, nervous energy on full display. "We wanted to follow Bay for the day."

"Really?" Mom's expression barely changed. "How do you feel about that, Bay?"

"I have other plans," I replied evenly.

"Uh-huh."

"I have no plans," Aunt Tillie said. "Follow me."

"That's an interesting thought." Mom slid the tray onto the table and focused on me. "What are your plans?"

She was really putting me on the spot, and I didn't like it. "I'm covering the dead body downtown."

"I thought we weren't sure yet if that was a murder."

Landon's head poked out from under the table. "It's a murder."

"Oh." Mom slid into her chair, barely looking up when Marnie and Twila emerged with the breakfast meats and doughnuts.

"Score!" Landon pumped his fist and climbed out from under the table. "Don't watch me eat, Peg," he admonished. "It will upset you, and the last thing I want is to break your little heart. It's just ... it's bacon. I'm addicted."

I watched Landon reclaim his chair. "I really need to get you a dog."

"I have you. I don't need a dog."

"Hey!" I lightly slapped his arm, earning a grin.

"I didn't mean that the way you took it," he said, laughing. "I just meant that I enjoy spending time with you, and I'm not sure our lives are conducive to owning a dog right now. We keep weird hours."

"Doing what?" Maya asked. Her eyes looked positively dreamy as she regarded Landon.

"Doing things." Landon frowned at her before turning back to me. "We have a lot of late hours, Bay."

I understood what he was saying. That didn't change the fact that I was seriously considering getting him—or rather us—a dog for Christmas. Just because we often ran out late at night didn't mean we couldn't take a dog with us. Or even drop it at the inn on our way to a crime scene. Landon liked having something to dote on. I figured it was best to feed that need before he really did start hounding me for a kid we weren't ready to take care of.

"We'll talk about it later. As for today, I don't want to be on your television show. Find someone else."

Debbie's disappointment was palpable. "But Mrs. Little insisted you were the one to follow."

I couldn't contain my frown. "Did she?"

"Oh, that's so Margaret." Aunt Tillie offered up a playful wave. "She loves playing games. Luckily for her, I love playing them too."

"Yes, speaking of that, I think it's best you help Bay with whatever she's working on today," Mom said. "It seems she's very busy—the run-up to Christmas is always busy in this town—and since you're not doing anything else, it's best you help her."

That was the exact opposite of what I wanted. "I object." I raised my hand, earning a grin from Landon.

"I do too." Aunt Tillie chimed in. "I'm going to be a television star. The film crew is going to follow me around all day and take shots of my pretty posterior."

"Now I'm going to have to object," Debbie said. "It was one thing when we thought Bay would be open to us using her as our central character. Unfortunately, Tillie doesn't best represent our demographic."

Aunt Tillie leaned closer to Landon. "Did she just say what I think she said?"

"Yup." Landon nodded without hesitation. He had a slice of bacon gripped between his fingers, which was surprising because I hadn't even noticed him reach for the meat tray. I was trying to watch his fat intake of late because he was a glutton, but he was a slippery devil when he wanted to be. "She said that you're too old to be a television star."

"I am middle-aged!" Aunt Tillie shook her fist. "I can't believe I'm being tossed out in my prime like this."

I risked a glance at the film crew and found almost all of them looked uncomfortable. The lone exception was Greg, who appeared amused and more than happy to continue watching the scene play out.

"I think we've somehow gone off the rails," Debbie said, her eyes pleading as she focused on Mom. "We didn't mean to offend anyone."

"Don't worry about it." Mom didn't look bothered in the least. "You're being victimized from all sides. I'm sure Margaret Little told you that Bay would want to be filmed to torture Bay ... because there's nothing Bay would hate more than being followed by your team all day. As for Aunt Tillie, she's just looking for attention."

"Look at this outfit," Aunt Tillie shot back. "Do I look too old for a prime demographic?"

Mom refused to play the game. "You're going with Bay today. She needs your help."

"How do you know that?" I demanded. "Maybe I don't need help today."

"Landon said you needed help when he texted me before breakfast," Mom replied. "He said you were going on a mission and that Aunt Tillie would be the perfect one to help you."

I pinned Landon with a dark glare. "What?"

"That was a secret text," Landon hissed at my mother. "*Secret.*"

"Oh." Mom looked taken aback. "I didn't realize. Ah, well, it's out in the open now. You get Aunt Tillie for the day, Bay. You need help, and she has nothing to do."

"I have plenty to do," Aunt Tillie shot back.

"And I don't need help," I added.

"What did I say?" Mom's tone told me she was done talking about the situation. "It's done. I don't want to hear another word about it. In fact, it's time to shut up and eat your breakfast."

Everybody—including the film crew—followed her orders and focused on their food. I was the only one who didn't immediately start shoveling it in.

"We're going to fight, aren't we?" Landon asked after a few seconds of silence, his mouth full of bacon.

"Probably," I replied.

"You still love me?"

"I'll let you know after I spend the day with Aunt Tillie."

LANDON FOUND ME WAITING FOR AUNT Tillie in front of the inn forty-five minutes later. I was under the impression he'd already left, but apparently, that wasn't the case. He was drying his hands with a paper towel as he exited the inn, and he brightened considerably when he saw me.

"There's my favorite girl in the world."

I refused to smile in response. "I believe that's Peg."

"No, she's my favorite pig. You're my favorite girl." He stopped in front of me. When I didn't immediately pick a fight or cuddle close for a hug, he let loose a heavy sigh. "Listen—"

"No, you listen." I wasn't in the mood to let him charm me. "You said we were compromising. I get that you didn't want me to visit the meth heads alone, but you said you trusted me."

"I do." Landon was matter-of-fact. "I also love you. I feel it's better for you to have backup."

"Even if that backup is Aunt Tillie?"

"Especially if it's Aunt Tillie. There's no way she's going to let a meth head best her. On top of that, you can use her as an excuse if the meth heads question why you're there. All they'll see is an eccentric old lady."

"I heard that," Aunt Tillie drawled as she appeared behind Landon, a huge bag slung over her shoulders.

"What's in the bag?" I asked, suspicious. Aunt Tillie only carried things if she had a plan.

"I thought we would stop by Margaret's store on our way to visit the drug dealers," Aunt Tillie replied. "She's due for a new curse."

"Oh, yeah?" I found I wasn't nearly as opposed to the idea as I would've been three days before. "What's the plan?"

"I was thinking I would go with Operation Dancing Rat."

"Do I even want to know what that is?" Landon asked.

"Probably not," Aunt Tillie replied. "All you need to know is that it will make for great television in a few hours."

Landon's lips curved. "Delightful." He rested his hand on Aunt Tillie's shoulder. "Make sure to keep an eye on my beautiful wife when you're messing with the drug dealers. I specifically requested you for this assignment because I knew you were the one person who could instill real fear in their hearts."

"I am good at that," Aunt Tillie agreed. "As for Bay, don't worry about her. She knows how to take care of herself. Something tells me she's going to take care of you too, later ... and not in the way you're hoping."

"I'm willing to put up with whatever punishment she doles out," Landon said. "I don't want to restrict her activities. I just want to make sure her bases are covered, even if that means adding you as her backup."

I hated to admit it but having Aunt Tillie as a sidekick on this one probably wasn't a bad idea.

"I'm going to punish you when I get home," I warned as I opened the passenger door for Aunt Tillie. "You're going to cry when I'm finished with you."

"Ah, something to look forward to." He leaned in for a kiss. "Remember to text me when you're done so I don't worry. That's a rough bunch out there. They won't go gooey at their core when they see you like I do."

"I know how to handle drug dealers. You have nothing to worry about."

"That will be a nice change of pace, won't it?"

Nine

I parked on the road outside the old river cabin location in case we needed to make a hasty escape. Aunt Tillie was excited about our excursion, and when she climbed out of my car, she made a big show of showing off her faux leather leggings under the sun.

"Nice, huh?" She waggled her eyebrows.

I couldn't decide if the new leggings were better than her old pair. "I don't know, I kind of miss the dragons."

"Your mother hid my dragon leggings." Aunt Tillie's expression momentarily darkened. "She's the devil."

"I believe she says the same about you." I was annoyed with my mother, so I took Aunt Tillie's side on this one. "There aren't that many places she could've hidden them. Have you tried the attic?"

"She has it warded."

I slowed my pace. "She warded the attic?" There was no way she'd done that simply because of Aunt Tillie's leggings. "What does she have up there?"

"I've been wondering that myself." Aunt Tillie was thoughtful as she slid her eyes to me. "You're probably strong enough to break the wards if you put some effort into it."

"Why should I break the wards?"

"Because I'm the alpha in the pack, and I say so."

"Whatever." I flicked my eyes to the huge field we were passing and frowned. "Since when is there a farm out here?"

"This was always farmland." Aunt Tillie said. I knew she wouldn't give up on the attic just yet, but it was time to focus. The attic could wait ... at least for now. "Arlo Jenkins owned the property for a long time. He was my age. He used to grow corn and ran the cabins for hunters and vacationers on the side."

"Huh." I knit my eyebrows as I studied the field. "That looks like corn on the perimeter, but not on the inside."

"No, that's pot," Aunt Tillie agreed.

I didn't bother questioning if she was certain. If there was one thing Aunt Tillie knew about, it was pot. She'd been cultivating her own field for as long as I could remember. "They're not really even trying to hide it," I mused.

"They're not, and that's way more than twelve plants."

"You have way more than twelve plants."

"Yes, but I follow the letter of the law and keep my pot in an enclosed area that only certain people have access to. This is a huge field that anybody can gain access to willy-nilly."

I could practically hear the gears of her mind working. "Don't steal their pot," I ordered.

"Oh, don't be a ninny." Aunt Tillie rolled her eyes. "Those plants are dead. Nothing can grow when it's this cold. They let their harvest wither on the vine."

She had a very good point. "Why would they do that?"

"My guess is that they want people to focus on the pot." Aunt Tillie's eyes narrowed in shrewd observation. "It's possible they're only growing hemp over there. That might be their loophole. Maybe they want people to focus on the pot so they can ascertain how many people are watching them without risking their true business."

It was an interesting theory. "Hmm."

"Yeah." Aunt Tillie bobbed her head, clearly warming up to her theory. "On top of that, maybe they have something else going on in all those cabins." She pointed for emphasis.

I followed her hand. There were eight cabins. Foot traffic was being funneled to what had served as the office years ago. The other cabins were spread out, and the pathways between the main cabin and the two farthest cabins were cut off by several rough-looking men clad in denim and leather.

"They're going to like my outfit," Aunt Tillie said with a grin. "They'll want me to join the gang. Just so you know, even if I say yes, it will all be for show. I'm not interested in meth."

"Where do you think they're doing that?" My gaze returned to the far cabins.

"Oh, don't be the one known as Thistle's dumbest cousin," Aunt Tillie groused. "That's something Clove would ask. You know darn well where they're cooking the meth."

I frowned at her. "Cooking?"

"Yes. I googled it. You cook meth. You smoke pot. You snort coke. You shoot heroin. I'm an expert on all of it."

"I know you cook meth." My irritation came out to play. "I just didn't realize you knew it."

"I know everything."

"Yeah, yeah, yeah." I waved my hand at her. "Let me do the talking."

"I already told you that I'm the alpha of the pack. I do the talking."

"No. I'm doing the talking." I was firm on that. "This was my idea."

"Let's flip for it."

"I'm not doing that. You cheat."

"I never cheat." Aunt Tillie sounded legitimately scandalized. "You take that back."

"You cheat all the time."

"Oh, you're totally on my list."

I did my best to ignore her as I focused on the burly man who moved onto the path in front of us. His shoulders were huge. He looked like he could be a professional wrestler. Despite that, I remained calm in the face of his obvious disdain when he lifted a hand to halt us.

"What business do you have out here?" he asked in a gravelly voice.

"Steroids shrink testicles," Aunt Tillie said.

I'd had a plan to get us in to see the main man, but Aunt Tillie's "fun fact" threw me. "What?"

"I was just stating the truth," Aunt Tillie replied blandly. "Steroids shrink testicles, and most guys can't get it up when they shoot up."

"Why are you telling me that?" the man demanded.

"I don't know." Aunt Tillie was the picture of innocence. "It just popped into my head."

"I'm not on steroids." The man was offended. "Why would you even assume something like that?" His eyes were on me as he asked the question.

"It totally boggles the mind," I replied. What else was I supposed to say? "Um, I'm here to see the leader of your group."

"He's not an alien," Aunt Tillie hissed. "This is not a 'take me to your leader' situation."

I was seriously regretting bringing her. Landon was totally going to pay for this. "You have a boss, right?" I refused to engage with Aunt Tillie. I had an agenda. "I would like to talk to him."

"What can I tell him this refers to?" the man drawled.

I couldn't help being surprised that he came across as mildly intelligent. I'd embraced a stereotype upon first seeing him, but there was intelligence in his eyes.

"A body was found in downtown Hemlock Cove yesterday," I replied. There was no sense dragging things out ... or lying. "I have a few questions."

"You're assuming we're responsible for a body in your town?"

I shrugged. "Let's just call it a hunch."

The man folded his arms across his chest. "And what happens if I don't let you go any farther? What will you do then?"

"I'll unleash Aunt Tillie on you." I inclined my head to the witch in question. "You won't like that."

"You really won't," Aunt Tillie readily agreed. "These leggings mean I'm a badass. See." She gestured to the leggings, which looked more wet than badass, but I didn't comment either way. "I'll make you cry if you don't give us what we want."

"Oh, yeah?" Amusement flooded the man's square face. "And how are you going to do that?"

"Pretty easy, actually. I'll just..."

My mouth dropped open when Aunt Tillie took two long strides forward and grabbed the man by the crotch. There was no hesitation in her movements, and the behemoth of a man obviously didn't expect her to go there, because he made no move to protect himself. His eyes went wide, and then crossed when Aunt Tillie began squeezing.

All around us, the men who had only been half listening stood at attention as the big man dropped to the ground. The air escaping from his lungs sounded like it came from a leaky balloon.

"Oh, crap," I muttered. I was still debating how to react—running seemed a feasible option—when the door to the main cabin opened, and a different man appeared.

He wasn't what I was expecting. His shoulders and waist were narrow. His hair was blond. There wasn't a hint of stubble on his chin. He wore khakis instead of denim. His eyes, however, were a peculiar shade of green, and when they landed on me, he almost looked as if he was fighting off a laughing fit.

"I'm Mickey Morton," he announced.

"Mickey Morton?" Containing my surprise would've been wise, but I couldn't manage the effort. "That's an interesting name."

"If you're living at an amusement park in Florida," Aunt Tillie countered.

"You really need to let him go." I slapped at her wrist to get her to release the man who was still writhing on the ground. "He'll never father children if you keep that up."

Mickey continued to surprise me as he calmly crossed to the fallen man and leaned over him. "Are you okay, Dane?"

Now Dane was a motorcycle gang name. It fit the big man. Mickey was still an enigma.

Dane grunted but showed no signs of getting up.

"I'm sure he'll be fine." Mickey waved off his friend's pain with a quick flick of his wrist and focused on us. "You're the first visitors we've had since our arrival," he noted. "I expected more from a small town known for its hospitality. Still, this is a fun development. Shall we go inside?" He gestured toward the cabin.

I was almost positive he didn't expect us to risk going inside. I decided that it was best to continuously keep him on his toes. "Sure." I flashed a smile when his eyebrows migrated toward one another. "Let's go inside."

"Okay then." Mickey took the lead, holding open the door for us like a gentleman.

The first thing I noticed when we entered the building was that somebody had purchased new furniture. There was a comfortable-looking couch and two chairs in the center of the room. In one of those chairs sat Kevin. He was dressed like a typical biker—maybe even a little too on the nose for my taste—and his eyes momentarily widened when he saw me. To keep him calm, I showed no signs of recognition and turned my gaze to the rest of the room.

"It's surprisingly homey," I said to Mickey as I plopped down on the couch. "I was expecting a trash heap to be honest."

"Oh, yeah?" Mickey's amusement was evident as he sat in the chair next to Kevin. His attention was solely for us. It was like Kevin wasn't even in the room. "Well, at least you're honest."

"That's our motto," I agreed.

"My motto is if you think you're too small to make a difference, try sleeping with a mosquito," Aunt Tillie offered.

Mickey focused on her for a beat, his expression frozen, and then he smiled. "That's ... lovely."

"Sometimes you're the windshield and sometimes you're the bug," Aunt Tillie added. "That's another of my favorites."

I desperately wanted her to shut up.

"My favorite is, if you can't convince them, confuse them. I live by that one on a daily basis."

Mickey touched his top lip with his tongue and focused on me.

"The word you're looking for is 'anyway.'" I said with a grimace.

Rather than admonish Aunt Tillie, he smiled. "Before we start, I should point out that I know who you are." Mickey leaned back in his chair and crossed his legs at the ankles. "Both of you."

"That's not really surprising," I noted. "We don't really try to hide our identities."

"Speak for yourself," Aunt Tillie countered. "I'm a superhero by day. I try to hide my identity all the time. That's why I only wear the cape for special occasions."

Mickey's lips quirked. "I see your reputation wasn't exaggerated, Ms. Winchester."

"I like living up to expectations," Aunt Tillie replied. "Just out of curiosity, how much meth are you cooking in those far cabins? The pot is an interesting distraction, but letting it die like that serves as a dead giveaway to anybody in the trade. You're protecting the back cabins for a reason. You should really consider changing your configuration with your men so it's not so obvious."

All traces of merriment fled Mickey's eyes. "Excuse me?"

"Ignore her," I said hurriedly. "She's in a bad mood because my mother has been hiding her favorite leggings. She feels the need to fight with someone, and because she's afraid of my mother, you're the unlucky individual who gets to face her wrath."

Aunt Tillie was incredulous. "Oh, you're definitely on my list. I am not afraid of your mother."

I pretended I hadn't heard her. "We're here because an individual without any identification or means of transportation as far as we can tell was killed in downtown Hemlock Cove yesterday."

"And you think that has something to do with us?"

"It makes sense," I replied, refusing to back down despite the obvious shift in his attitude. "The dead guy was dressed just like your other ... soldiers." I flashed a wan smile. "It would be easy to remove a motorcycle from downtown without anybody noticing."

"Well, as long as you have proof." Mickey shook his head. "I have no idea what you're talking about. That goes for the meth, too." He glared at Aunt Tillie. "As for the pot plants, we left some of them out because we couldn't harvest them in time. It's hell getting good help these days."

"That might work on randos in town, but I know better," Aunt Tillie replied. She was clearly enjoying herself, and I didn't know if I should let her continue to irk him or try to rein her in. For now, I opted to sit back and watch. "Those two plants closest to the path were Northern Lights. I'm guessing you picked them because they lack bright colors."

Mickey looked momentarily impressed. "You can identify pot strains?"

Aunt Tillie bobbed her head. "It might be trite, but Purple Haze is still my favorite. I'm also a big fan of Blue Dream and Acapulco Gold, but good luck growing the latter in this climate. I've opted for Sour Diesel a time or two, and it's proven pretty hardy."

I didn't realize I was rubbing my forehead until Mickey turned his attention to me.

"Your aunt is pretty interesting," he said.

"She's ... something," I agreed.

"That doesn't change the fact that I can't help you." It was with a great deal of calm restraint that Mickey pushed himself to a standing position. "We're just trying to stay out of the way and get on our feet here. We don't want to cause trouble."

"We don't want to cause trouble either," I said.

"That's where you're wrong, Ms. Winchester." His eyes lit with amusement. "Trouble seems to follow you everywhere. It follows your aunt, too." He inclined his head toward Aunt Tillie. "We don't need your sort of trouble finding us out here."

It was a warning. "Okay." I stood. "I guess we'll get out of your hair."

My response obviously surprised Mickey, because lines appeared on his forehead. "Just like that? I thought you'd push a bit harder. You have a reputation as a dogged reporter ... something that must drive your husband crazy."

He wanted me to know that he'd done his research. Not only did he know who I was, he also knew who I was married to. It wasn't a test as much as a statement of facts. Everybody was aware of everybody else, and we were in a stalemate.

"I didn't come here because I expected you to bow to my whims," I replied as I helped Aunt Tillie stand. "I'm not surprised at how things went."

"Why did you come out here?"

"I wanted to gauge your reaction to news of the body."

"How did I do?" Mickey looked amused.

"You failed," I replied. "You know who the dead guy is, and you're annoyed I had the audacity to come out here. You're wondering how much I've told my husband and if you can get away with an overt threat. You can't, for the record, so don't even bother."

A muscle worked in Mickey's jaw. "It seems you've developed quite the opinion," he gritted out.

"Yeah, I'm good like that." I grabbed Aunt Tillie's elbow. "Let's go."

"I'm not done," Aunt Tillie complained. "I was about to explain why Northern Lights is a poor choice to disguise the property."

"I'm sure he can figure it out," I replied.

Mickey's footsteps were heavy on the wooden floor as he moved behind us, but I refused to give him the satisfaction of looking over my shoulder. Once we were on the pathway heading out again, a sigh of relief escaped. The momentary feeling of euphoria, of getting away with something, lasted only another three feet when Mickey called out to us.

"Why is Northern Lights a poor disguise?" he asked Aunt Tillie.

"Because it's highly flammable," Aunt Tillie replied. I didn't miss the evil glint in her eye when she turned ... or the way she raised her hand.

"No!" I tried to grab her wrist, but it was already too late. The pot plants were already engulfed in flames. The fire was spreading to the filler plants they'd used to disguise the property.

Flames raced through the plants, growing in scope until the entire field was ablaze. It was a cold morning, and yet I could feel the heat of the flames.

Mickey stood among his soldiers, his jaw swaying in the breeze, and the fury I'd been trying to tamp down kindled with a vengeance.

"You just had to do it, didn't you?" I growled.

Aunt Tillie's response was a shrug. "He decided it was a good idea to send the first warning. I just wanted him to know I could do it better."

"You know we're in trouble, right?"

Aunt Tillie didn't look bothered in the least. "I won. My message was better. That's all I care about."

"I don't think Landon will feel that way."

"I'm not afraid of him."

"What happens if he tells Mom what you did?"

It was impossible to miss Aunt Tillie's audible gulp. "I'm not afraid of her either," she lied.

"Yeah, you keep telling yourself that. We're both in big trouble, and you know it."

Ten

Emergency personnel flooded the scene, and Landon looked furious when he found me standing next to my car, arms crossed, twenty minutes later.

"Nice fire," he drawled.

Chief Terry was with him, looking confused. "What are you doing here?" His tone was accusatory.

"I take it you didn't get a chance to catch him up before the call came in," I said. "Sorry about that."

"You're going to be sorry." Despite his bold words, there was a glint in Landon's eyes I couldn't quite identify. "Where's Aunt Tillie?"

I pointed down the road, where Aunt Tillie stood with Evan, the day-walking vampire who had taken over one of the farms down the way. He was friends with another witch I'd met—Scout Randall—and was struggling to lay claim to a life he didn't yet know how to live. He'd developed a rather interesting relationship with Aunt Tillie since relocating to town, and I was glad for his presence.

"What is he doing here?" Chief Terry hissed, his eyes narrowing. He was less excited to see Evan than I had been when the vampire had appeared on the dirt road and immediately drew Aunt Tillie to him. I figured if Mickey ordered his men to attack, Evan would risk life and limb to get Aunt Tillie out of harm's way.

"He was drawn by the fire," I replied. "He thought it might be some sort of accident. As soon as he saw Aunt Tillie, he realized what it was."

"She did this?" Chief Terry looked caught between fury and confusion.

"She was sending a message."

"To whom?"

I inclined my head toward the khaki-wearing gang leader. "Mickey Morton. Have you had the pleasure of meeting him yet? We have, and he's all sorts of weird."

"Did he threaten you?" Landon asked. "Is that why she did it?"

"I believe she did it in an attempt to show him that her balls are bigger than his. He was a bit condescending when we questioned him. He's also a really poor liar. He knows who the dead guy is. He just won't tell us."

"Well, we figured that out ourselves." Landon rolled his neck and focused on the fire. "Will it spread?"

I shrugged, noncommittal. "Probably not. I believe Aunt Tillie's strike was precise. She actually told Mickey she was going to do it right before it happened."

"Run it down," Chief Terry ordered with a grimace.

I filled them in, and by the time I'd finished, the fire department had arrived. Nobody made a move to extinguish the flames, however. Instead, everybody simply stood and watched the field burn.

"That doesn't sound like a smart move," Chief Terry said after a few seconds of grumbling. I couldn't make out all of what he was saying, but I was convinced I'd heard the words "stupid" and "trying to kill me" more than once.

"I have no idea if it was smart or not," I replied. "I just know it's done."

"It definitely wasn't smart." Chief Terry was having none of it. "Have you looked that way?" He pointed down the road, in the opposite direction of where Evan and Aunt Tillie had their heads bent together. When I saw what had him so annoyed, I sucked in a breath.

"That's right." Chief Terry was furious. "The call went out on the scanner, and we weren't the only ones who heard it. Our friendly neighborhood paranormal television crew heard it too. They're filming everything."

I had to bite back a sigh as I watched the excited crew point at various people as they filmed.

"Don't worry about it," Landon said after I'd spent a couple seconds silently fretting. "There's no way they can blame this on you."

"Except that she is to blame," Chief Terry said. "Do you really think they won't hear about a spontaneous fire? Give me a break." He looked furious, and for a change, some of that anger was directed at me. I wasn't used to being on his list, and I didn't like it.

"It was Aunt Tillie," I complained. "I was minding my own business."

"Young lady, you were not minding your own business." Chief Terry was stern when he lodged his hands on his hips and glared at me. "If you were minding your own business, you wouldn't have been out here sticking your nose in their business. I know what you were doing out here ... and you're in trouble."

My cheeks heated under his fury. "Landon knew what I was going to do," I said.

"Thanks for that, baby," Landon growled, shaking his head.

"Oh, he's in trouble too," Chief Terry sputtered. "Do you have any idea how messy this is going to get? How am I going to explain a spontaneous fire? We're all screwed, and it's your fault."

I balked. "Hey." I loved him, but I could only take so much. "I had no intention of bringing Aunt Tillie. That was all Landon. He arranged for it to go down the way it did."

"He's in trouble too."

"I don't think it's so bad," Landon argued. "It's Aunt Tillie. She has a certain reputation. I guarantee that these guys had already heard of her. Now they'll be afraid to go near her. How is that not a good thing?"

"Because that camera crew is questioning the foot soldiers," Chief Terry shot back, his finger jabbing toward Falcon and Elle as they happily chatted away with two men in leather jackets. "What do you think they're telling that crew right this very second? I guarantee it's not a science lesson about spontaneous combustion. No, it's a conversation about a little old witch in leather leggings who issued a threat and then backed it up without a lighter."

"They're not really leather," I replied before thinking.

Chief Terry's glare was incredulous. "Really? Is that what's important right now?"

I shrank in the face of his fury. "I don't like when you're angry with me," I whined.

Landon, ever protective, slid his arm around my shoulders. "Don't give her grief," he ordered Chief Terry. "She didn't cause this."

"She shouldn't have been out here in the first place," Chief Terry growled. "That's why you didn't tell me what she had planned. You knew I would put my foot down and forbid it."

"I forgot to tell you," Landon said. "As for putting your foot down, you're not her boss."

I shot Landon a dubious look. He often made demands when it came to my presence at crime scenes. "Really?"

"Don't. There's no sense arguing about who's to blame. Now we need to pick up the pieces and mitigate the damage."

"How are we going to fix this?" Chief Terry demanded. "They know we're watching them now."

"They already knew," I replied. "I mean ... Mickey Morton recognized me. He recognized Aunt Tillie too. That means he's boned up on all the players in town. I'm willing to bet he can identify every Winchester by sight. He even mentioned my husband, but not by name."

"I don't like that." Landon dropped his arm from my shoulder and rubbed his chin as he regarded the man in question. Mickey was on the porch of the main cabin, Kevin at his side. I had no doubt about what they were discussing. The meth cabins had to be protected.

"We should at least make noise about searching all the cabins," Landon said. "If we don't, he'll be suspicious."

"Oh, he's already suspicious," Chief Terry argued. "Come on. The second Bay and Tillie showed up, he knew he was in trouble."

"I think he was more amused at first," I offered. "He looked at us as if we were adorable kids selling cookies. That feeling didn't last long, and when I pointed out I knew he was lying about the dead guy we found, he didn't take that well. But he thought it was funny when we first arrived, and Aunt Tillie grabbed the big guy by the testicles."

Chief Terry changed his stance, telling me I'd made another mistake.

"Oh, crap. I forgot to tell you about that part." I was sheepish as I finished filling them in. "When we first got here, the big guy was in our way. He didn't seem helpful." I pointed to the minion in question, who was back on his feet. "Aunt Tillie grabbed his testicles, gave them a bit of a squeeze, and that was enough to garner Mickey's interest."

"Well, that's just great!" Chief Terry threw his hands in the air. "You guys are unbelievable." Rather than continue ranting, he stalked in Aunt Tillie's direction. I had no doubt a fight was going to erupt between them.

"He'll be okay," Landon assured me. "Just let him calm down."

I attempted a smile. "I really didn't know things would turn out this way."

"I know." He pulled me in for a hug and exhaled his angst on the crown of my head. "It's not good that the television crew is here, Bay. I'm not going to lie. It's very bad."

"Yeah, but ... what are they going to do?" I'd been thinking about this since they arrived. "Even if they get the meth guys to say on the record that Aunt Tillie somehow started the fire, nobody will believe it. They're in a gang, and she looks like a harmless old lady in faux leather leggings."

"You have a point," Landon acknowledged, his hand moving to my shoulder. "What do you want to do, Bay?"

I appreciated that he wasn't barking orders. Unfortunately, I had no idea what to do. "I want Chief Terry to stop being angry with me to start."

"He'll be fine. He can't stay angry with you. He's like me on that front."

"I still don't like it."

"You'll live." Landon gave me a serious look. "You need to make a decision. This is a precarious situation."

"Yeah." I glanced back at Mickey. "I guess I'll go offer my apologies."

"Do you think that's wise?"

I held out my hands. "Nothing about this was wise. I need to gauge his mood."

"Knock yourself out." Landon made a sweeping motion with his hand. "It's not like he's going to be stupid enough to attack you in front of a camera crew, the entire fire department, and your FBI agent husband."

"No, he'll leave that until it's dark and he can approach from the woods," I said.

Landon's frown was instantaneous. "That's not funny."

"I'm just letting my imagination run wild."

"I'll call your mother and have her check the wards on the property." He removed his phone from his pocket, resigned.

"Good idea." I patted his shoulder and started up the walkway. When Mickey saw me approaching, he shook his head. "I'm not here to cause trouble," I offered, raising my hands.

"You've already caused trouble," Mickey said dryly. "How much more trouble could you manage in one morning?"

"You might be surprised." I shot him a rueful smile. "I just want to apologize. I had no idea that was going to happen."

"I think you had some idea." Mickey folded his arms across his chest. "It was a neat trick. It's put us in a precarious position. Did your husband put you up to it?"

"Believe it or not, my husband rarely puts me up to anything." That was mostly true. Sure, we often conspired, but it was rare for Landon to ask me to intervene on one of his cases. In fact, it was usually the opposite.

"If you say so." Mickey clearly didn't believe me. "What do you want?"

"To warn you that they're going to ask to search the cabins." It wasn't a lie. It also wasn't a betrayal of Landon. I wanted Mickey to think I was trustworthy—or maybe just a little less dangerous—and the best way to ensure that was to offer him something.

"I figured."

"I just wanted to make you aware."

"They're going to be disappointed. We're not going to allow them into our cabins."

"I didn't figure you would." I rubbed my hands over my jeans, uncertainty gnawing at the pit of nervous energy pooling in my stomach. "I really am sorry. I didn't intend for any of this to happen."

"That doesn't change the fact that it did." Mickey tapped his foot on the porch before turning on his heel and disappearing inside. Apparently, he was done with me.

"How much trouble am I in?" I asked Dane. He was the only one still around. "Is he going to move on my family to return the favor?" I was going for levity, but the question was too serious.

"Probably not." Dane didn't smile. He was still holding a grudge thanks to Aunt Tillie's wandering hands. "You live with an FBI agent. The police chief shares a roof with your mother. And your crazy freaking aunt can apparently start fires without matches."

"Fair point," I murmured. "He seems angry."

"He's dealing with a lot."

"Like what?"

"Like his men going missing."

I froze. Was Dane supposed to tell me that? Probably not. "His men are going missing?"

"Not officially, so if you tell your husband that little tidbit, Mickey will deny it. Unofficially, we've had three people go missing in the last few weeks."

I didn't know what to make of that, but my mind flitted to the shadow. "Have you seen anything ... weird ... in the fields?"

One of Dane's eyebrows winged up. "What sort of weird?"

"Oh, I don't know, like ... maybe footprints have been appearing in the fields."

"The ground isn't soft right now. No footprints show up. Besides, we spend very little time in the fields these days. Harvest season is over."

"Right." I let out a breath, my mind busy. "Have you reported them missing?"

"What do you think?" Dane shot me a pitying look. "We're not in the sort of business in which you can report to the cops."

"Fair point, but why tell me?"

"Because you wander around visiting people you shouldn't be getting close to, and the only person you bring with you is your crazy freaking aunt who knows way too much about pot, by the way. What is up with that?"

"She's a woman of eclectic interests," I replied. "Were all these men alone when they disappeared?"

"Yeah. Is that important?"

"I was just wondering if there were witnesses."

"No. If there were witnesses, the person responsible would already be dead."

"So, they were alone, and they've gone missing over the course of a few weeks. Did you ... um ... sense anybody watching you before the disappearances?"

"Did we sense anybody watching us? Are you trying to be funny?"

"It was just a question." I held up my hands. I couldn't stop the wheels in my mind from turning. "Have any other bodies turned up?" I was making a leap. I had no proof the body in the alley was taken out by the shadow.

"No."

"Okay." I started back down the walkway without uttering another word.

"What are you going to do?" Dane called to my back.

"Figure things out," I replied simply.

"How are you going to do that?"

"I have no idea. I probably won't inform you when I figure it out. No offense, but this is something I have to do alone."

"It's not like I was bucking for a position as your sidekick."

"Good to know."

"Whatever," Dane growled. "That aunt of yours is a menace," he added after a few seconds. "She should be locked up in a home."

"Oh, we know."

"Why do you keep her around?"

I motioned to the flames, now diminishing because there was nothing to fuel the fire. "Wouldn't you? It's a trade-off. She starts fires, but she also puts them out. We've learned to balance the two."

"If you say so."

"I'll be around if you have more information you want to share."

"That's not going to happen."

"Never say never."

Eleven

Thankfully, Landon was chatting with the fire chief. I texted him to keep his distance and to meet me at the diner when he was finished. His response was a heart emoji, followed by a smiley face making a kissy face. He was such a goof sometimes.

Evan walked Aunt Tillie over to me. He seemed amused by the turn of events even as I shot Aunt Tillie the most powerful scowl in my arsenal.

"You're in big trouble," I warned her. "Chief Terry is going to ground you."

"I'm not afraid of Terry." Aunt Tillie waved off the warning.

"You will be when Mom takes his side."

"How many times do I have to tell you that I'm not afraid of your mother?"

"Until I believe it." I turned my attention to Evan. "I don't suppose you've been watching these guys?"

Evan shook his head. "I didn't know I was supposed to be watching them."

"They're cooking meth," Aunt Tillie offered. "Feel free to chomp on them with impunity."

I sighed. "You're free to spy on them if you're ever bored."

"Okay." He bobbed his head without hesitation. "Do you think they're responsible for the body found in town yesterday?"

"You heard about that?" I couldn't contain my surprise. Evan wasn't much for town gossip.

"I keep my ear to the ground. I heard you found the body."

"That honor goes to Cady and Carla. They own the hat store. I just followed the sounds of their screams."

"I also heard the body was glowing."

"That is true." I still had no answers on why. "There's some rogue shadow in town, too. It attacked me outside the greenhouse last night. If you can track that thing down and behead it, we'd all be grateful."

"I love having a to-do list." He rubbed his hands together, his gaze thoughtful. "Are you okay? I see some bruising around your neck."

My hand flew to the soft skin there. I'd thought the bruises were hidden thanks to the mugwort lotion I'd rubbed on the area after my nap the previous day.

"Don't worry," Evan reassured me. "Most people can't see it."

"He took me by surprise," I admitted as I lowered my hand. "I won't make that mistake again."

"I'll keep an eye out." He shoved his hands in his pockets and rocked back on his heels. "This is a weird place to manufacture meth."

"It is," I agreed. "I'm not entirely certain that they're not doing a little more than that."

"I'll keep an eye out."

"Thank you." I motioned for Aunt Tillie to get in the car. "Come on. We're going to town for lunch."

"Oh, yeah?" Aunt Tillie checked her phone screen. "Huh. Look at that. It's perfect timing."

"Perfect timing for what?"

"Margaret's curse."

"Oh, right." I smiled. "I forgot about the curse. Are you ready to tell me what form it will take?"

"Not so much. I think everybody will enjoy the surprise, though."

I could think of one person who wouldn't enjoy it. Mrs. Little was partially to blame for our current plight, so I didn't have much sympathy for her. "Let's get going. I have some information to share with Landon and Chief Terry. I don't want to risk it in front of Mickey the Mouth. They're already suspicious of us."

"What sort of information?" Evan asked.

"It seems three of the meth heads have gone missing the past few weeks."

"Dead?"

"I'm pretty sure the body we found downtown was one. As for the others, I don't know. Dane wasn't overly chatty."

"Who would be hunting meth dealers?"

"That's a good question. A better one is why the body was glowing. That suggests some sort of paranormal activity, but I've never known paranormals to hunt drug dealers."

Evan rolled his neck. "I'll be on the lookout. If I find anything, I know how to reach you."

"I really appreciate it."

"I like staying busy."

It was more than that, but I didn't push him. He was still settling into his new reality after years of living without an intact soul and an inability to quench his bloodlust. He was doing his best, and I was growing quite fond of him ... and not only because he kept Aunt Tillie busy several days a week.

"I'll see you around," I offered.

"It certainly seems to end up that way," he agreed.

LANDON AND CHIEF TERRY ARRIVED at the diner about ten minutes after Aunt Tillie and I claimed a table. Chief Terry's glare was dark when it landed on Aunt Tillie, but Landon was all smiles when he greeted me with a kiss.

"Did you miss me?" he asked in his flirtiest tone.

I arched an eyebrow. "How can you possibly be in the mood after what happened?"

"Believe it or not, Bay, I'm always in the mood around you."

"He is," Chief Terry agreed in a solemn voice. "It's disgusting, and I want to thump him good."

I swallowed hard as I turned my attention to Chief Terry, sitting directly across from me. "I take it you're still mad."

"Of course I'm mad." Even as he did his best to maintain his glare, the lines around his mouth softened. "But it has come to my attention that this might not be your fault."

"Does that mean you're mad at Aunt Tillie?" I asked hopefully.

"Definitely." Chief Terry slid the darkest look in his repertoire to her. "Would you like to explain to the class why you set that field on fire?"

"Not so much." Aunt Tillie had chosen her seat so she would have a clear view of Mrs. Little's store through the window.

"Well, I think I'm going to have to request an explanation regardless," Chief Terry pressed.

"He was bugging me." Aunt Tillie was a master at not making eye contact when she was trying to escape punishment, and today was no exception. "How do we feel about rats?"

Chief Terry pretended he hadn't heard the question, something I was fairly certain he would regret when the clock struck noon. "You've put us in a bad position."

That drew Aunt Tillie's full attention. "How so?"

Chief Terry kept his voice low. "You set their pot field on fire."

"So?"

"So now they know that we know about the pot."

"Actually, all the evidence of pot went up in flames. It seems to me you could just say, while doing that weird pointing thing you do, that you'll be watching. That will be enough to keep them from suspicion ... and convince them they dodged a bullet. They'll be feeling full of themselves, which will likely have them making a mistake."

I was impressed. "She kind of has a point," I noted.

"You just got off my list," Chief Terry reminded me. "Do you want to go back on?"

"Not so much." I was sheepish.

Landon rubbed my back. "It's done," he reminded Chief Terry. "We can't un-ring that bell."

"Maybe not, but we can make her think before doing something this stupid next time."

That sounded unlikely. I decided to change the subject. "That Dane guy let something slip. Or maybe he wanted me to know for reasons I don't yet understand. Either way, he told me that three of their workers have gone missing in the last few weeks."

Landon snapped his head in my direction. "He told you that?"

I nodded.

"He just volunteered that?" Chief Terry asked.

"Yeah." Suddenly, I was uncertain. "Why is that such a big deal?"

"He's a drug dealer, Bay," Landon replied. "Drug dealers don't usually volunteer information to newspaper reporters, especially ones married to FBI agents."

"He seemed to want me to know for a very specific reason."

"And what reason is that?"

"I think he wants help."

"Help to do what? It's not as if you can find these men."

"I was pretty close when one of them was found yesterday. I'm convinced that guy was part of the gang."

"Yeah, and I'm hopeful that knowledge will help us track down a name for him," Chief Terry said. "But even if we get a name, I'm not convinced it will lead us to Mickey Morton. We'll know they have ties but knowing it and proving it are two entirely different things."

"And even proving it does nothing for us, because I think it's unlikely that a meth dealer made a body glow like that," Landon noted. "It's possible we have two things going on here."

"Meaning that the dealers are cooking meth, and somebody else is hunting them," I said, leaning my head against Landon's shoulder as I considered what that could mean.

"It's the shadow, right?" Chief Terry asked, keeping his voice low. "That thing attacked you. It can't be a coincidence."

"I'm not a dealer," I reminded him. "Why go after three men who are likely cooking meth and then go after me?"

"That I can't answer." Chief Terry held up his hands and then frowned at Aunt Tillie, who was back to staring out the window. "Maybe it was looking for Tillie. She has a certain reputation, after all."

"That doesn't seem likely to me."

"Or me," Aunt Tillie agreed. "There's no way I was the target. It was definitely Bay."

"How can you be sure of that?" Landon demanded.

"Because she was attacked."

"That doesn't prove anything."

"It does to me." Aunt Tillie pointed at the clock on the wall. "Are you ready?"

"Ready for what?" Landon turned his confused gaze to me. "What is she talking about?"

"I might've stopped in town long enough for her to cast a curse before heading out to Sand Lake," I admitted. "It seemed like a good idea at the time," I whined when Landon pinned me with a dirty look.

"Crap, Bay." Landon pushed himself to a standing position. "Stop whatever this is right now," he hissed at Aunt Tillie. "I mean it."

"Shh." Aunt Tillie held a finger in front of her lips. "You're ruining my fun."

A series of screams rippled down Main Street. Aunt Tillie hopped to her feet, a sly smile sliding across her face as people began to run down the sidewalk. They headed in a variety of directions. The only thing they had in common was that they seemed desperate to put distance between themselves and the Unicorn Emporium.

"What did you do?" Landon growled.

Aunt Tillie didn't answer. She didn't have to. At that exact moment, a pack of about twenty rats appeared on the sidewalk. They moved in tandem, like a small gang, lunging at anyone who neared Mrs. Little's store.

As for the woman of honor, Mrs. Little appeared on the step at the store's door, screaming at the top of her lungs as the rats surrounded her.

"Why would you do this?" Chief Terry dropped his forehead into his hand. "There's a film crew out there."

I was about to remind him the crew had stayed behind at the fire, but then I caught sight of two men with cameras. They were in the middle of the road, their attention focused on the rats, filming the mayhem.

"It's not so bad," Landon said as he craned his neck to watch the action. "I mean ... it's focused entirely on the other side of the street."

"Yes, and as soon as she manages to escape from her store, who do you think she's going to blame?" Chief Terry demanded.

"Good luck proving it," Aunt Tillie muttered.

"In this particular instance, it doesn't matter what she can prove. It matters that she's going to sic that television crew on you."

Aunt Tillie fluttered her hand over her curly hair. "I've always fancied myself a star."

"Oh, I don't believe this." Frustrated, Chief Terry gripped the edge of the table and glared at me. "I can't believe you helped her do this."

Under different circumstances, I might've apologized. I hated when he was angry with me. I refused to do that today, however. "She set this in motion. She brought those people here in an attempt to expose us. I'm not just going to sit back and do nothing."

Incredulous, Chief Terry worked his jaw. "Bay, you're supposed to be the smart one."

"And she keeps trying to hurt the people I love." I refused to back down. "I'm not sorry."

Terry turned his imploring gaze on Landon. "Do you want to do something here?"

"Actually, I don't." Landon shook his head. "Bay's right. She keeps coming for this family. She deserves whatever Tillie doles out. And before you get worked up, it's just rats ... and they all seem to be coming from Mrs. Little's store. She can blame that on Tillie all she wants. People won't believe it. They'll think she's a filthy pain who had a bit of karma smack her across the face."

"Listen to you guys." Defeated, Chief Terry sank back in his chair. "I can't believe you're okay with this."

"It's going to be fine, big guy." Aunt Tillie clapped him on the shoulder. She was wiggling her hips excitedly when she turned back to the window. "Oh, look, they're about to dance."

I froze in my chair. *Did she just say dance?*

Landon had obviously picked up on the same word. He jumped to his feet. "Oh, holy hell."

I had to drag myself to a standing position. It took me a few minutes to focus, but sure enough, the rats were moving in tandem in front of the unicorn store. They were clearly being choreographed.

"You just had to go there, didn't you?" I mused when I realized Aunt Tillie's smug smile was fixed on me.

"It's neat," she replied.

"And when it makes national television?"

She shrugged. "That will be Margaret's problem. I was at a fire ... and then I was here eating lunch ... with local law enforcement at that. Somebody had their eyes on me at all times."

And that's when I realized why she'd really started the fire. "Oh, you're diabolical."

"And I was filmed on the record at the meth house." Aunt Tillie's smile was benign. "Good luck proving I did this, Margaret. She's going to look like a laughingstock." Aunt Tillie lowered her voice. "Or maybe even something worse," she added. "Maybe she'll be seen as the real witch."

I was numb when I returned to my chair. She really was diabolical. "You're paying her back with karma," I mused. "She tried to out us, and now you're painting her with our favorite colors. You're going to make sure the world believes she's the witch."

Aunt Tillie was the picture of innocence as she met my gaze. "Does that sound like something I would do?"

"Um ... yeah. You're already doing it."

She was ecstatic as she sat on her chair and rubbed her hands. "So, who's ready to order lunch? I've worked up quite the appetite today. I'm thinking I want a cheeseburger and fries. Why not celebrate with grease, right? Winnie monitors how much grease I eat, and I can't stand it for one more second."

"What do you think?" Landon asked as he rested his hand on top of mine. "Is this going to work?"

I knew what he was really asking. He didn't care if Mrs. Little was painted as a witch. He just wanted to make sure it wouldn't backfire on us.

"I have no idea," I replied. "It will be interesting to watch, though."

"It sounds frightening."

"It's also intriguing."

"There is that." He forced the conversation back on track. "Now, let's talk about where these missing meth heads might be. If we can find them, they might provide some clues."

I didn't have any ideas. "I don't know. I need to think."

"For how long?"

"Until I'm done."

"That's pretty vague, sweetie."

"There's nowhere else to look."

Twelve

C hief Terry did his best to pretend he was still angry, but he wasn't good at it, and gave me a side hug before he left. Aunt Tillie scampered across the road without saying goodbye to anyone—a festival was opening, and she looked as if she had mayhem on her mind. She left Landon and me to talk privately in front of the diner.

"What are you going to do?" His expression was challenging as he leaned against my car, arms crossed.

"I'm not sure yet. What are you going to do?"

"I figured we'd run a deep search. If we know that three individuals have gone missing, that means someone somewhere has to have reported that information."

"Wouldn't you have already heard if that were the case?"

"Not necessarily. We don't know that they're missing from Hemlock Cove. In fact, I'm willing to bet that they're not from here. They could be from anywhere. Flint and Detroit are high on my list."

It made sense. "Well, good luck with that."

"You still haven't told me what you're going to do," he prodded.

"Not that you're keeping tabs on me or anything, right?" I teased.

He smirked. "I'm concerned your plan is to head back to Sand Lake Motor Inn and start asking questions."

"Would I do that?"

"Yes."

"Well ... that's not the plan." I opted for the truth. "They're not going to talk to me. Dane blabbed, but that feels strategic."

Landon's eyes narrowed. "Like he was trying to manipulate you?"

I shrugged. "Is that so hard to believe?"

"No, but I'm curious why he would go that route if it's not true."

"I'm not saying it isn't true. In fact, I think it's most likely true. I just think it's a means of distraction. He wants me looking closer to home for missing meth heads, so I'm not focused on what they're doing out there."

"Which means you won't be breathing down their necks," Landon said, nodding in agreement. "It makes sense when you really think about it. He wants you looking elsewhere."

"The question is ... why." I rolled my neck and stared at the festival. Our festival foot traffic was always heavy, even in down tourism months. "Do you think it's possible they'll move the meth out of those cabins when they think we're distracted?"

"Anything is possible. I guess we'll just have to play it by ear."

I focused on him, smiling when I found him watching me. "What?"

"I was just thinking how tenacious you are. You're like a dog with a squeaky toy when you decide you want to chase a story."

"Are you any different when you have an investigation?"

"No. We're quite the pair." He gave me a hug. When he pulled back, concern crinkled at the corners of his eyes. "Just one thing."

"I figured there was something."

"I'm worried that Aunt Tillie is going to push things with Mrs. Little until everything explodes, and we're in even bigger trouble than we are now."

I'd been thinking about that too. "Her determination to make Mrs. Little look like a witch could backfire," I agreed. "If it does backfire, it's possible that it will backfire in such a way that it will make Mrs. Little look bad."

Intrigue glinted in his eyes. "How so?"

"Well, Mrs. Little called them. She's been steering them our way, to the point it might look suspicious. If magic starts backfiring around her, I can see Debbie questioning the entire thing. She might accuse Mrs. Little of trying to manufacture buzz for the town."

"I don't think that will stop Debbie from getting her episode," Landon argued. "She seems tenacious too."

"She does, but if it's framed in such a way that the attention is directed at Mrs. Little, everybody will focus on her. She'll be the one bearing the brunt of the gossip and mean comments online."

He reached over and lightly brushed his fingers over my cheek. "You know we're not out of the woods yet? Mrs. Little won't just let this go. I mean ... we have talking rats."

"Dancing rats."

He smirked. "It was kind of cool, but we can't encourage Aunt Tillie to act out. That will only make things worse."

"I think I'm going to track her down and give her some grief. She has to know this is a dangerous line she's walking."

"I don't think she cares."

"She cares, just not in the same manner we would like her to. That's the problem."

"Well, I'm sure you'll figure it out." He gave me a light kiss. "Don't spend too much time worrying about it, Bay," he said. "We can't control what she's going to do. She is who she is. Giving yourself an ulcer over things beyond your control won't help anybody."

"I can't help it. I'm a worrier."

"I'm well aware." He raised a hand as he started across the street. "I'll be in touch when I have something."

I watched him go for several seconds, sighing at the fine figure he cut. He was ridiculously handsome, something I'd noticed the first day I'd met him, even when I wasn't certain if he was on the side of good or evil. Now I knew, and it made him even more attractive.

"You're so lucky." The words were uttered with a feminine gush, and when I glanced to my left, I found Maya admiring Landon. "He's so hot."

I couldn't be offended that she felt the need to tell me. Landon was indeed hot. He'd made more than one heart go pitter-patter. "He's a handsome man," I agreed.

"And he's all yours." Maya's eyes sparkled. "Do you feel lucky?"

"Because he's hot?"

"Because he's devoted to you. That's the stuff of romance novels. He doesn't even look at other women."

I wanted to ask how she knew that—had she been testing him?—but it seemed unnecessary. "He's a loyal guy. That's one of his greatest assets."

"But you haven't been married all that long, right?" Maya asked. "It's kind of like you're still in the honeymoon phase."

It could've been taken as an insult. I opted against lowering myself to react negatively. "It's only been a few months, but we've been together for years. He's always been a romantic fool."

"So, so lucky."

She sounded so wistful, I was starting to feel uncomfortable. She was young, but it was rude to ogle my husband right in front of me. "I tell myself that every single day." I raised my fingers in a lazy wave. "I'll see you around."

"Where are you going?" Maya scrambled to follow. "You're not leaving, are you?"

I stilled about a quarter of the way across the street. "And if I am?"

"I'm just asking."

She was watching me. I flicked my eyes to the diner and found Debbie and Falcon sitting in window seats, their attention on me. "I'm going to the festival," I replied. "You can tell your boss that's where I'll be when she decides to be invasive and follow me."

Maya balked. "Nobody is following you."

"That's good, because I'm not going to be interviewed for the show. You won't be able to wear me down or change my mind. I have no interest in your show."

"Most people jump at the chance to be on television," Maya argued.

"I'm not most people. I don't need attention from people I don't even know. I get more than enough attention from the people I do know."

"Like your husband." Maya was back to wistful.

"Like my husband," I confirmed. "You can tell Debbie I'll be at the festival. You guys should head over when you're finished with your lunch, catch some of the local color. There's nothing Hemlock Cove does better than festivals."

"We plan to right after lunch."

"Awesome." I kept my smile in place until my back was to her, and then I frowned for the rest of the walk to the fairgrounds. The fact that Debbie and her pack of busybodies were focused on me wasn't good in the least. I had to wonder if Mrs. Little had told them more than she'd let on. It would be just like her to go that route.

I was so lost in thought I almost didn't notice when two figures slid in front of me. One of them was abnormally large. When I glanced up, an apology for not paying attention on my lips, I found Scout Randall and Gunner Stratton watching me with unreadable eyes. Per usual, Gunner had food in his hands and looked perfectly happy to be eating.

"What are you guys doing here?" I blurted. I was happy to see them, of course—they were fun and entertaining—but fear was my initial reaction because of the television crew. "You shouldn't be here."

"And a happy hello to you too," Scout drawled. "What's up?"

My second reaction was one of relief. I needed someone to bounce ideas off of. Scout was a witch ... with a little pixie thrown in for good measure. Her powers were off the charts. She might have ideas on the missing meth producers.

"We should talk." I motioned to one of the picnic tables on the far edge of the food truck spread. In addition to a lack of eavesdroppers, the table provided a clear view of the diner so I would know when the camera crew left. Even though I wanted to keep my distance, there was no harm in watching them ... discreetly, of course.

"Oh, this doesn't sound good." Gunner bit into his hot dog and looked me up and down. "Am I going to need ice cream for this?"

"Maybe." Honestly, ice cream didn't sound so bad despite the brisk weather. "Maybe we'll both get some after I've filled you in."

"Sure," Scout said as she sat at the picnic table, Gunner sliding in next to her. She appeared to be bracing herself for Armageddon when she gripped her hands into fists. "Tell us what's going on."

It didn't take me long to catch them up. Because they were both paranormal—Gunner was a shifter—I didn't have to go into depth when I explained the glowing body or Aunt Tillie's pyrotechnics at Sand Lake. When I was finished, Gunner was doubled over in laughter, and mirth danced in Scout's eyes.

"It's not funny." I sounded surly, but there was no holding it back. "She could've gotten us in big trouble."

"Oh, it's a little funny," Scout insisted. "Come on. She started a pot field on fire."

"I'm more interested in the dancing rats," Gunner said. "How did she manage that?"

"It's her Cinderella spell," I replied darkly. "Or probably a modified version."

Gunner arched an eyebrow. "Cinderella spell?"

"When we were kids, we would get bored, and she would use a Cinderella spell to make us think that the animals were talking to us."

"Wait ... so the rats weren't real?" Scout looked pensive.

I shook my head. "It was just a very elaborate glamour."

"Oh, well, that's a bummer." Gunner looked disappointed. "I like the idea of dancing rats."

He always made me smile. "So do I," I assured him. "The thing is, Aunt Tillie never does anything halfway. That glamour will keep growing. People will see the rats around town. Some might even think the rats are talking to them. And since Aunt Tillie is trying to make life difficult for Mrs. Little, it's likely the rats will be pointing the finger at the Unicorn Emporium."

"That's ingenious." Gunner beamed. "Have I mentioned that I love her? She's fantastic."

I shook my head. "She happens to believe that too."

"You're worried," Scout noted when I was silent a few seconds. "You think that this camera crew is somehow going to catch you guys in the act."

"It's a really bad time for a glowing body to show up," I conceded. "I just wish it wasn't happening right now. Not that I want someone to die at a different time or anything."

"I've got it." Scout bobbed her head. "You're convinced the dead guy was one of the meth cookers."

"Yes, and if Dane was right, there are two other individuals from this area missing."

"And there's an aggressive shadow running around," Scout added.

"The camera crew just adds an air of worry to everything," I said. "We're careful when we fight, but we don't always have the luxury of choosing between saving ourselves and exploding our family. I don't know what to do."

Scout's eyes drifted to the kissing booth, and when I looked in that direction, I saw Elle and Reid talking to some of the locals. Everybody looked to be having a good time, but I didn't miss the occasional glances Elle darted toward me.

"They want me to be the star of their show, so to speak," I said. "It's becoming very uncomfortable."

"I'm guessing that the more you deny them, the more fixated they become," Scout mused. "They're used to people falling at their feet. The fact that you won't makes them suspicious."

"Well ... I don't want them following me."

"I don't blame you. But you can't blame them for wanting you."

"Oh, I can blame them." I looked to the right. Debbie and Maya stood looking at a tablet, their heads bent together, plotting. When Maya glanced up, our gazes immediately locked. She gave a small wave, but her attention was quickly diverted to Gunner, and I swear I could see the drool forming from fifty feet away.

"Landon is going to be crushed when he realizes Maya's devotion isn't just for him," I said with a laugh.

Gunner, ketchup on his cheek, followed my gaze. "Who is she?"

"The production assistant. She's been drooling over Landon for days. Now she appears to be drooling over you."

"What can I say? Women love me." Gunner shot Scout a cheeky smile. "Don't worry, baby, I'm hopelessly devoted to you."

Scout merely blinked. "You have ketchup on your face," she said before shaking her head. "Have you considered searching the woods for the other missing guys? It makes more sense to drop a body in the woods than it does in a downtown alley."

"I've been considering it," I said. "It has to wait until after dark. I can't risk the camera crew following me."

"We'll help." Scout was matter-of-fact. "We can use a locator spell and Gunner's sniffer." She gestured to his nose. "If there are bodies out there, we should be able to find them."

I nodded. "I appreciate the help, but are you sure you want to risk getting on the crew's radar? The last thing you want is them following you back to Hawthorne Hollow."

"That's true, but I'm not too worried about it." Scout's grin was cheeky. "People don't naturally like me. I come across as overbearing and terrifying. They won't want to be my best friend—or even a casual acquaintance—by the time I'm done, even if the young one wants to rub herself all over Gunner and lick his ketchup cheek."

"Oh, she wants to lick my ketchup cheek," Gunner replied in a husky voice. "I'm just that hot."

He was joking, so I didn't allow myself to get annoyed with his bravado. In truth, he had a giving heart and only talked big about his looks in a superficial way. He loved Scout with his whole heart. He only mentioned his looks when bored or trying to get a rise out of Landon.

"You can join us for dinner at the inn," I offered. "I chatted with Evan earlier. He saw the fire and wandered over to check it out. He promised to watch the meth dealers. He might come in handy for the search."

"We need to be smart about it," Scout said. "We'll park our bikes at the guesthouse. We don't want to give the camera crew an easy opportunity to follow us. We'll start searching as close to the meth compound as possible and work our way out from there." Scout sounded determined. "If there's something to find, we'll find it."

I wasn't worried about that. I was worried about the shadow. If we found the bodies, would we find it? And, if we did, would we be able to fight it off?

"Sounds like a plan." I flashed a smile. "So, while we're waiting, catch me up on your lives."

"That's a great way to waste a year," Scout drawled.

"I still want to hear."

"Then I guess we have no choice but to oblige you."

Thirteen

I texted Landon that I had Scout and Gunner in tow for dinner. He replied that he would meet us at the inn but didn't add anything about his research. I figured it wasn't going well. Scout insisted on seeing the greenhouse, and she strengthened the wards I'd so studiously drawn right before being attacked.

"I'm just making sure," she offered when I shot her a questioning look.

"Of what?"

"Oh, you know." Her smile was sly. "Has the television crew tried to get inside?"

"Not to my knowledge. Mom warned them the first night that it was Aunt Tillie's private space, and they should steer clear. She tried not to put too much emphasis on it because she was afraid that would encourage them, but I'm convinced they have no interest in respecting people's boundaries."

"It doesn't sound like it," she said. "What about Hollow Creek? Do you think they'll head out there?"

"I'm pretty sure that the only reason they haven't gone yet is because the fire and festival drew their attention."

"So, it's only a matter of time." Scout scuffed her feet against the hard earth. "It's too bad your shadowy friend doesn't return right now, huh? We could snuff him out and hit the pot roast with no worries."

"Except for the meth heads."

"They're probably not a worry when you take the shadow out of the equation."

I didn't believe that. "Mickey acted as if he knew me. That means they've been doing research. I don't like him."

"He cooks meth. What's to like?"

I shrugged. "The whole thing feels off."

"When don't things feel off here?"

She had a point.

Aunt Tillie was on the couch in the family living quarters yelling answers at Mayim Bialik as she watched *Jeopardy*. Peg was asleep on the couch—something I was fairly certain my mother had forbidden—and Aunt Tillie didn't bother sliding a glance in our direction when we entered.

"I miss Alex Trebek," she lamented. "I can't believe he died and ruined my show."

"Yes, I'm sure that was his biggest worry," I drawled. "He didn't want to ruin your show."

"Whatever." Slowly, she tracked her eyes to Gunner and Scout. "You have something planned," she surmised.

"We're hitting the woods by Sand Lake after dinner," I replied. "And, no, you can't go."

"I can do what I want. You're not the boss of me."

"You can't go," I insisted. "If you disappear, the television crew will be suspicious. The last thing we need is them following us."

"Oh, please." Aunt Tillie let loose a bored hand wave. "Once we're gone, it won't matter. They can't follow us. I'm going."

"No, you're not."

"I think you should let her," Gunner said. "She is helpful in a pinch."

I murdered him with a glare. "How about you stuff it?"

He didn't look bothered by my tone. "I'm just saying."

"Shh. It's quiet time," Scout chided. "This is Bay's show."

"I just want you to know that I would totally take you with me," Gunner told Aunt Tillie. "You're my favorite."

"And that's why Bay and Scout are on my list and you're not," Aunt Tillie replied on a winning grin.

Gunner brightened considerably. "Landon says you cast spells that make people smell like certain things."

Scout jerked her head and stared directly at Gunner. "Don't," she warned.

Gunner ignored her. "If you're taking requests, I have a thing for gas station chicken."

Aunt Tillie winked at him. "Consider it done."

"Well, great." Scout threw her hands in the air. "This is exactly how I saw my night going."

"It'll be great." Gunner slid his arm around her waist. "Just think of the possibilities."

"I'm thinking about the possibility of you sleeping on the couch."

"It will be worth it."

Mom, Twila, and Marnie were working in the kitchen when we left Aunt Tillie to rage at her show. The smell of pot roast permeated the kitchen, and Gunner made an excited slurping sound.

"All my favorite women in one room," he announced as he stood next to Mom and nudged her with his hip. "Did you miss me?"

Mom was genuinely fond of Gunner—he was a hard guy to dislike —and the smile she graced him with should've been accompanied by angels singing. "I always miss you."

"I'm missable," Gunner readily agreed.

"I'm curious what you're doing here, though." Mom slid her eyes to me. "Are you doing something I don't want to know about this evening?"

"That depends on what you want to know," I replied. "We are going on an adventure after dinner."

"What sort of adventure?"

"One that won't be carried out here. I need you to make sure the television crew is properly distracted once dessert is finished. It's best they don't follow us."

Mom hesitated and then nodded. "I heard about the fire."

"What did you hear?"

"Terry called." Mom made a face as she said it. "I believe I have all the pertinent details."

"She did it on purpose," I supplied. "She wanted an alibi for the rats downtown."

"Yes, I heard about that too." Mom looked none too happy. "I'm going to sell that still if she doesn't get it together."

The back of my neck suddenly startled prickling, and when I looked around, I found Aunt Tillie watching me, retribution in her eyes. She was quiet like a cat when she wanted to sneak up on people.

"You're definitely on my list," she barked.

"Scout helped her tattle on you," Gunner volunteered. "You should definitely make her smell like chicken before we go."

"And now you're on my list," Scout gritted out.

Mom's lips curved. "Why don't you hit the dining room and check on the film crew? I want to make sure they're happy. This could be a boon for the inn."

Since The Overlook was almost always booked, I didn't understand why she was so excited. But rather than ask questions, I nodded. "Sure. We can do that."

Scout and Gunner followed me into the dining room. I thought Aunt Tillie might join the party, but Mom stopped her for a lecture. Aunt Tillie's tone told me that she wasn't happy. She picked her battles when it came to my mother, however, and apparently this wasn't a hill she wanted to die on. She stood there and took it as Mom rattled off all the ways she could've ruined our lives.

The entire television crew was in the dining room. Debbie and Maya had tablets, showing footage to the other members of their team. Greg and Reid looked intense as they watched, and whatever Debbie was explaining—something about the lighting—had their full attention.

"Oh, new faces." Maya broke into a huge grin when she caught sight of us. She nodded at Scout and me, but Gunner drew her full attention. "I think I saw you at the festival."

"Oh, yeah?" Gunner oozed charm. Sometimes I wondered if it was the shifter in him. Other times, because of his rough childhood, I believed it was a defense mechanism. His own mother had tried to kill him, after all. It wasn't surprising that he went out of his way to schmooze people in the aftermath. It was his way to exert control. "I'm sorry I missed you."

He moved to the drink cart and surveyed the offerings. "Anybody want a cocktail?"

"I'll take some whiskey and 7-Up," Scout replied. She sat in one of the open chairs—the one my mother normally occupied—and eyed the television crew. There was nothing friendly about her countenance.

"These are my friends Scout and Gunner," I said. "They live in Shadow Hills."

"Oh, yeah?" Reid perked up, tearing his gaze from the tablet Debbie held. "That's where I grew up."

"Oh, yeah?" Gunner looked at Reid with fresh eyes. The cameraman appeared to be a few years older than Gunner. "What's your name?"

"Reid Prentiss."

Gunner's forehead creased. "Are you related to Dale Prentiss?"

"He's my uncle."

"My father is Graham Stratton," Gunner volunteered. "He's the chief of police."

"I haven't been back to Shadow Hills in a long time," Reid said. "I was only there a few years when I was a kid. My parents moved to Grand Rapids when I was eight. I can only remember bits and pieces."

"Nothing has changed." Gunner handed Scout her drink and then glanced at me. "What do you want?"

We were going on a mission after dessert, and I didn't want to get tipsy, but it couldn't hurt to look relaxed. "I'll have a rum and Coke. Thank you."

"No problem." Gunner set about making the second drink. "Do you talk to Dale much?"

"Not really," Reid replied. "He and my father talk every few weeks. I keep up on his family through my dad, but I haven't seen him in years."

"You should stop in and see him. He still owns the hardware store. I'm certain he would like to see you."

"I'll consider that."

The room lapsed into silence. It didn't last long.

"So ... you're all friends?" Maya glanced expectantly between Gunner and me. I could practically hear the gears in her mind working as she tried to figure out Gunner's status. I opted to put her out of her misery.

"Gunner and Scout live together in Shadow Hills. We visit and share meals. Kind of like double dates."

Scout shot me an amused look but didn't comment.

Gunner was smiling when he handed me my drink. "Yes, I love spending time with Bay and Landon. One of my greatest joys in life is being more handsome than him." His eyes drifted to the door just as Landon and Chief Terry appeared. "Isn't that right?"

Gunner boasted a heightened sense of hearing, so I had no doubt he'd heard Landon and Chief Terry as they walked down the hallway. The scowl Landon shot him made it obvious he'd heard the dig.

"I'm way better looking than you." Landon dropped a kiss on top of my head and then looked inside my glass. "We're drinking?"

"It's a relaxing night," I replied. "Scout and Gunner want to play cards at the guesthouse after dinner." It was a ridiculous lie, but the *Haunted Traditions* crew would have no way of knowing that.

"That sounds fun." Landon's smile was easy. "How was your day?" His gaze roamed my face. "How was the festival?"

"The festival was the same as all the festivals."

"The hot dogs were great," Gunner enthused. "I'm also a big fan of that kissing booth. I mean ... what is up with that? Who has a kissing booth in this day and age?"

"Hemlock Cove," I replied. "It's one of Landon's favorite booths."

"It's almost winter," Landon countered. "The kissing booth will be left in the dust when the hot chocolate and whipped cream booth shows up. When is that, by the way?"

"Probably the next festival," I replied.

"They have a whipped cream booth?" Gunner's eyes went wide. "Are you serious? I totally want to visit the whipped cream booth."

"You would," Scout said. She was slouched in her chair, studying our guests. "So, you guys are filming a television show?"

I was curious where she was going with this, but I figured it was best to give her some leeway. She knew what she was doing and was a master at sussing out information … even if her personality often bordered on abrasive. People couldn't stop themselves from gravitating toward her. I figured it must be the pixie.

"*Haunted Traditions*," Debbie replied, her smile on full display.

"It's a reality show," I explained, even though Scout already knew that. "They pick locations around the country and then hunt for ghosts, vampires, and witches. I bet you can guess why they're in Hemlock Cove."

"I can," Scout easily agreed. "I've always been curious about how this stuff works. I mean … why choose a town full of fake witches for a television show about paranormal activity?"

I pressed my lips together to keep from reacting. Scout was a master of getting under people's skin. Part of me wanted to laugh. The other part wanted to tell her to stop. If she painted a target on her back with some of these people, I had no doubt they would shoot.

"Ah, but that's why it's fun," Falcon replied with a wink. He looked as if he were engaging the flirt machine when he leaned closer to Scout. "This is a town with fake witches, but what happens if real witches are living among the fake ones?"

Scout snorted. "Seriously? That's how you think this is going to work?"

"We've already seen a bunch of stuff," Maya offered enthusiastically. "There was a fire earlier, and nobody knows how it started."

"Actually, people are saying your great-aunt caused it," Greg said. His gaze was fixed on me. "They say she's a regular firebug."

"Is that what they say?" I had to force down my nerves. "Well, if people say it, it must be true."

"We don't have a cause for the fire," Landon interjected.

"The guys who live out there said it was Tillie," Greg persisted.

"You mean the meth cookers?" Landon leaned back in his chair and folded his arms across his chest. "They seem like a solid source of information."

"Meth?" Debbie leaned forward. "How do you know they're cooking meth?"

"More importantly, if you know, why haven't you arrested them?" Falcon demanded.

"We haven't finished our investigation," Landon replied. "By all means, though, believe the meth heads." He rolled his eyes until they landed on Gunner. "Right?"

"I love meth heads," Gunner replied. "They're fantastic."

"What about the rats?" Elle asked. "People say there were rats dancing downtown today."

"Did you get that on film?" Scout asked dubiously.

Elle shook her head. "No, but a bunch of people described what happened. We'll get it on film next time."

"Then I would stick close to Margaret's store," Aunt Tillie said as she slid into the room. She didn't look happy, which meant Mom had gone hard chastising her regarding the afternoon's events. "The big rat always draws the small rats."

"Have the rats been sighted in front of her store before?" Elle asked eagerly.

"Not that I've heard, but I'm betting you'll luck out if you play your cards right." Aunt Tillie plopped down in her usual chair. "I need a drink."

Gunner obediently returned to the drink cart. "What would you like?"

"Throw some hooch in a glass and surprise me," Aunt Tillie replied.

"The crew thinks you started that fire out at the old motel," Scout volunteered. She was clearly trying to rile Aunt Tillie up.

"Oh, it was totally me." Aunt Tillie cast a "come and get me" glare at Mom as she appeared with a huge platter of roast. "People often underestimate me. That's to their detriment. I like to set things on fire."

"Really?" Greg's eyebrows hopped, and his grin was instantaneous. "How did you do it?"

Aunt Tillie waggled her fingers. "Magic."

I cringed as I slid my eyes to Landon. He shrugged. We had no control over this.

"That looks amazing." Gunner plopped down in one of the open chairs. "This is my favorite place to eat. I'm telling you, gas station chicken is amazing, but this is sublime." He offered up a chef's kiss as Mom regarded him with more fondness than she normally reserved for her own family.

"Let's eat," Mom suggested. "There's no need to talk about that fire. It's terrible, but nobody was hurt. That's the important thing."

"Yeah, the fire is old news," Scout agreed as she ceded Mom's chair to her and crossed to Gunner on the opposite side of the table. "I want to hear what working on a television show is like."

"Oh, it's not that interesting," Debbie replied. "I'm pretty sure that what you're imagining is exactly how it plays out."

"I have a terrible imagination," Scout replied as she sat. "I want to hear everything. Lay it on me."

Fourteen

D inner was tense. The table was full, every chair taken, and nobody trusted anybody from outside their group. Mom did her best to keep the conversation light despite Scout's constant questions, but there was no denying that things were starting to spiral.

There was chocolate cake and ice cream for dessert. When it was time to sneak out of the inn, I reminded everyone that we needed to fly under the radar. Scout seemed to find that funny, but she didn't argue. She helped Mom pack baggies of pot roast for Landon and Gunner—they wanted snacks for the excursion—and left me to organize our escape.

"Do you think you're up for it?" I asked Twila, who was busy finishing the dishes.

"Do I think I'm up for it?" Twila let loose an unladylike snort. "Of course I'm up for it. I was born for this." She fluffed her hair. "It's time for my close-up."

Mom smirked as Twila swept through the swinging door. "Those poor people won't know what hit them."

"I just need time to slip out the back with my group," I explained. "That group does not include Aunt Tillie, for the record."

"Definitely not. She's grounded."

I pursed my lips. "You're grounding her?" I tried to picture how that would play out and heard horror movie screams inside my head. "Have fun with that."

Landon was the last to join us in the kitchen. He moved behind me and rested his hands on my hips. "They're in the library. Twila just went in and has them completely blocked in. If we're going to go, now is the time."

I nodded.

"Here." Mom handed Landon one of the pot roast baggies. "It's enchanted to stay warm."

"You're too good to me." Landon forgot he was halfway to feeling me up and leaned in to kiss Mom. "I love that you're my mother-in-law."

I made a face, something that had Scout grinning, and then gestured to the door. "Let's go. At some point, the film crew will make a break for it. I want to be long gone by then."

"I love that you're Bay's mom, who she doesn't appreciate enough and that you spoil us," Gunner offered my mother before falling into line. He gripped his bag of pot roast tightly. "You're my absolute favorite person in the world."

"Hey!" Scout's annoyance was on full display. "Where did the love go?"

"Into my stomach," Gunner replied on a grin. "Thank you for being my best friend, Winnie," he called out as Scout dragged him to the door. "I'll never love anyone more."

"You're definitely sleeping on the couch tonight," Scout growled. "I hope you love that just as much as Winnie."

EVAN MET US ON THE ROAD BY THE field. He was a lurker by nature—maybe he had been even before he became a vampire—but his face was awash with worry.

"Not a sound. Not a hint of movement. Nothing." He held out his hands. "Something is going on."

"Were you here the whole day?" I asked.

He shook his head. "They caught sight of me and tried to hunt me in the trees across the road. I hung around for a bit, but they were armed, and I didn't want to risk them accidentally shooting some innocent out here hiking."

"How long ago did you leave?"

"Hours."

"So, they could've done something."

The sound of crinkling plastic caught my attention, and I glared at Landon and Gunner as they happily took out their pot roast baggies and dug in.

"Seriously?" Scout shot them dirty looks.

"Hey, this isn't my thing," Landon replied around a mouthful of food. "This is my wife's thing. I'm just here to offer emotional support."

"It is my thing," Gunner said. "But until you find something, I'm useless. Call me when you need me." He leaned against Landon's Explorer, shoulder to shoulder with my husband, and focused on his second dinner.

"Well, fine." Scout growled and tugged the sleeve of my coat. "Let's check out the field. These guys are useless."

"I love you too," Gunner called out in singsong fashion.

"I'll go with you," Evan offered. He was always serious—though he'd been loosening up a bit of late—but he was completely focused this evening. "I don't like this."

We left Landon and Gunner to stuff their faces. In truth, there was very little they could offer until we had a magical trail to follow.

The field, which smelled of burned plants, reminded me of a graveyard. These monuments were of the dead plant variety, but that didn't make them any less creepy.

"I can't stand men sometimes," Scout muttered. "They're just so ... male."

"You'd better not be including me in that statement," Evan groused.

"I haven't decided how I feel about you today," she fired back. "You did leave."

"I thought it was best. I assumed I would be able to return this evening to spy on them. Apparently, that wasn't the case."

I slowed my pace. "It is weird that it's so quiet." I took a moment to study the cabins. "Why don't they have guards outside? If ever they needed to protect themselves, today is the day."

"I don't know." Scout slid her eyes to me. "Should we search the cabins?"

I hesitated and then pointed at the two at the far end of the uneven pathway. They were the units that had piqued my interest on our first visit. "That's where they're cooking. At least that was my guess earlier."

"Then let's head that way." Scout didn't cast a look over her shoulder to see if Landon and Gunner were monitoring our progress. I did, of course, but there was nothing to see. The two men still had their heads bent together and their forks out.

"I'm going to have to talk to my mother about feeding them in circumstances like this. It's so stupid."

"They're fine."

Scout's response caught me by surprise. "You were the one just complaining."

She waved off the comment. "They're doing what we need them to do, which is take a step back. If they were hovering, we would be irritated about that. We can't have it both ways."

I rocked to a standstill. "Since when are you the reasonable one?"

She smirked. "I've been doing a lot of thinking the past few weeks. With Gunner's mother on the loose..." She trailed off.

She kept conversations about Gunner's mother—who had just escaped from an asylum—to a minimum. If she did mention her, it was only in passing. To bring her up now, she had to be feeling the pressure.

"Any word on her?" I asked.

She shook her head. "She's out there somewhere, hell-bent on hurting him. I haven't been able to track her down. I've been casting locator spells, but they keep leading me to dead ends. I think she's messing with me."

I didn't know what to say to her. If Landon's mother had tried to kill him as a child and was hunting him now, I'd be a ball of tears and a mess of moods. Instead of telling her she was doing all she could, I took another route.

"If you find her, call us. We'll be more than happy to help take her down."

Scout managed a small smile. "I just might do that. Subjecting Yolanda to a couple hours with Tillie sounds like karma." She blew out a sigh. "I don't want to talk about it right now. There's nothing I can do to fix that situation. This is at least something tangible to focus on."

We fell into silence. Evan kept close to Scout but never crowded her. Their friendship, which had been lost so many years before, seemed to be on solid ground again. I was happy about that because I didn't have a doubt that Scout would need him. When the war with Yolanda came, Scout would be in the center of it. Evan would be at her side, which not only felt reasonable but necessary.

We made it to the first of the remote cabins without anybody intercepting us. The lights in all the cabins were out, and there wasn't a hint of movement to tell us that the dealers were hiding to lull us into a false sense of security before jumping us.

"This just isn't right." Scout made a disgruntled sound deep in her throat before extending her hands. She rested her palms on the door, purple fire erupting. The magic rippled over the building, a glowing wave twinkling under the moonlight.

"Anything?" Evan asked after a few seconds.

Scout shook her head. "There are no wards here, if that's what you're asking. I don't sense anyone inside."

"Hold on." Evan held up his hand to stop Scout from turning the door handle. "Just hang here for a second." He moved off the dilapidated porch and toward the window on the side of the cabin. He was gone about thirty seconds, and when he returned his expression was even darker. "I don't think this place is boobytrapped, but I also don't think that anybody is here."

"Would they just pack up and leave?" Scout asked me.

I held out my hands and shrugged. "I didn't think so, but maybe what happened earlier—the fire, the cops hanging around—threw them. It's possible they ran because they didn't know what else to do."

Scout didn't look convinced. "It feels off." She shoved open the door and waited before entering, likely to make sure that Evan had been right about a lack of traps. Once she was reasonably assured that an ax wasn't going to fly at her, she cast a magical net inside the building to illuminate things.

"There's a switch on the wall," I noted. "The place has electricity."

"Yes, but I wouldn't put it past meth heads to rig the switch, so something explodes. I think we're better off with magic."

I started looking around. I had to breathe through my mouth because of the overwhelming smell, and I shook my head at Scout when she reached out to touch the wall.

"Don't," I warned. "It could get in your system. I've read stories about babies becoming addicted because they licked the walls in a kitchen where meth was being cooked."

"I'm a little smarter than a baby," Scout shot back. "I have no intention of licking the wall."

"Just don't."

"It smells like they had cats in here," Evan noted, his nose wrinkling and eyes watering. His sense of smell was more developed than a normal human's. In a situation like this, that was a detriment.

"It's the meth. When you cook it, there can be a strong ammonia smell afterward. When you smoke it, the scent is sweeter. They were definitely cooking in here."

"How do you know all of that?" Evan looked impressed.

I shrugged. "For a time, I was a reporter in Detroit. I happened across my fair share of meth labs covering stories."

"The scent is here but nothing else," Scout noted as she opened the small cupboards in what could loosely be referred to as a kitchen. "No pots or pans. No utensils. Everything is gone."

"The beds have been stripped too," Evan said, pointing.

I followed his finger with my eyes. "If they were smart, they didn't have anybody sleeping in this cabin. It could've been dangerous, especially if a fire broke out. The bed might've been stripped before they left."

"And yet it appears they did indeed leave," Scout mused.

Something occurred to me. "I wonder if Kevin is still with them."

"The undercover agent?" Scout asked.

"Yeah. I don't know how often he checks in with his handlers."

"I'm not sure there's a reason to panic yet." Scout left the cabin and appeared grateful for the fresh air as she sucked in huge mouthfuls of oxygen.

We checked the second cabin. It was almost exactly like the first. It reeked of ammonia. The bed was nothing more than an ancient mattress. There were no personal items or cooking utensils. It had been stripped bare.

The other cabins were empty, but they didn't smell. There was nothing to suggest that anybody had ever lived in them.

"They cleared out," Scout said as we emerged from the last one. "They're gone."

"Where did they go?" I asked. "Do you think they had a backup location in mind or just fled willy-nilly?"

"I have no idea." Scout was just as pensive as me and fell silent as we started across the burned field to rendezvous with Landon and Gunner. "They must've packed up in record time. I'm guessing they were afraid the feds might raid them. Still, they moved faster than I would've thought possible."

"Yeah, I..." My gaze drifted to the ground when I felt something under my boot. It was almost as if the ground was moving. Frowning, I tilted my head and shuffled my feet, my heart leaping when a shadow emerged from beneath the ground. I reacted on instinct and threw out a burst of magic to freeze the shadow. At the same time, I hopped backward, essentially throwing myself into Evan.

"What's wrong?" Evan caught me around the waist and held me tight.

"Shadow," I barked in a hoarse voice.

"Where?" Evan studied the ground where I pointed. Once I threw out the magic, the shadow had beaten a hasty retreat. Nothing was moving, and the ground felt solid under my feet.

Still, I knew something bad was about to happen.

Landon. His name was a scream ripping from my soul, and when I jerked up my eyes to search the darkness—we'd traveled well east from where we started, so the Explorer was no longer directly in front of us—I realized he wasn't leaning against his vehicle eating pot roast.

"Landon!" I yelled his name while trying to keep the beat of my heart down. Now wasn't the time to panic, and yet I couldn't stop myself. "Landon!"

"I'm here." His response was a grumble. He was somewhere off to my right. "Don't get worked up."

"Also, maybe don't yell so loudly?" Gunner groused. "We don't want the meth heads to hear us."

"The meth heads are gone," Scout snapped, "but I think they left something behind." She made a strangled sound, and Evan released me and bolted in her direction.

I turned just in time to see Scout grab something and yank it upward, her head cocking as she regarded a shadow creature with keen eyes.

"What are you?" she demanded.

The shadow struggled against her grip, lashing out with what looked like claws—had the first shadow creature boasted claws?—and catching her wrist.

Scout hissed as she dropped it, frowning as she cradled her wrist to her chest. I was breathless when I made it to her side.

"Let me see," I ordered.

"It's fine." She held up her wrist so I could see the ugly marks. The creature had broken the skin, but she didn't look as if she was in danger of bleeding out. It did bring to mind another concern, though.

"What if the claws were poisonous?"

"I think it's fine." Scout's eyes were trained on the ground. "It's best we get out of here. There's more than one."

"There are quite a few," Evan confirmed. "We can't stay here." He was intent as he pushed us toward the Explorer. "We need to leave. Right now."

I swallowed hard but nodded. "Okay. We can go." I lifted my eyes to search for Landon and was relieved when he appeared with Gunner at his side. He didn't look concerned in the least. Well, until he caught sight of Scout's wrist.

"What happened?" he demanded, rushing forward.

"There are shadow creatures throughout the entire field," Evan replied in a low voice. "One attacked Scout."

"It's more apt to say that I grabbed it, and it tried to escape," Scout corrected. "Either way, we can't stay here. It's not safe, and I'm not sure what we're dealing with."

"Then let's go." Landon grabbed my hand and gave me a tug. "There's no reason to stay a second longer."

I shot him a small smile. "Oh, well, now I'm more important than the pot roast."

"You were always more important than the pot roast. I had no idea we were going to run into this sort of trouble." He looked alarmed now. "We're out of here. Right now."

I was right there with him and nodded. "Let's go. We can talk about what we're facing once we're clear of this place. This is ... not normal."

"Oh, what was your first clue?" Evan drawled.

"We need to get to safety." I refused to be drawn into an argument. "After that, we can figure out our next move."

If we had a next move.

Fifteen

Nothing attacked during our escape, but the feeling of dread —we were definitely being watched—tied my stomach in knots for the ride home. Scout said she would do some research, but she seemed as lost as I felt. This entire situation was weird. Heck, weirder than normal. When you lived in a world that included Aunt Tillie, that was pretty frightening, because "normal" was already a slippery slope.

Evan stayed behind to monitor the shadows. I didn't like the idea of him being alone, but he laughed when I voiced my concerns.

Landon checked the locks ten times before we shut down for the night. The guesthouse was warded, so I promised him we would be fine. I didn't sleep well despite my comforting words to him. I was far too agitated, and my dreams were a hodgepodge of dark shadows and screaming meth dealers, and I was still exhausted when I woke the next morning.

"Five more minutes," Landon mumbled when I moved to slide out of the bed. His arm slipped around me, and he snuggled me tightly against his side. "Stay with me."

I acquiesced, turning so I could bury my face in the hollow of his neck and listen to his rhythmic breathing.

"Tell me what you're thinking," he said after a few moments of silence.

"I don't know what I'm thinking." That was the truth. "The shadows last night didn't attack, but they could have. So why didn't they?"

"Maybe they were afraid of you."

"I didn't do anything to fight off the one at the greenhouse. It attacked me, and there was nothing I could do to stop it. I was only saved by a fluke."

"Well, thank you for putting that in my head so early in the day." His eyes were dark when he pulled back to look at me. "I didn't need to hear that."

I couldn't help but laugh. "You're so dramatic sometimes." I poked his cheek. "Spending so much time with my family has turned you into a bit of a drama queen."

"Spending so much time with your family—which is now my family—simply allowed my inner drama queen the opportunity to come out and play. No matter how ridiculous I am, there are always people in the inn who are worse."

"True story."

"Word." He bopped his knuckles against mine and grinned. The smile lasted only a few seconds. "I don't like hearing that you were saved by a fluke. You're a superwitch and nothing can take you out."

"Oh, if only that were true."

"I need to believe it's true, because the alternative is too much to bear."

I pressed my hand against his chest, reassuring my inner worrywart with the steady beat of his heart, and then forced myself to focus on our current predicament. "Maybe it was Scout," I suggested. "Maybe they were afraid of her, and that's why they didn't attack."

"She grabbed one by the throat. Seems it was about to attack her."

"Maybe." I wasn't convinced. "Or maybe they were just curious."

"The one that attacked you outside the greenhouse was a little more than curious. It said it was going to kill you."

"It did, but there's more than one of them. Maybe, just like people, some of the shadows are nicer than others."

"Is that just wishful thinking?"

"Probably." I puffed out a laugh and closed my eyes. "None of it makes sense. I mean ... how does it all fit together? Where are the meth heads? Did they know the shadows were in the field? Is that why they fled? What about the missing meth heads? Did the shadows kill them? Why was one of them killed downtown? Why was his body glowing?"

"That's a lot of questions, Bay."

"Are you telling me you don't have the same questions?"

He shook his head. "I have the same questions ... and maybe a few more. Unfortunately, I don't have your witchy background to fall back on to fill in some of the gaps. For example, what could create a shadow like that? We've fought shadows before, but they always seemed to have magic behind their appearances. What sort of magic are we dealing with this time?"

"I have no idea." And that bothered me a great deal. "When I first saw the shadow outside of the greenhouse, it was flat. My initial instinct was that somebody had come outside, and I hadn't seen. Of course, there was no sun ... and there was no reason for some huge guy to be in the yard behind the inn, but my mind tried to rationalize it."

"Maybe that's how they manage to keep from being detected," he mused, his fingers lightly tracing over my back. "If they're constantly appearing as two-dimensional shadows, most people wouldn't pay them any heed. The only reason you noticed is because you were alone. The lack of sun didn't enter your mind in those first moments."

"That's true. If I'd been at the festival, I wouldn't have even registered the lack of sun because I would've been distracted by all the activity."

"The shadows are only one of our problems," Landon pointed out. "The meth heads were firmly entrenched on that property. They bought it, but now they're gone."

"You're worried about Kevin," I surmised.

"He didn't make contact yesterday."

"He might not have been able to. If they packed everything up and took off as a group, he might not have been able to slip away."

"I know, but he had to figure that we would be worried." Landon scrubbed his cheek and stared at the ceiling. "Back when I was under-

135

cover, I did my best to make contact at regular intervals. Big moves had to be reported. Why couldn't Kevin slip away for three minutes and call with his burner phone?"

"Perhaps they were watching him."

"Maybe." Landon didn't look convinced. "If I were in his position, I would've found a way to make contact."

We didn't often talk about Landon's time undercover. He'd tossed that part of his life when we got together.

"Let's say Mickey started freaking out the second the emergency vehicles left his property," I prodded. "How would you make contact if everybody was supposed to be working together to move the operation?"

"Well, in the initial rush, he wouldn't be able to make contact," Landon replied. "They would've had a plan in place to move fast. You said all the equipment is gone."

"Yeah. The cabins are empty. We checked the back two first because we assumed that's where they were doing the cooking. You could smell the ammonia, but they were empty. Even the beds were stripped."

"That doesn't necessarily mean anything. Nobody would be able to sleep in those cabins if they were cooking. At least not safely."

I smirked. "That's what I said."

"Such a genius." Landon tickled my ribs and then went back to contemplating Kevin's lack of contact. "They were likely all staying in the other cabins. Were there bunk beds?"

I shook my head. "Double beds in each cabin."

"That's not enough beds. Even if they were sleeping two in a bed they wouldn't have had enough beds for everybody."

"I'm sure they had roaming sentries," I said. "Maybe they slept in shifts."

"Still doesn't feel right." Landon's forehead creased. "They have to have another base."

The assumption caught me off guard. "Near the cabins?"

"It would have to be. It's something we missed."

"Why wouldn't Kevin tell you?"

"He wasn't with the group more than a few days. He might've planned to tell us and then everything turned to crap."

"How do we find the secondary location?"

"We need that big map at the inn," Landon replied. "It contains old houses."

"You think they took over one of the old homes too."

"It makes sense."

I rolled out of bed. "Let's get showered and dressed. We can look at the map before breakfast."

"It would probably be quicker if we showered together," Landon supplied on a cheeky grin. "I mean ... just to streamline the process."

"Oh, that *would* be convenient." I couldn't stop from laughing. "Even in a crisis you like to flirt. I think that might be my favorite thing about you."

"I have fifty favorite things about you, and this is just one of them." He moved to follow. "Do you think your mom will cook bacon for breakfast? I might need the boost. Something tells me it's going to be a long day."

"Doesn't she always make you bacon?"

"Yes, but you've been limiting my bacon intake. Are you going to do that today?"

I hesitated and then shook my head. "You can have as much bacon as you want this morning."

"Thank you, dear. You're too good to me." He lavished an exaggerated kiss on my knuckles.

"I'm trying to make sure you live a long life," I complained as we padded to the bathroom. "I'm not trying to be bossy."

"I'm well aware."

"But you see me as bossy."

"Just a little. As it happens, I like women bossy. It works out well for both of us."

"I guess that's why you love this family so much."

"It's only one of the many reasons. Now, come on. I'd like to show you how much I love you and then get to that map. I think we're definitely on to something."

· · ·

LANDON AND I WENT STRAIGHT TO THE library when we arrived at The Overlook. We drove, leaving both our vehicles in the parking lot, and avoided the family living quarters. The library was empty, but that didn't last long.

"What are you doing?" Aunt Tillie demanded when she appeared in the doorway. "Are you plotting without me? You know I don't like that."

"We're trying to figure something out," I replied, casting her a sidelong look. "Actually, you might be helpful. The map shows three houses at Sand Lake. What can you tell us about the houses?"

Aunt Tillie didn't immediately respond. Instead, she moved to stand between Landon and me. Her eyes were keen as she watched Landon peer at the map. "What am I missing?" she asked. "Why do you care about houses out there?"

"The meth heads are gone," Landon replied. "They packed up yesterday afternoon and disappeared."

"There weren't enough beds in those cabins for them to sleep comfortably," I added. "We believe they had a secondary location. You're familiar with the area. You used to be friends with Beverly McKinney. I remember you guys drank cocktails on her dock."

"Who is Beverly McKinney?" Landon asked.

"She's gone now," Aunt Tillie replied. She looked thoughtful. "She was fun. I liked her a great deal ... and not just because she hated Margaret. Cancer got her about eight years ago."

"What happened to her house?" I asked.

"It was sold to some auto executive from the south," Aunt Tillie replied. "They used it as a summer getaway. They came maybe twice a year, but otherwise left the house to rot."

"That's something to consider," Landon mused. "Maybe they invaded a house somebody else wasn't using. Which house would that be on the map?"

I pointed.

"So, Beverly McKinney's house is less than a mile from the cabins," he said. "That's convenient, especially if nobody is using the house."

"It might be convenient, but I don't think that's it," Aunt Tillie replied. "Beverly's house was at most fifteen hundred square feet. That's not much room when you're dealing with meth heads. Bob Johnson's house is probably a good five thousand square feet when you include the boathouse."

Landon straightened. "Five thousand square feet? That's a mansion."

"The boathouse is more than a thousand feet of that, and there's a walkout basement," Aunt Tillie replied. "It's big, but I think there are only four bedrooms."

"Bob died this summer," I explained to Landon. "His children moved from the area years ago. I heard they were letting the house sit through the winter before putting it on the market in the spring. I thought we might even go see it when they list it."

"I thought we were building on the old campground," Landon complained.

"We are," I reassured him, biting back a laugh. He was definitely dramatic. "Bob's house has a lot of cool features. I thought we could get some inspiration for when we design our house. We don't need a boathouse, but that recreation room is amazing. I remember seeing it when I had to stop there as a kid to drop off a casserole for the previous owners. Mom sent me with the food, and I saw the house. It's amazing."

"And it's big enough to house a bunch of meth cookers," Landon said. "Where is that on the map?"

I pointed toward the opposite side of where the cabins were located.

"About a mile," he said.

I nodded. "It wouldn't be that far from the cabins … and it's much more space."

"What are you doing?" Chief Terry asked as he joined us in the library. "Why are you looking at the map?"

"The cabins are empty," Landon replied. "They've been cleaned out."

"What?" Alarm rippled across Chief Terry's face. "How is that possible? Where did they go?"

"That's what we're trying to figure out."

"What about Kevin? Did he check in?"

"No, and we're worried." Landon pressed his lips together and glanced between the map and me. "We think we have an idea where they are. Bob Johnson left a big house there when he died, and it's empty until at least spring. It's worth checking out."

Chief Terry rubbed his chin. "That house is just sitting there, and because of the location, nobody will check on it during the winter. There are no neighbors. They'd be able to set up shop without anyone noticing."

"That's exactly what we were thinking," Landon agreed. "But we have a problem. If we drive out there, and they see us coming, they might feel trapped and start shooting or something. We can get help from the state police, but it would be better if we had confirmation they're actually there first."

"Okay." Chief Terry's expression was impossible to gauge. "What do you plan to do?"

"I thought maybe Bay could take a look around." Landon looked as if he would rather swallow glass than utter those words, but he barreled forward. "She can use her magic to camouflage herself. We need confirmation. Once we have it, we can call the state police and set up a raid."

Chief Terry immediately started shaking his head. "I don't like it. Since when do you want to put your wife in unnecessary danger?"

Landon glared at him. "Don't ever phrase it like that again," he warned in a low voice. "I don't want to put my wife in danger. I do, however, acknowledge that she can get closer than we can. She's strong and smart ... and she can do things we can't."

"Oh, you say the sweetest things." I beamed at him. "You're also getting really good at being the husband of a witch. I love it."

"Well, you gave in on the bacon this morning." He gave me a serious look. "Compromise, right?"

I nodded. "Compromise."

"Well, I think it's a bad idea, and I don't want to risk it," Chief Terry huffed.

"It will be fine," Aunt Tillie assured him. "I'll go with her."

"That doesn't make me feel any better," Chief Terry fired back.

Oddly, it made me feel better. If the shadow monsters moved on us near the house, Aunt Tillie might have a few ideas on how to tackle them.

"You can go with us and wait in the truck," I said. "We can take a walkie-talkie since cell service is spotty out there. It will be fine."

Chief Terry folded his arms across his chest. "What if something goes wrong?"

"What if something goes right?" I challenged.

"How often does that happen?"

I refused to acknowledge he had a point. "I've got this. Trust me."

"Fine, but if things go sideways, I'm going to say 'I told you so' until the day I die."

That seemed fair. "I would expect nothing less."

"Let's eat breakfast first," Landon said. "I get to go nuts on the bacon for the first time in weeks. After, we'll make sure the film crew is pointed elsewhere. We don't need them following us."

Sixteen

"You're back."

Debbie beamed at us as we made our way into the dining room, but there was a glint in her eyes that made me nervous. I returned her smile—we were always pleasant with the guests even if we didn't like them—and sat in my regular seat between Landon and Chief Terry.

"We eat breakfast here almost every morning," I replied. "As my mother likes telling me—repeatedly—I'm not much use in the kitchen. I let her dote on Landon when it comes to food."

"It must be convenient living on the property," Reid noted. "You can wander in and out when you feel like it. Take last night, for example. You and your friends managed to slip out without anybody being the wiser."

The statement was pointed, and when I slid my eyes to my mother as she emerged from the kitchen with a huge platter of waffles and pancakes there was a warning in her expression.

"I don't know that I would say we slipped out," I countered. "We simply headed back to the guesthouse for a few drinks and games."

"Games?" Reid arched an eyebrow. "What sort of games?"

"Euchre," Landon replied. He placed a glass of juice in front of me and then reached for the coffee carafe. "We're big euchre players."

"I don't know what euchre is," Maya said. She stared at Landon with adoring eyes. "Is it a board game?"

"Cards," Reid replied. "It's a regional thing. It's big in Michigan and Ohio."

"We do love our euchre in Michigan," I agreed.

Twila brought the meat platter out, and Landon was all over it before bothering with the pancakes. "Who played euchre?" she asked as she settled in her chair. "Why wasn't I invited to play?"

"We played at the guesthouse last night," I lied. "That's what we did when we left the inn."

"Oh, and here I thought you guys were leaving to skulk around and mess with the meth heads." Twila, ever oblivious, didn't meet my warning gaze. "I can't picture Scout playing euchre. Was she any good?"

"She was fine," I gritted out.

"Why would they skulk around the meth heads?" Reid asked.

"They do it all the time." Twila let loose a haphazard wave. She never could read a room, one of the qualities that drove me crazy. "They like having adventures. You know ... fighting monsters and stuff."

I was going to kill her—with intense pain. At the very least, I was going to gag her.

"Fighting monsters?" Debbie leaned in. "What sort of monsters?"

I glared at my mother, silently demanding she somehow fix this situation. In truth, there was no fixing it. We all knew that.

"Trouser snakes," Aunt Tillie volunteered. She'd been so quiet for the duration of the conversation I'd almost forgotten she was present.

"Trouser snakes?" Falcon choked on a laugh. "I think I'm missing something."

"It's a running gag," Aunt Tillie replied. "Twila just doesn't get it."

Twila was obviously annoyed by the statement. "Excuse me?"

"I guess we must be missing something," Debbie said. "What are trouser snakes?"

Next to her, Reid laughed again. "Think about it."

"I'll lay it out for you because you appear slow," Aunt Tillie offered. "Landon and Bay are sex fiends. They should get treatment for sex addiction they're so bad. One day Landon said he had a monster to show Bay—a trouser snake—and it became a running joke. Twila's brain doesn't work fast enough to understand the joke."

"Hey!" Twila's fury was palpable. "I know what a trouser snake is, and that's not what I was talking about."

Mom was on her feet in a flash. "We need more syrup." She grabbed Twila's arm and ruthlessly tugged her toward the kitchen. "Why don't you help me get some?"

"There's syrup right here." Reid held up the bottle for proof. "I think we can all share."

"No, we need more."

Twila was still sputtering when Mom pushed her through the swinging door. The pall left over the room was heavy enough to weigh down a body.

"Do you spend a lot of time talking about trouser snakes in front of your mother-in-law?" Reid asked. He seemed desperate to get a reaction out of Landon, and I was terrified he would get his wish.

"Like Aunt Tillie said, it started as a joke," Landon replied evenly. He sipped his coffee, likely to buy himself enough time to organize his thoughts. "Now the joke has taken on a life of its own."

"It's beyond frustrating," Chief Terry agreed. He looked as if he wished he was talking about anything but trouser snakes, but we'd committed to the lie at this point. "I threaten to kill him on a weekly basis because of that joke."

"But you're not Bay's father," Reid pressed. Why was he so interested in our family tree?

"I'm not," Chief Terry confirmed.

"He is," I countered, frustration getting the better of me. These people were invading my home, and I didn't like it. I wanted them to go. Maybe if I was rude enough, they would get the hint. "He's always been there for me, ever since I was a kid. He and my father gave me away at my wedding together. Blood doesn't make a family."

"I wasn't suggesting otherwise," Reid said. "The dynamics here are hard to wrap my head around."

"Well, maybe you don't need to understand them." I stabbed a fork into the pancake stack and transferred some to my plate. "You're here to find witches, right? I would think you'd focus on that."

"We can multitask," Falcon said. "In fact, we're on the hunt today. We're going to that creek that's so famous. Supposedly witches dance naked around it."

I narrowed my eyes. "Who told you that?"

"We had coffee yesterday morning with Mrs. Little," Maya volunteered. "She had a group of women with her. She called them the heart and soul of the town. They were full of interesting tidbits."

I didn't have to ask who Mrs. Little referred to as the "heart and soul" of the town. She had minions, and that's who she'd clearly unleashed on the film crew yesterday. "And she told you that witches dance naked at Hollow Creek?" I demanded.

"She did." Falcon bobbed his head. Much like Twila, he seemed to have trouble reading a room. He was either oblivious or playing a game. "She said that rituals are performed there."

I slid my eyes to Aunt Tillie. She seemed as baffled as I felt. "Well, have fun with that."

"What are you doing today?" Debbie asked. She'd opted for one pancake and two sausage links, which seemed a waste when there was a veritable feast in front of us.

"I have work," I replied.

"What sort of work?"

"I run the newspaper largely on my own. I have to okay the layout for this week's paper, talk to a variety of advertisers, and get the art for this week's edition from our photographer. It's all very boring."

"Still, it must be nice to own your own business," Maya said. "Is that why you fell in love with her?" she asked Landon. "Did you like that she was an entrepreneur?"

Landon froze with his fork halfway to his mouth. "I guess." A smile played at the corners of his mouth. "I didn't know she was an entrepreneur the first day I met her. I thought she was a mouthy blonde who enjoyed pushing all my buttons."

"You clearly liked having your buttons pushed," Reid noted.

"I'm a perverse creature." Landon winked at me and then sobered. "Bay is a hard worker. She does everything at that newspaper, and she does amazing things with very few resources. It takes a lot of her time, but that's one of the reasons we decided to stay in Hemlock Cove. It's easier for me to work remotely."

"You inconvenienced yourself for her." Maya pressed her hand to her chest and sighed. "That is just ... so hot."

Landon forced a smile. "I'm not inconvenienced. This is what's best for us as a couple."

"What are you doing today?" Reid asked. "While your wife is working at the newspaper?"

Reid was digging for information. They didn't trust us ... and rightfully so.

"We're still trying to dig up an identity for our dead guy," Landon said. "We got distracted because of the fire yesterday. That's the main order of business today."

"What will you do when you know who he is?"

"Hopefully, we'll find answers. Until then, we're stuck ... and I hate being stuck."

Reid didn't blink. "Don't we all?"

LANDON AND CHIEF TERRY PARKED ON A TWO-TRACK about a quarter of a mile from Bob Johnson's house. It was the closest they could risk without being seen.

"I don't know if I like this," Landon complained as Aunt Tillie and I prepared to approach the house from the woods. "We're not close enough to race to your rescue should you get in trouble."

I had to stifle a laugh. "Just out of curiosity, if we did get in trouble, what would you do? I mean ... racing to our rescue. What would that look like?"

"I would shoot the meth dealers."

"And when they shoot back, and we're caught in the crossfire?"

Landon's glare was dark. "Listen, I didn't say it was a perfect plan. I don't like being separated from you."

"I get it." I did. "We're going to cloak ourselves magically."

"Yes, we're going to make ourselves look like bears," Aunt Tillie readily agreed.

I shot her a sidelong look. "No, we're not."

"Coyotes?"

"I was thinking we would just do that chameleon spell, so we fade into the foliage. We're not crossing into the yard. We're just getting close enough to the house to see if there's any activity outside."

Aunt Tillie looked less than impressed. "You're zero fun. I don't understand how I went so wrong with you."

"We'll be fine," I assured Landon. "We have the walkie-talkie and our cell phones."

He gave me a kiss. "Be careful."

"I'm always careful."

"Be way more careful than that."

I led the way into the woods, being careful to check the ground for shadows. Aunt Tillie followed, throwing up the camouflage spell.

"Your husband is a nuisance," she complained.

I picked my way through the bushes. Once temperatures dropped in mid-October, all the green disappeared until spring. That had me thinking. "Did you make sure we meld with the current colors? We're not going to look bright green to anybody watching the woods from the house, are we?"

"Am I new?" Aunt Tillie demanded. "I've got it under control."

"I was just asking." We stopped speaking for the rest of the walk. The woods were quiet—too quiet—no noise from scurrying animals or blowing fern fronds. The only noise emanated from our footsteps, and it made me leery. Thankfully, it didn't take us long to close the distance to the house.

"There it is," I said in a breathy whisper as I extended my arm to keep Aunt Tillie behind me. If we broke from the cover of the woods, we would definitely be seen.

"It's a nice house," Aunt Tillie mused after several seconds, cocking her head. "If it wasn't out in the middle of nowhere, I'd consider moving here."

"You would consider leaving the family property?" I was dubious.

"Your mother is being a pain. I want to teach her a lesson."

"What lesson?"

"She's not the boss of me."

I pressed my lips together and moved a bit to my right, my attention fixed on the house. There were no curtains drawn, and even though we had a clear view into the house, it was too dark to make anything out.

"There's nobody here," I said after a few seconds.

"You don't know that." Aunt Tillie raised her hands and sent out a magic pulse before I could warn her to stop. "They could be hiding."

Her magic rolled over the property before disappearing into the woods on the other side. "Huh," she said after a moment. "There's nobody here."

"You don't know that," I challenged on an eye roll, perfectly mimicking her voice.

"Don't be you, Bay," she warned. "It's been a long day, and I can only take so much."

"It's not even ten," I pointed out.

"Well, it's still been a long day." She ran her tongue over her lips and scanned the yard again. Then, before I realized what she was about to do, she popped out from behind the tree we were using as cover and started across the lawn.

"What are you doing?" I hissed at her back. "That's not part of the plan."

"Oh, stuff it."

She was twenty feet ahead of me before I got my head together and gave chase. By the time I caught up with her, she had her hands on the windowsill and was peering inside.

"This is not stealthy," I growled.

"Will you look at that?" She made a tsking sound with her tongue and shook her head. "Who needs that much wallpaper? It's such a waste. He should've gone for the log cabin look in the rec room. That's just tacky."

I shot her a death glare but didn't say anything. Instead, I fixed my attention inside the house. "There are blankets," I said. "And cots."

"I'm betting all the bedrooms have been taken over too," Aunt Tillie said. "There's just one problem."

"No people."

"Yeah."

"No Kevin." I glanced to the driveway. "Let's see if it looks like motorcycles have been here. It's possible they're out running errands."

"Yes, entire groups of meth cookers often run to the grocery store together," she agreed.

"Nobody needs the sarcasm." I stepped lightly rounding the house, convinced this could still be a trick. When we arrived at the dirt driveway, two things became obvious. The first was that motorcycles had indeed been running up and down the driveway. The tire tracks were obvious. The second was that none of them were present now.

"What do you think?" Aunt Tillie asked as she scanned the ground. "Do you think they decided against staying here? Maybe they worried the cops were getting too close and decided to run."

I wasn't convinced that was true. I retrieved the walkie-talkie from my back pocket. Cell service this deep in the woods would be nonexistent. "I need to call Landon."

"I'll do it." Aunt Tillie snagged the walkie-talkie from me before I could object and pressed the button. "Breaker, breaker, Big Momma is in the house. I'm looking for Bacon Lover and Constant Whiner. Hit me back."

I didn't want to laugh, but it took everything I had to swallow my chuckle.

"Which one of us is Constant Whiner?" Landon asked.

"That could work for either of you," Aunt Tillie replied. "Also, Bacon Lover isn't fun. Let me try again. Breaker, breaker, Big Momma is in the house. I'm looking for Major Buzzkill and Bane of His Mama's Existence. Hit me back."

"Give the radio to Bay," Landon barked.

Aunt Tillie smirked before handing over the walkie-talkie. Then she headed for the garage.

I kept one eye on her as I spoke. "There's nobody here. They've been here. There are tire tracks in the driveway, and cots are set up inside."

"What did I say?" Landon complained. "You weren't supposed to risk going close to the house."

"Yes, well, I've been a bad girl. You'll have to spank me later."

"I'm about to be Constant Whiner if you don't shut up," Chief Terry groused. "Are you sure they're not there?"

"We haven't gone inside, but there's no movement. We can't detect anybody with our magic. The place looks abandoned."

"But ... why?"

"I don't know." I watched with grim curiosity as Aunt Tillie raised the garage door. "I think this is their meth equipment. It's been stowed in there."

"Where did they go?" Chief Terry asked. I was guessing the question was directed at Landon.

"I don't know," Landon replied. "Where is Kevin? Did he go with them? Did they figure out who he was and make him go with them? Maybe they didn't leave of their own volition."

It was a thought. "What do you want us to do?"

It was silent on the other end for several seconds—probably so Landon and Chief Terry could confer. Landon answered me when it came time.

"Close the garage door and meet us at the end of the driveway. We'll pick you up. Let's not give them a reason to be suspicious if they return."

"I don't think they are going to return. This place feels abandoned."

"Let's just see."

"Okay. See you in three minutes."

"I'll be the one Big Momma warned you about."

Seventeen

A unt Tillie didn't want to be dropped back at the inn—a definite red flag—but Landon didn't balk when she asked that he leave her on the corner near Hypnotic. It was obvious she had plans. Nobody doubted those plans revolved around Mrs. Little. There was no point in arguing with her. She would find her way into town regardless.

"I'm kind of curious about what she'll do," Landon admitted as we climbed out of his Explorer in front of the police department. Chief Terry had insisted on being driven back to The Overlook so he could reclaim his official vehicle and was several minutes behind us.

"You just want to watch her torture Mrs. Little," I surmised as I leaned into him. It was cold, and my mind was swirling with possibilities regarding the gang.

"It's not like she doesn't have it coming." Landon kissed the crown of my head as he hugged me tight. "What are you thinking?"

"I'm thinking we should go away somewhere after Christmas, just the two of us."

He stilled. "Are you serious?"

"Yup. I want a vacation from my family."

"That can be arranged. Do you want to go someplace specific?

151

Would you want to go back to Moonstone Bay?"

It was an interesting offer. I'd enjoyed our time on the island despite Aunt Tillie crashing our honeymoon. It wasn't what I had in mind, though. "I was thinking someplace on the West Coast. Aunt Tillie hates fog."

Landon barked out a laugh. "I'll go wherever you want. Just give me time to put in for my vacation, and we'll take off and not tell your family where we're going."

I smiled against his chest and then sighed as I pulled back. "I think they might be dead, Landon."

He didn't look surprised by my declaration. "The meth cookers?"

I nodded.

"I was thinking that myself." He dropped his arms from around my waist and dragged a hand through his hair as he turned to survey Main Street. "How would that work, Bay?"

Was he seriously asking me that question? "How should I know?"

"You're the expert." He turned back. "You know more about this than I do. What are we dealing with?"

"If I knew the answer to that question, I would've stopped this by now."

"Theorize."

"Oh, geez." I rolled my neck. "They were conjured somehow. Someone magical conjured the shadows to stand as sentries. That explains why they were by the cabins. They wanted to protect the meth, make sure nobody could spy on them, and they created guards."

"You were out there. Did anybody feel magical to you?"

I considered the question for a long time. "No," I said finally. "They didn't feel magical. That doesn't necessarily mean anything, though. I've been bamboozled before."

"Mickey was in charge. Could he be magical?"

"Anybody can be magical, Landon. It's all in how they hide it. You had no idea I was magical when we first met."

"I knew you were magical the moment I laid eyes on you. I just didn't think you were magical in such an overt way."

That made me laugh ... and then groan. "You're so corny."

"That's why they call me Constant Whiner with a Heart of Gold."

"I'm pretty sure you were also Bane of His Mama's Existence."

"I can live with that." His lips curved as he brushed my hair out of my face. "If they're dead, what happened to their bodies?"

"Maybe they turned into the shadow people."

"So, the three people who went missing initially were all shadow monsters after the fact. Is that why the body we found glowed?"

"It's a possibility. This is all still a hunch. I don't suppose you've checked to make sure the body is still there?"

Landon hesitated, looked concerned for a moment, and then he pulled his phone from his pocket. "Hold on."

I moved away from him as he placed the call, my attention on the Unicorn Emporium across the street. Aunt Tillie usually timed her spells for noon because she wanted the maximum number of eyes on Mrs. Little's meltdowns. We still had an hour and a half before her next showing ... whatever form it would take.

Landon was on the phone a full five minutes. The medical examiner's secretary found his request that she check to make sure a body was still there ludicrous, but she did as she was asked. I could only hear Landon's side of the conversation, and I was lost, so I had to wait until he hung up to question him.

"So?" I prodded.

"The body is still there. It's no longer glowing. According to Meredith—she's the crabby woman who answered the phone—they're running extensive tests for any compounds that could possibly light up a body and then disappear. She mentioned something about bioluminescence."

I frowned.

"That's when living organisms glow," he said.

"I never would've guessed," I muttered.

"It wasn't an insult," he said. "I was just making sure you'd heard the word before."

"I saw it in an old episode of *SeaQuest* when I was a kid. There was an oversized squid that was attracted to bioluminescent fish."

"It's not just a water thing," he said. "Bugs can be bioluminescent."

"Yeah. Bugs." I rolled my neck. Was that important? Part of me thought it might be. The shadows weren't bugs. They didn't even resemble bugs. "So, the body was glowing, but now it's not. It's still there, and we don't know what happened to the other bodies."

"We don't know that there are bodies," Landon reminded me. "It's possible that Mickey saw the writing on the wall and fled. He might've originally decided setting up shop in Bob Johnson's house was the smart move but then thought better of it."

"Maybe." That didn't sound right. "Why leave all that stuff behind?"

"Maybe he's coming back for it."

"How can he be guaranteed it will still be there?"

"I can't answer that, Bay." Landon held out his hands.

I turned back to Mrs. Little's store. She was visible through the window—Connie Daughtry and Sara Boudreaux were bent close and listening to whatever she was ranting about.

"Landon, if the gang is dead..." I couldn't finish it.

"Then Kevin is probably dead too," he said when I didn't speak for several seconds. "I know, Bay."

"It might explain why he hasn't called." I felt sick to my stomach for even suggesting it.

"It might. Or they could've run, and he had no choice but to go with them. If he feels his life is in danger, his orders are to stay under until he's certain he can escape. Kevin might have to stick with the group until they pick a new location to settle in."

"What are the odds he would stick with them through that?"

Landon hesitated and then held out his hands. "I don't know, but he's a dedicated agent. I know he came across as gung-ho when you met him, but he's a good guy. He's just young and green."

"I didn't dislike him," I said quickly. "I don't want you to think that."

"Okay."

"I was just worried that you were having a problem with his assignment because you wanted it."

"Sweetie, I'm exactly where I want to be." He was earnest. "I was a boy when I met you. You made me a man."

It was a nice sentiment, but it could be taken several ways.

"Stop smirking," he ordered. "I didn't mean it that way. When I met you, I knew you were going to change my life. I know it's weird to say because we fought at the start, but I had this feeling. I don't miss being undercover. That was a fun life for a few years, but this is a better life."

I squeezed his hand, grateful for the words. "Thank you. It's nice to hear, but I know how you feel. You tell me with words and deeds every single day."

"Do you want to go to your office and take a 'nap' to reward me for my words and deeds?"

"Maybe later." My eyes were drawn back to Mrs. Little's store. She looked as if she was still ranting. "I'm worried about Kevin," I admitted. "He seemed dedicated to the job. He wanted to do things the right way. I don't think he would've gone this long without making contact unless something very serious happened."

"We don't know he's dead."

"No, and we don't know that the missing men are being transformed into shadows. It's just a hunch."

"What else could it be?"

"It's possible the shadows are ghosts. I mean ... they could be dark souls. Maybe there's another necromancer in town, and he or she is appropriating souls to hunt the meth dealers."

"Why?"

"It's possible whoever it is lost a child to drugs or something."

"That sounds a little Movie of the Week, Bay."

"It does, but that's the world we live in. Somewhere out there right now, Aunt Tillie is plotting to ruin Mrs. Little's life. She's going to do something worse than dancing rats at noon."

"I'm kind of hoping for a return of the farting unicorns." Landon took on a nostalgic expression. "That was honestly my favorite prank."

It was a good one. "She doesn't like to do repeats. She prefers to one-up herself."

"Maybe the unicorns could make little rainbow poops all over the store. That's worse than farting."

"Don't ever mention that to Aunt Tillie," I warned. "She would totally go nuts with something like that. I know she's plotting something. The dancing rats were cute, but people have already forgotten. And because it was a glamour, nobody is complaining about vermin leaving droppings everywhere, and the whole thing has already been forgotten for the most part."

Landon moved his hands to my shoulders and rubbed them up and down my arms. "Both ideas are valid. I'm leaning more toward the first. If that thing that attacked you outside the greenhouse was a ghost, your instincts would've allowed you to fight it off right from the start. You're too good for it to go the other way."

"I'm flattered by your assumption, but I'm not sure I believe it. I was flustered that day. I was ... afraid. I couldn't think clearly."

"I'm sorry you were afraid." Landon pulled me tight against him. "I still don't think it's ghosts. I know I don't get a vote because this isn't my world, but that doesn't feel right to me."

"You get a vote. You might not have been born into this world, but you live in it now. You're much more knowledgeable than you give yourself credit for."

"I'm dreamy," he agreed on a smug grin. "I'm the perfect man. I still don't believe it's ghosts."

He wasn't the only one. "There's just one problem with the first scenario," I said. "If we're right, and the gang members are being killed and turned into shadows, who is moving on them?"

Landon shook his head. "I don't know."

"It has to be someone powerful."

"Which means a new face? You would know if someone in town had that power."

"Maybe, but I don't want to pin everything on that assumption. It's possible it's a local. It's also possible we're not dealing with someone from Hemlock Cove. Sand Lake is halfway between Hemlock Cove and Shadow Hills. Maybe the magical person we're looking for lives there."

Landon pursed his lips. "Is there a way to find out if you're right?"

"Not off the top of my head. I need to give it some thought ... which I plan to do back at my office."

"After taking a 'nap' with me on the couch?"

"No nap." I was firm on that despite how adorable he was. "You'll have to wait to play that game until we're alone tonight."

"Ugh. You're zero fun, just like Aunt Tillie says," he complained, a small smile playing at the corners of his lips.

"Whatever. I..." All thoughts of finishing the banter died when I saw Connie crossing the street in our direction. She looked fueled by righteous indignation ... and maybe something a little extra, like fear.

"This doesn't look good." Landon pushed himself away from his Explorer. "How much do you want to bet Mrs. Little sent her to be obnoxious?"

That wasn't a bet I was willing to take.

"Agent Michaels," Connie said primly when she reached us. She was slightly out of breath, which wasn't surprising because she'd booked it across the street. "I would like a word with you."

"Knock yourself out," Landon said blandly.

"In private." Connie cast a disparaging look in my direction. "This is not a conversation I want to have in front of ... her type."

Landon offered a lazy grimace. "Listen, I'm not a police officer in this town. If you have a complaint, you need to take it up with Terry Davenport. If you have a specific concern, you can tell me now ... but Bay isn't going anywhere."

"It's a private conversation," Connie insisted.

"I'm really gossipy and tell Bay everything," Landon said. "So, you can tell her now or you can wait for Terry to get to his office. Those are your options."

Fury flitted through Connie's eyes. Part of me was convinced she was going to storm off, but she kept it together. "Fine. We have a situation."

"What sort of situation?"

"There are monsters on the loose in Hemlock Cove."

"Monsters?" Landon's eyebrows hopped.

"Monsters," Connie insisted. "The sort of monsters in horror movies." She leaned forward and said the next part in a conspiratorial whisper. "I believe that your wife's great-aunt is the source of these monsters."

Landon didn't as much as blink. "How did she do that?"

"She's horrible. Everybody knows it."

"Everybody knows Mrs. Little is horrible too," Landon pointed out. "Maybe she conjured the monsters. I still don't know what sort of monsters you're talking about."

Connie sounded exasperated now. "Is there more than one kind? All I know is that Margaret is a kind and decent woman, and now she's being haunted by some sort of weird shadows. She thinks Tillie cut them off of people and sent them to haunt her."

I froze in place, and it took me a full five seconds to loosen my tongue enough to speak. "She's being haunted by shadows?"

"I'm not talking to you." Connie's glare was full of hate. "I can't stand you or the rest of your family. If people weren't snowed so easily and bamboozled into believing you're entertaining, I would vote to evict you from this town."

"Well, then I guess we're lucky it doesn't work that way," Landon said. "What did Mrs. Little say about these shadow monsters?"

"That they were harassing her all night. Apparently, they were in her yard and tried to entice her outside. They were lewd and crude to boot. You know darned well that was Tillie. She's responsible for the farting incident. Everybody in town knows it."

I didn't care about the farting incident. The shadows haunting Mrs. Little were another matter entirely.

"I'll talk to her," Landon said, forcing a smile. "I'll head over in just a minute."

"Talking to her doesn't solve the problem," Connie argued. "Tillie Winchester is a menace."

"I'll talk to Mrs. Little," Landon reiterated. "That's the best I can do right now."

"Whatever." Connie left in a huff, her head down as she stalked toward the coffee shop.

When I was certain she was out of earshot, I spoke. "That can't be a coincidence."

"I should think not."

"Maybe we should talk to her together."

Landon didn't look thrilled at the notion, but he nodded. "Can't hurt."

It could, but I decided not to start listing the litany of ways this could work against us. If the shadows were haunting Mrs. Little, we were dealing with a whole new ball game ... and I didn't understand the rules to this game any better than I did the last one.

Eighteen

I was determined as we crossed the street. Sara was still with Mrs. Little, and I gave her a pointed look as I walked through the doorway.

"What do you want?" Mrs. Little demanded.

"We want to talk to you," Landon replied. He raised his chin to Sara. "You don't mind letting us have a few moments with Mrs. Little, do you?"

Sara looked caught. "Um..." She slid her gaze to Mrs. Little, seeking permission.

"Go." Mrs. Little waved her off. "It's fine. They won't do anything to me ... at least not in the middle of the day. When I go home tonight, they might send their monsters to mess with me again, but I'll be expecting them."

I managed a bemused smile. Sara took her time leaving when it became apparent nothing more would be said until she made herself scarce.

"What do you want, Bay?" There was no warmth in Mrs. Little's voice. That was normal for her, but part of me felt bad we couldn't even pretend to be pleasant any longer.

159

"Connie said you were attacked by monsters last night." I saw no point in dragging things out. "What sort of monsters?"

"Connie said I was attacked by monsters last night?" Mrs. Little's voice ratcheted up a notch. "And you believed her? How very odd."

Mrs. Little was many things, but a proficient actress wasn't one. Every emotion registered on her face if you cared to watch for them. The one emotion taking precedence today was fear.

"Don't play games." My agitation was on full display. "What did you see?"

"Why do you care?"

"I'm a concerned citizen."

"And I'm an FBI agent," Landon added. He stood several feet away from me, the picture of a professional. "If something happened, I need to know about it."

Ever petulant, Mrs. Little folded her arms across her chest. "Since when are you in the monster-hunting business?"

"For as long as I can remember," Landon replied. "It was a childhood dream of mine. I always wanted to hunt monsters, and look at me now, I get to do it for a living. Not all monsters look like those in books."

"What about the family of monsters you married into?" Mrs. Little demanded.

Landon extended a warning finger in her direction. "Don't."

"Don't what? Don't tell the truth?"

"We need to know what happened to you last night," I snapped. "It could be important. We're not asking because we enjoy torturing you."

"Although that is an added bonus," Landon muttered.

"We need to know what happened," I insisted. "I know you care about this town. If you won't do it for me ... or even for yourself ... do it for the town."

Mrs. Little bit her lower lip then blew out an exasperated sigh. "I don't know what it was. Or, I guess, what *they* were. I heard them after I'd gone to sleep. They woke me. At first, I thought I was dreaming."

"What time?" Landon asked.

"After ten o'clock I guess. Closer to eleven."

Apparently, that was late in Mrs. Little's world. I wasn't surprised that she was in bed before ten. There were nights I was more than happy to climb between the sheets with a good book before nine. The time frame was important.

"We were at the cabins then," I said to Landon.

He nodded, thoughtful.

"What cabins?" Mrs. Little's forehead creased. "What are you talking about?"

Rather than answer her question, Landon pressed forward. "Have you had any interactions with the individuals who were living at the Sand Lake Motor Inn lately?" he asked.

"You mean those druggies?" Mrs. Little's distaste was obvious. "No, I haven't been hanging out with them. They're not exactly my cup of tea. They're probably your wife's cup of tea—she fell in love with you when you were pretending to be a druggie if I'm not mistaken—but I don't hang around with the dregs of society."

"Did you fall in love with me when I was pretending to be a drug-gie?" Landon asked me in teasing fashion.

"I think it took a little bit longer than that," I replied. "But when you took a bullet for Aunt Tillie, I think our fate was sealed."

"Yes, if only you hadn't arrived in time," Mrs. Little groused.

"You don't want to go there either." Landon pressed his palms on the counter. "You knew what they were up to out at the lake. Why didn't you make a report?"

"I told Terry. He said he couldn't do anything without proof."

"I hadn't realized." Landon licked the seam between his lips. "He didn't tell me you stopped by to complain."

"I'm betting he didn't think it was news," I said. "She stops in at the police station to complain every day. He's used to it."

"I'm a concerned citizen," Mrs. Little barked. "I have a right to complain when the world is going to hell in a handbasket. It's my duty to protect this town."

"So you've said on many occasions," Landon said. "Did you ever have words with anybody at the cabins? It's important."

"I stopped in a few days ago, said that we would be filming a television show, and asked them to make themselves scarce."

My mouth dropped open. "You have more guts than brains some-times," I muttered. "Do you know which one you talked to?"

"He said his name was Dane."

I nodded. "Did he threaten you?"

"No. He was actually decent. I wouldn't go so far as to call him reasonable, but he wasn't awful."

That was high praise coming from her. "Did he say they would stay out of town?"

"He didn't respond, and I didn't hang around to wait for a response. I said what I wanted to say and left."

"Nothing weird has happened since then?"

"As compared to what?" Mrs. Little snapped. "Weird things happen to me all the time now. If it's not unicorns passing gas, it's people claiming rats danced on the sidewalk in front of my store. If that's not weird, I don't know what is."

She had a point.

"Tell me about last night." Landon's voice was soft as he prodded her. "You said you were sleeping. Did their voices wake you?"

"Yes. They were outside, in the yard. I assumed it was Tillie being Tillie and was about to go out there and give her what for, but when I turned on the floodlights there was something off about the situation."

"Meaning?"

"Meaning that ... they didn't appear to have faces." Mrs. Little looked distinctly uncomfortable now. "It was like they were shadows. Like ... Peter Pan's shadow. You know how in the movie he has a personality all his own? It was like that. I saw shadows but no people to go with them."

"Did they speak to you?" Landon asked.

"They said that I was in the way and had to go. Why are you ques-tioning me like I'm the criminal? We all know Tillie sent them. You should be interrogating her."

I couldn't blame Mrs. Little for believing that. Aunt Tillie had been torturing her for years. I doubted shadow monsters had been part of the deal, but from Mrs. Little's perspective, there was no reason to believe the shadows weren't part of an elaborate plan by my great-aunt to slowly drive the store owner insane.

"You stayed inside," Landon said. "What made you decide to do that? If you thought it was Aunt Tillie, why didn't you go out and confront her?"

"Maybe because I didn't want to die," Mrs. Little shot back.

That was enough to jolt me out of my deep thoughts. "You know darned well Aunt Tillie wouldn't actually hurt you. Not that way. She might embarrass you and enjoy a good verbal spat, but she wouldn't do anything dangerous."

Mrs. Little shifted from one foot to the other, and for the first time in ...well, perhaps ever ... she looked earnest. "If you want to know the truth, there was a small part of me that questioned if it was Tillie. I know it was, but it wasn't..."

And that's when I realized the truth of it. Mrs. Little knew the shadows weren't Aunt Tillie's doing. She might hate my great-aunt, but she recognized real danger when she saw it.

"Don't let the shadows draw you out of your house," I said, making up my mind on the spot. "I promise you they're not Aunt Tillie's doing. Whatever happens to your store at noon, that you can blame on Aunt Tillie. But the shadows..." I shook my head.

"What are they?" Mrs. Little's voice was barely a whisper.

"We don't know," Landon replied. "Whatever you do, don't leave your house if they show up again. Obviously, they couldn't get inside, so you're safe there."

I had an idea why they couldn't get inside, but I didn't mention it until we were back out on the street. "Aunt Tillie warded her house."

Landon led me toward the diner. "I wondered."

"It's the only thing that makes sense."

"Why would she do that?"

"She probably did it when Mrs. Little was cursed and didn't tell us. It was an added safety measure."

"Why not remove the wards?"

"She probably forgot."

"Okay." Landon took a breath as he held open the diner door for me. "Why would those ... *things* ... go after her in the first place?"

It was a good question. I spied Chief Terry at a table when we entered and headed toward him. "Maybe they didn't like what she had to say."

"I can't see them caring. There's nothing she could do to them. They wouldn't want to keep drawing her attention. Wouldn't it make more sense to leave her alone?"

"Who are we talking about?" Chief Terry asked as we settled across from him.

"Mrs. Little." Landon calmly launched into the tale she'd just told us. When he finished, he raised his hands. "We're trying to figure out why she would be a target."

Chief Terry rubbed his chin. "Any ideas?"

"Other than her telling them not to come into town, I can't see why they'd care," Landon offered. "They wouldn't want to deal with her on a regular basis. It makes more sense that they'd want to avoid her."

Chief Terry kicked back in his chair. "So, what are we dealing with?"

"Bay and I have been talking about it, and I think we're dealing with some sort of magical being who is turning the gang members into monsters."

I jerked up my chin. Landon hadn't lowered his voice when delivering the answer. Thankfully, we were early for lunch, and the tables around us were empty.

"Don't worry." Landon bumped his shoulder against mine. "I wouldn't mention shadow monsters in front of an audience."

"Just making sure."

His smile didn't diminish. "It could be a mission-based killer," he said as he sobered. "Just because we're likely dealing with a magical being doesn't mean we can throw other motives out the window."

"You mean like a cleaner," I mused.

"A cleaner?" Chief Terry looked confused.

"Back in Detroit a few years ago," I said, "there was a serial killer who started offering homeless people free drugs to lure them in. They shot themselves up without asking what was in the syringes. They died after injecting themselves with caustic cleaning chemicals."

Realization dawned on Chief Terry's face. "I remember that."

"That was a mission-based killer. The guy—he used to be a doctor

—believed that homeless people were a scourge on society and decided to clean them up his own way."

"Well, that is just lovely." Chief Terry looked disgusted.

"How do you know the terminology?" Landon asked.

I didn't bother to hide my smirk. "Impressed?"

He nodded.

"I used to work in Detroit," I reminded him. "I interviewed a few profilers."

He rested his hand on my knee and squeezed. "I don't know why I ever lose sight of the fact that you're the smartest woman in the world."

"I have no idea, but it is distressing."

"You're saying that in this case, the killer is going after drug dealers," Chief Terry mused. "Part of me thinks we should be applauding them instead of hunting them."

"Did you forget the part where the shadow tried to kill Bay?" Landon demanded.

Chief Terry gave me an apologetic smile. "Sorry about that, kid. I would never want to gloss over that."

I had to laugh. "You don't have to apologize. Frankly, that throws a kink into our leading hunch. If the shadows are going after Mrs. Little and me, we can't be dealing with a mission-based killer."

"Unless the shadows are hunting you on their own," Landon countered. "Isn't it possible that they're afraid you and Mrs. Little could somehow put an end to their lives? If a magical being created them, maybe they're worried you will have a hand in ending them, and they're trying to get ahead of that."

"I can see that being the case for Bay," Chief Terry said, "but not for Margaret though. By her own admission, she went out there to make sure Hemlock Cove wouldn't look bad in front of the television crew."

"That's true," I agreed. "Say what you want about her, she does put the town first. If push came to shove, she would choose herself over the town, but she hasn't had to make that choice. She has Hemlock Cove's best interests at heart."

"Why would someone want to end her because of that?" Chief Terry idly scratched his chest.

"I'm going to think about that. What about the dead guy in the morgue?" Landon asked. "Do we have an identity yet?"

"No, and it's getting a bit ridiculous," Chief Terry said. "You would have to think that somebody involved with meth distribution would have a record."

"Unless it was his first time," I said.

"Someone has to be missing this guy." Chief Terry was adamant. "He's been dead for days. I've been watching reports from all over the state. Nobody has reported anyone who sounds remotely like our dead guy missing."

It was another conundrum we couldn't find a way around. "What about other states?" I asked. "Or Canada?"

"I haven't opened up the search that far, but I can." Chief Terry didn't look thrilled at the prospect. "If he's from Canada, it could take months to identify him."

"We don't have that kind of time." My mood was taking a definite downturn. "I wish I'd pressed Dane on the issue yesterday. Now I might never get the chance."

"You don't think they'll show up somewhere?" Chief Terry asked, reminding me he hadn't been present for my conversation with Landon regarding the likelihood of the gang already being dead.

"I hope they will." I couldn't lie to him, but I didn't want to foist my opinion on him before he was ready. If he wanted to believe Kevin was still out there struggling to find a way to get in touch, I couldn't take that possibility away from him just yet. "It just seems odd that they disappeared the way they did."

Chief Terry looked to Landon. "What do you think?"

"We need to get ahead of this." Landon was firm. "I'm not sure what that's going to take, but we need to start with another outing this evening."

"To where?" Chief Terry looked horrified.

"Mrs. Little's house," I replied. "There's every reason to believe those shadows will be back at her place tonight."

"Can you fight them?"

"I can try."

"I don't like this." Chief Terry hitched his thumbs in his gun belt.

"Why can't we have a normal week? Just one normal week. It's not too much to ask."

"We don't live normal lives," Landon replied. "It is what it is."

"Since when are you the calm one?"

"Since I married a badass witch." Landon shot me a fond grin. "She can do anything, including solving this case. We just need to give her a little room to navigate."

Nineteen

Landon was leaning one way—and I didn't disagree with him—and yet I couldn't shake the feeling that we were missing something big. Tonight, we had to stake out Mrs. Little's yard. If we could catch one of the shadow creatures and interrogate it, we might find answers.

Or, if we were really lucky, we might be able to eradicate them all at the same time and put an end to this. Eliminating the threat was the most important thing. I couldn't find all the shadows myself, so I needed reinforcements. That meant recruiting Thistle, who I had no doubt would be crabby about the entire thing.

I figured it was best to get it out of the way and headed to Hypnotic, pulling up short when I found Reid standing outside the store smoking a cigarette.

"Hey," I said dumbly.

Reid blinked twice and then grinned. "Is that your lame way of hitting on me? If so, your approach needs work."

I frowned. "I have a husband."

"So I've noticed." He took another drag on his cigarette. "You seem to be joined at the hip."

"We do our best."

"Doesn't that make solving crimes difficult? For him, I mean. I can't imagine that it's easy to save the world from evil one criminal at a time when you take your wife everywhere you go."

Reid had been full of pointed statements since I'd met him. He seemed to have an attitude, one that wasn't in line with the other people on the film crew. "We make it work."

I crossed my arms over my chest and shifted from one foot to the other. It was rare to get members of the crew on their own, and I had questions. "You grew up in Shadow Hills, right?"

"I spent part of my childhood there," he corrected. "I don't remember much about the town. There was a pretty good diner. My grandparents took me there for breakfast Sundays after church, even though they lived in a different town. Other than that, I remember a lot of trees ... and maybe a park somewhere. My memory is fuzzy."

"You must have been very young."

"Yeah. We left when I was a kid because my father wanted more work opportunities. We moved south, and then left the state three years after that. My mother wanted a warmer climate. She was never one for snow."

"I can see that. A lot of people hate snow."

"Do you hate it?"

"I don't hate it, but I don't love it. It's fun to cuddle up with some hot chocolate and a good book in front of the fireplace on a snowy day. Aunt Tillie has a plow truck she likes to take out. I never got into skiing or anything, so the climate up here is wasted on me. Fall is my favorite season. I'm a big fan of summer, too."

"Your aunt has a snowplow?" Reid looked tickled at the idea. "Does she volunteer her time to plow out the neighbors or something?"

"More like she volunteers to plow in her enemies. That's far more her speed." I didn't mention her penchant for yellow snow. "How is the filming coming?"

Reid lifted one shoulder in a shrug. "It's fine. The footage will be pretty if nothing else. I honestly wish we would've come three weeks earlier when the trees would've been in full color."

"But the town would've been crawling with tourists then. That might've hampered your efforts."

"That's true. You need some people to fill out the frames, but too many become a distraction." He took one final drag on his cigarette and then stubbed it out. "We went to Hollow Creek this morning. That place is trippy."

"Trippy?" It was an interesting word choice.

"Falcon and Elle were gushing on air about how haunted it felt. They insisted you could feel ghosts watching from the shadows."

Shadows? "Should I take that to mean you didn't feel the same way?"

"I'm not a true believer." Reid gave a wink that felt smug. "I'm just here for the paycheck. And, well, I love to travel. The others might get off on this stuff. I'm bored by it. I have to say, though, if there was ever a haunted place in this area, that creek does feel like it would be the place."

Was he playing with me? Was he trying to get me to say something that would somehow incriminate my family or the town? Before I could respond, the sound of Hypnotic's door opening drew my attention, and when I turned, I saw Debbie and Greg exiting the store.

"Bay." Debbie clapped her hands. She was a little too excited for my taste. "I'm so glad we ran into you. We just finished our interview with Thistle. She is a real hoot by the way. The viewers are going to love that bad attitude of hers."

"We all love her bad attitude," I said. "It's the stuff of legends."

"It's ... something." Debbie looked momentarily perplexed and then shook her head. "We have an appointment at the Dandridge to interview your cousin Clove next. We can make space for you if you're ready."

Clove was probably racing around like a moron to make sure the Dandridge was spotless and her makeup was on point so she would be Kardashian camera ready at this very moment. I didn't bother mentioning that, however. "I don't think I need to do an interview," I said.

Debbie's expression faltered. "You're the local newspaper reporter, Bay. That makes you a historian of sorts. We need you for the episode."

"I'm not comfortable talking on camera." That wasn't a lie. I didn't want to help them on pure principle, but the idea of talking on camera tied my stomach in knots.

"You're thinking about it too much," Debbie insisted. "It's not like a production. It's just a conversation that the camera happens to catch."

"I'm still not comfortable."

"But Mrs. Little promised we could get an interview with you."

"Perhaps she should've broached the topic with me."

"She said you would be fine with it. Your family is at the heart of the piece. We've already got your mother and aunts locked down. Thistle, while reluctant, said a few things we can use. I don't foresee a problem getting Tillie on camera."

Getting Aunt Tillie on camera would be easy. Getting her to play nice when she was in a bad mood was another thing entirely. That was their problem. "Then you shouldn't need me."

"We need you more than the rest of them combined," Debbie insisted. "You're the reporter. You're the one people will most believe."

"That seems unlikely."

"It's true."

She wasn't going to give up. She was tenacious to a fault, something I normally respected. Not today though. "I'll give it some thought."

"That's not good enough."

"Oh, geez." Reid swore under his breath and pinned Debbie with a dark look. "You can't force her to be on camera, Deb. I know that you're used to bullying people to get what you want, but it won't work with her. Give it a rest."

"I have to agree with Reid, Deb," Greg offered. His gaze was intense as he looked me up and down. "She won't back down, and the more you push her, the more she'll dig her heels in. If she wants to talk, she will." The smile he sent me suggested I should be grateful for his interference.

"You guys have been doing this for a long time, right?" I decided to change tactics.

"More than a year," Greg confirmed.

"Then I'm sure you have contingency plans. I don't see why people would want to hear from me. I run a tiny newspaper. I'm guessing you'll have more than enough footage with Mrs. Little leading the charge, so maybe focus on her."

"Oh, we'll have plenty of footage of Mrs. Little," Debbie intoned.

She looked momentarily frustrated. "She's already sat for three interviews, with three changes of clothing, and wants to set up two more."

I smiled. "She's an expert on the town. She knows the history. I'm sure she's been a source for a great many stories."

"She has," Debbie agreed. "Unfortunately, most of those stories involve your family."

A cool sense of dread rolled into my stomach and took up residence. It was like a brick of meatloaf that refused to digest. "Oh, yeah?" Keeping my face placid took work. "What sort of stories?"

"Most of them are absurd," Debbie acknowledged.

"I'm a big fan of the yellow snow story," Reid offered.

I froze. He hadn't mentioned yellow snow when I brought up Aunt Tillie's plow. "Yellow snow, huh? That sounds fun." I let loose a hollow laugh. "I remember those days well."

"That's one of the reasons we want to talk to you on camera," Debbie pushed. "Magical yellow snow will have our viewers howling."

I needed to kill this storyline. "It wasn't magical. It was food coloring." That was a lie. Aunt Tillie's yellow snow assaults on Mrs. Little were definitely of the magical variety.

"How did she manage to cover the entire yard in food coloring?" Greg asked.

It felt like a trap. Of course, everything the film crew did these days made me feel as if I was under assault. I could readily admit that I didn't want them here, which made me defensive, but I refused to let them bulldoze me.

"She didn't buy the food coloring from the grocery store. Well, actually I think she did a time or two. She had to dilute it so much she was disappointed with the result, so she began making her own dye."

"How did she do that?" Greg looked smug enough that I had no doubt he believed he was catching me in a lie.

"Saffron threads," I replied. "It's a spice. You can order it almost everywhere. Aunt Tillie used to buy it in bulk, and a little saffron goes a long way making color. If you can't find saffron, turmeric will work ... although turmeric turns everything yellow, including your hands. It's hard to get rid of, so Aunt Tillie prefers saffron."

Greg blinked then flicked his eyes to Debbie. He didn't come right out and ask if that was true, but he wanted to.

"Sounds ... interesting." Debbie's disappointment was palpable. "Mrs. Little seemed certain that your great-aunt is magically torturing her."

"I'm sure she did." I graced the producer with what I hoped would pass for an easy smile. "Mrs. Little has always been a little excitable, and Aunt Tillie goes out of her way to feed the delusions."

"I wonder if that means the big finale she promised us will fall through." Debbie chewed her bottom lip as she darted her eyes to Reid. "Maybe we should brainstorm a backup plan."

I had questions, and lots of them. "Big finale?"

"Oh, yes." Debbie bobbed her head. "It's a reality show, but we need to plan certain things. Mrs. Little has promised us a finale that will thrill our fans. Something about a magical explosion and exposing the town witches for what they truly are."

It took everything I had not to race across the road and start ruthlessly questioning Mrs. Little all over again. I had no doubt we were the target of her big finale. How did she plan to trick us into performing on camera? That's what she wanted. If we were exposed, we would have to draw back from public life or leave entirely. Hemlock Cove would then be hers to run.

"Well, that sounds fun." I flashed a fake smile bright enough to fuel the sun. "I can't wait to see what she comes up with. Hopefully, it's not as bad as the time she tried to pretend all her unicorns were farting thanks to a magic spell. We're still picking up glitter from that debacle."

Debbie's frown grew darker. "That was fake too?" She looked anguished. "Our viewers would've loved that story."

"Have you ever seen ceramic unicorns fart?" I asked pointedly.

Debbie, dejected, scuffed her foot against the pavement. "Well, this sucks." She focused on Greg and Reid. "We need to do some brainstorming."

"May I suggest getting peppermint lattes across the street." I pointed to the coffee shop. "They're delightful, and you have a clear view of the town. They always help me think when I need to come up with enough material to fill the paper."

"What are you going to do?" Reid asked.

"I'm going to do what I always do in the middle of the afternoon when I want to kill time," I replied. "I'm going to flop on Thistle's couch and complain about our family."

Reid cracked a smile that didn't touch his eyes. "Have fun with that, I guess."

"That's the plan." I waved them off with a sunny grin and stepped into the store. I waited until the door had drifted shut to speak. "I can't stand them, and I'm going to kill Mrs. Little. And it's going to hurt."

"Are you channeling Aunt Tillie?" Thistle looked more amused than worried. "And here I thought I was the one who was going to turn into her. Whew." She wiped the back of her hand across her forehead in exaggerated fashion. "What a relief."

I pinned her with the darkest glare in my repertoire. "We have a problem."

"You should get a shirt made that says that. It would save time."

She was far too blasé for my liking. Of course, she'd been purposely avoiding the inn for days, so she wasn't up on the gossip. "I'm serious. Mrs. Little has promised them a big finale."

Thistle stilled. "What does that mean?"

"I have no idea, but we both know it's not good."

"Definitely not."

"There's more." I caught her up on everything she'd missed.

"So, the dealers are gone, along with Landon's undercover agent?" Thistle's expression was blank.

I nodded. "I think they're dead, Thistle. I also think it's possible the shadows are the dead men."

"Well, that's not good."

"It's not. Why they're focusing on Mrs. Little is beyond me. It makes sense—at least in a roundabout way—for them to go after me. Going after Mrs. Little is a different story. What do they hope to accomplish by luring her out of her house?"

"Maybe they want to make a shadow out of her."

The thought hadn't occurred to me, and in hindsight, that was obviously a mistake. "Oh, geez."

"They might want her knowledge," Thistle continued, oblivious to the change in my demeanor. "She does know everything about the town. Maybe there's information they think only she can provide."

"That would make her a genuine target they'll keep coming back for."

"That would be my guess."

"Well, crap." I threw my hands into the air, disgusted. "I can't believe we have to save her two months in a row when she's so terrible to us."

"Nobody says you have to save her."

I shot her a withering look. "Really? Do you think I'm just going to sit back and let her die?"

"No. You're a hero. But heroes don't complain about the people they have to save."

"You need to come with me tonight." I got directly to the heart of matters. "We need to spy on Mrs. Little's property, and I need some form of backup that isn't Aunt Tillie. She gets too easily distracted around Mrs. Little."

"I guess I can do that." Thistle didn't look thrilled. "If one of those shadow creatures kills me, I'm going to totally blame you."

"I can live with that."

"You might change your mind if I turn into a vengeful ghost."

There were worse things ... and one of them was across the road plotting a finale that I knew wouldn't be good for us. For once, Mrs. Little was way ahead of us.

Twenty

T headed to the newspaper office once I was finished at Hypnotic. The film crew was inside the coffee shop when I passed, and Falcon waved enthusiastically. I nodded and kept going. The crew was a worry, but Mrs. Little was the bigger concern. Not only did she have something planned, but she was also in danger. The woman never ceased to be a menace.

"There are monsters hanging around town," Viola announced when I walked into the lobby. "Also, where have you been? I've been looking for you for days."

Viola was prone to dramatic fits. "You couldn't have been looking very hard because I haven't gone anywhere out of the ordinary. Well, other than Sand Lake, but I've been home and at the inn between trips, so you could've tracked me down there."

"That's so far to walk," Viola groused. "You should really come to me."

"You're a ghost and can basically poof wherever you want to go," I reminded her.

"Yes, well, that's neither here nor there." Viola's gray ghost eyes sparkled as she leaned closer. "There are monsters in town."

"I'm well aware. Where have you seen them?"

"They're everywhere. They're hiding in the shadows. Heck, they're made of shadows."

"Have you talked to them?"

"Why would I talk to them?"

"Because they're monsters, and you're a ghost. You might have a few things in common."

"I'm not a monster."

"You're not a Kardashian either, and yet you talk to them when you're watching television. I've heard you."

"They have such poor taste in men." Viola looked legitimately upset. "They're such pretty girls, and yet they keep picking terrible partners. That one keeps getting cheated on, and it's horrible."

"I'll take your word for it."

"One of them just married a tattooed gentleman who looks like he was a snake in another life. And that other one is dating a penis with ears."

I spent a few seconds trying to figure out who she was talking about and then brushed the comment aside. "That sounds terrible."

"It is. He was on *Saturday Night Live*, but he's not funny. I miss the days of Eddie Murphy and Will Ferrell."

"Don't we all?" I had an idea and decided to broach it while Viola was taking a breath. If I didn't redirect her attention now, I would be stuck listening to reviews of the *Saturday Night Live* cast for hours. "I have a mission for you."

Viola looked suddenly suspicious. "Am I going to like this mission? I have to be honest, the past few missions you've sent me on have been real downers."

"I don't know if you'll like it, but it's important."

"I guess I'll consider it." Viola's stance told me she was ready to shoot me down in an instant. As a necromancer, I could force her to do my bidding, but I always felt guilty when going that route.

"I need you to spy on Mrs. Little."

Viola's eyes went wide. "Are you planning to kill her? She always said this would happen. Was she right?"

"If I wanted to kill her, she'd already be dead. We don't want her to die. Well, mostly. Her attitude makes it very hard to root for her most days."

"She does have the personality of a pickled pig's foot," Viola said. "Why do you want me to watch her?"

"Because your shadow friends paid a visit to her house last night. They were trying to entice her outside, an invitation she thankfully declined. I need to make sure she doesn't change her mind. I'd also like to know what she's working on with her little cadre of jerks. She has a plan to deliver a grand finale for the television crew, and I'm worried it involves us."

Viola looked thoughtful. "Is she trying to be a television star?" she asked. "If so, she really needs to embrace her inner villain."

"That's exactly what I'm worried she's doing," I admitted. "Her plans for the television crew aren't as important as her safety. If you could find information on both, I'll be forever in your debt."

"Enough so that you'll upgrade the television in the kitchen? I hate watching my stories on that tiny screen."

I considered the request for several seconds and then nodded. "I'll get you a bigger television if you manage to get information from those shadows and figure out what Mrs. Little has planned for the television crew."

"I can do that." Viola's smile was bright. "In fact, it sounds fun. I was going to spy on her anyway. Whatever embarrassing spell Tillie plans to unleash on her today should hit any moment now."

I'd almost forgotten about that. My eyes moved to the clock on the wall. It was after noon, and Aunt Tillie was late.

"Tillie likes to mix it up occasionally," Viola volunteered to my unasked question. "She sometimes moves her attacks later so Margaret isn't expecting them."

"Good to know."

ONCE VIOLA HAD LEFT TO MONITOR Mrs. Little, I stopped in my office long enough to check emails. There was nothing of vital importance to steal my attention—when dealing with a weekly newspaper there rarely was—so I headed to Main Street in anticipation of the show.

I planted myself in front of the police station, snuggled into my jacket on the bench, and waited. Landon and Chief Terry found me five minutes later.

"I guess I don't have to ask what you're doing here." Landon sat beside me and slung his arm around my shoulders, tugging me in tight at his side. "Are you cold?"

"Winter is almost here." I was rueful. "I think that's part of the deal when living in Michigan."

"I would suggest a nap so I can warm you up, but your expression tells me you're not up for that."

I hesitated and then shook my head. "We have some things to talk about."

"We do," Chief Terry agreed as he sat on the other side of me. He wasn't up for a snuggle, but his burly frame offered warmth all the same. "We have news."

I slid my eyes to him and waited. The set of his jaw told me it wasn't good.

"We found Kevin's bike," Landon volunteered when Chief Terry didn't continue. "It was abandoned at the gas station store in Hawthorne Hollow. The one Gunner and Scout like to get their chicken from. The owner assumed the bike belonged to a member of their group and called them to pick it up. It had been there since yesterday. Graham Stratton ran the license plate, and it led him to us."

I took a moment to consider the information. "Well, that's not good."

"Not good at all," he agreed.

"Do you think the bike was abandoned in Hawthorne Hollow on purpose?" I asked. "With Scout's group being the dominant force in town, it's possible whoever dumped the bike thought they would be able to buy time before anybody noticed it."

"We don't know." Landon's voice was soft. "It doesn't bode well for Kevin, Bay."

"You think he's dead."

Frustration rippled across Landon's face. "I was leaning toward that assumption before the bike was found. I didn't want to admit it, but it's one of the only scenarios that makes sense. He would've found a way to make contact by now."

My heart went out to him. He'd acted jealous of Kevin the day I'd met him, but Landon was too good of a guy to hold a grudge. "I'm sorry."

"It's not your fault."

"No, but we've done nothing to stop these shadow things, and I was attacked before Kevin went missing. If we'd managed to..." I didn't finish. We all knew how much better things would've gone if I'd managed to fight off my attacker.

"Don't take this out on yourself, Bay," Landon chided. "You might be a superwitch, but you're not omnipotent. There's no way you could've known what was going to happen."

"But we've been spinning our wheels for days. People have gone missing. A lot of people. How can we still know nothing?"

"We're doing the best we can."

It didn't feel like enough. Then, something occurred to me. "They found Kevin's bike. What about the bikes of the other gang members?"

"Nobody has found them ... at least not yet."

"Why would Kevin's bike be separate from the others? If the gang realized Kevin was undercover and killed him, they would've fled as a group after the fact. I'm guessing they were all taken together."

"Bay has a point," Chief Terry noted. "Why was Kevin's bike separated from the others?"

"Could one of the shadows have realized after the fact that Kevin was different from the rest of the group?" Landon asked. "Could this be a way to send a message?"

There were a lot of different messages that could be sent in this scenario. "What if Kevin put the bike there?" I asked.

"Why would he leave the bike there if he knew he was in trouble?" Landon asked. "Wouldn't he have fled to us on the bike so we could protect him?"

"Maybe he's not Kevin any longer. Maybe he's a shadow that retains some of Kevin's memories. This might've been his attempt to warn us."

"Warn us how?" Frustration oozed out of Chief Terry as he fixed his eyes on me. "If he was transformed into one of those shadow things—and I'm not ready to go there just yet—why wouldn't he approach us and tell us what happened?"

"He might not be fully in charge of his new reality," I replied. "We're operating under the assumption that we have a genuine enemy—a witch, warlock, or mage maybe—creating the shadows. Maybe Kevin couldn't do anything but leave his bike somewhere he knew it would be discovered."

"Does that mean they're hiding in Hawthorne Hollow?" Landon asked. "Should we start a search?"

"It's a big area, and you can't very well tell your boss about the shadows," I reminded him. "I think it's better to let Scout and Gunner handle the search there. They know what they're doing."

"They said they were already starting," Landon acknowledged. "I feel so helpless. I don't know what to do."

I patted his knee. "I sent Viola to spy on Mrs. Little. At the very least, she'll be able to tell us if the shadows are watching her all of the time."

"Landon filled me in on that." Chief Terry stared into my eyes. "Why would those creatures be hunting Margaret?"

It was a question I'd asked myself more than once over the last hour. "I don't know."

"You must have an idea."

"Well, I don't." I held my palms out. "All I can do is theorize, which might not be our best option."

"Your theories are better than the facts we don't have so far."

"Ugh." I leaned forward and rubbed my forehead, sighing when Landon's hand landed on my back to massage away the tension. "Someone is creating and controlling the shadows. At first, only three people went missing, and over a much longer stretch of time. Whatever happened to most of the gang happened quickly."

"We're assuming that the gang packed their equipment and moved to Ben Johnson's house on their own, right?" Landon pressed.

I nodded. "There were multiple tire tracks in the driveway. They'd clearly been using the house, and the garage was full of meth cooking equipment and chemicals."

"So, whatever happened, happened at the house."

I took a moment to consider it and then nodded. "It makes the most sense. The problem is the motorcycles."

"Except you just posited that Kevin somehow maintained himself enough even though he was a shadow that he managed to take that bike to a neighboring town to send us a message."

Well, when he put it like that, it didn't make much sense. "I have a headache." I rubbed my forehead and then jolted when a loud sound reverberated down the street. It sounded like a gurgle, or a really loud burp. I glanced between Landon and Chief Terry. "What have you guys been eating?"

Landon gave me a dirty look. "That wasn't us. It was way too loud." He looked up and down the street. "I don't see any cars."

"Would a car make that noise?"

The sound echoed again. It seemed to come from everywhere and nowhere at the same time and was accompanied by a very distinct odor.

"Oh, geez." I pinched my nose and breathed out of my mouth. "Is it a gas leak?"

"It does smell like rotten eggs." Chief Terry's face turned an odd green. "Man, I think I might throw up."

"That's awful," Landon agreed, grabbing my hand. "We need to move downwind of whatever that is."

The belching came again, louder, and I swear the ground under my feet reverberated. My first thought was that we were about to be plunged into Armageddon. Maybe a hellmouth was opening under Main Street—hey, stranger things had happened—and we were about to be overrun by shadow creatures bent on killing everybody in town.

When the burping repeated, an odd suspicion took me over, and I jerked my eyes to the Unicorn Emporium. The scent was so strong, we couldn't outrun it. I knew that the instant store doors started opening on Main Street and owners began stepping outside. Everybody was gagging and waving their hands in front of their faces.

I was watching the unicorn store, seeing the door open in time with the sound. The smell that followed could've felled a lesser witch. Once I knew what we were dealing with—it certainly wasn't a hellmouth—I dropped my hand from my nose.

"That is foul," Chief Terry complained. "Is it possible somebody stuffed the bodies of the dead gang members in the sewer and they're bloating?"

"That isn't it," I replied grimly.

Chief Terry turned his curious eyes to me. "If it's not bodies, what is it?"

"Aunt Tillie."

Chief Terry's eyebrows knit, and I recognized the moment realization washed over him. His mouth dropped open, and he turned just in time to see the Unicorn Emporium belch again. He caught the flapping door and everything. "Oh, son of a witch," he bellowed.

Next to me, Landon bent at the waist, rested his hands on his knees, and started laughing. Unfortunately, the scent turned his laughs into heaves.

"This is the worst thing she's ever done," Chief Terry whined. "The whole town stinks."

"There aren't any tourists now," I reminded him. "It's just us ... and the film crew." I turned to the coffee shop and saw Greg and Reid on the sidewalk filming the phenomenon. They didn't look any happier with the smell than we were, but the footage obviously delighted them.

"This is going to reflect poorly on Margaret," Chief Terry noted. "It's going to look like she's doing it to get attention for her store. It *is* the center of the action right now, for better or worse."

"I'm sure that's what Aunt Tillie was aiming for," I acknowledged.

"How long will it last?"

I leaned forward and stared down the street. Sure enough, two blocks down, Aunt Tillie stood on the street corner watching her handiwork play out. She looked thrilled if her hip wiggle was to be believed. "Not long," I replied. "Ten minutes tops."

"How can you be sure?"

"Call it a hunch."

"You'd better be right. I can't stand this stench much longer."

Twenty-One

The belching building was the talk of the town. I was mobbed by whispering residents as I returned to The Whistler, but I didn't linger to talk to them because the stench was still over-whelming. I didn't want to throw up on the sidewalk. Cady Falls, who barged into my office when I was busy editing copy, said several people hadn't been as smart, and apparently, there was a vomiting epidemic on Main Street ... and everybody was blaming Mrs. Little.

Aunt Tillie's plan was working, something I had no doubt she would brag about later.

I forced myself to focus and finished most of the work for the next edition. Viola wasn't back by the time I needed to lock up, so I set a reminder in my phone to check in with her later. She would have to make the trip to the inn whether she liked it or not. Then I headed out. I didn't have a vehicle of my own, so I had to ride with Landon. He was quiet for most of the drive.

"I'm going to get a drink," he said after we entered the inn's lobby. "In the library."

He wanted to be alone. "Okay." I patted his arm. Because I didn't know what else to do for him, I said the one thing that I shouldn't have said. "We don't know he's dead. He could still be alive."

"We don't know that he's dead?" Landon's eyes flashed hot to match his temper. "Of course we know. There's no other explanation."

This was Hemlock Cove. There could be eight different explanations, each of them more ridiculous than the previous, so I opted to keep them to myself. There was nothing I could do to ease his burden. I hated feeling helpless, but I watched in silence as he trudged toward the library.

When I turned to the left, I found my mother sitting on her stool behind the desk, looking concerned.

"Do I even want to know?" she asked.

I shook my head. "You don't. What are you doing up here? I thought you'd be prettying yourself up for your interview with the film crew." There was a bite to my tone that I wouldn't normally use with my mother, but I was feeling too much pressure to fake being pleasant.

"First, I don't need to pretty myself up. I'm perfect as I am." She patted her hair by way of proof, her eyes narrowed. "Second, I wanted to talk to you about the incident downtown today."

"You'll have to be more specific. There were several incidents downtown today."

"You know what I'm talking about." Her expression was grave. "Aunt Tillie went after Margaret Little. Again."

"You can't possibly be surprised." I had to force myself not to snap at her. "Aunt Tillie has been torturing Mrs. Little for months." Actually, Aunt Tillie had been pulling her torture routine for decades. The only thing newsworthy about today was the way her efforts kept growing in scope.

"I'm not surprised, but we need to gain control of the situation. Burping buildings won't help tourism in Hemlock Cove. The whole reason I got on board for this television program was because I knew it would help the town."

Was she trying to fool herself or me? "Are you serious?"

"I am."

"Then you need to get your head in the game. Mrs. Little brought that film crew here to mess with us. She told them she has a big finale planned for the episode. They don't know what it is, but I think we can hazard a guess."

Mom's forehead creased with worry. "She plans to out us."

"She does, and the timing sucks, what with shadow monsters taking over the town. They appeared at her house last night. They tried to entice her outside. I think Aunt Tillie has the house warded. That's the only thing that saved her. Well, that and Mrs. Little's self-preservation skills. She was smart enough to stay inside instead of going outside to investigate the noise."

"Why would the shadow creatures go after Margaret?"

"I have no idea, but there's more." I rested my hands on top of the desk and lowered my voice. "All of the guys in that gang, the meth cookers, have disappeared. We think they were using Ben Johnson's house as a second base. There are tire tracks all over the driveway and a bunch of equipment and chemicals in the garage. They're gone though."

"I can't get worked up about a bunch of drug dealers going missing."

"Landon and Chief Terry had a man undercover with them." I had no idea if she'd been informed of that fact, but she needed to know now because Chief Terry was going to be just as upset as Landon, if not more. "His motorcycle was found abandoned in Hawthorne Hollow today."

"Why was it found there?"

I held out my hands. "I don't know, but he's gone. He should've checked in by now. If my hunch is correct, if the shadows really are the gang members, he's already gone."

Mom's face drained of color. "Are we certain that's what's happening?"

"No, but it doesn't look good. You might not care about the drug dealers, but Kevin seemed like a good guy. He was trying to do a good thing."

"And he's gone." Grief washed over Mom's features. "Poor Terry."

"Poor both of them. Landon is upset."

"Of course he is. Landon is a good guy too. He wants to protect everybody. He can't always manage it—especially when things spiral out of control—but he's a very good man."

I blew out a sigh and stretched my back. "The film crew adds an extra layer of stress to an already tense situation," I said. There was no way my mother would boot the crew now, but I had to vent, and I blamed her for at least part of what was happening.

"Not this again, Bay." Mom's frustration was obvious. "They're just doing a job, and the final product will help all of us."

"Will it? Because if Mrs. Little gets her way, we're going to be exposed. We're now backed into a corner with a battle on our doorstep, and there's a camera crew with access to that doorstep for what's sure to be a loud and obnoxious finale. This won't end well for us."

"Do you have to be such a downer? Things will work out. They always do."

"You won't be fighting the battle while trying to keep everything afloat, so I guess it's easy for you to say that." I pushed away from the desk. "Why can't you be on my side for this?" I knew I sounded whiny.

"Why can't you stop looking at the downside of everything?" Mom shot back. "This will benefit us all, Bay. The town is thriving. This will increase tourist traffic."

"I hope you're right." I meant it. "But if you're wrong, we might lose everything."

"We won't."

"Okay." I turned to leave the lobby. "I'm going to check on Landon. You might want to show a little sympathy to Chief Terry when he gets here. He's blaming himself. They're both blaming themselves."

"They couldn't have known."

"No, but we knew there was a problem when we found that glowing body. The film crew showed up that day and threw us. We were behind right from the start. When the shadow attacked me, we should've gone on the offensive. We've been on our heels for the entirety of this one, and now we're all going to pay."

"That's a great mindset you've got there, Bay," Mom chided. "Your pessimism won't help you figure things out today."

"I don't think blind optimism will help either. Just FYI, I'll be taking Aunt Tillie with me tonight. I'll need her if things turn ugly at Mrs. Little's house. Thistle is going too."

"I can go if you need more backup."

"Somebody has to stay here and keep the film crew busy."

"Nobody needs the attitude."

"True, but just once, I would like you to take my side simply because I ask. I made a very clear case for why I didn't want them here. I can't help but feel you should've listened to me."

"This is my property. I make the decisions."

"So I've noticed." I turned my back to her. "Just because you own the property doesn't mean the rest of us shouldn't get a vote. We're in trouble, Mom, and I have no idea how to get us out of it."

With that, I left her to stew and headed toward my husband. I couldn't help him ease the burden he was carrying, but I could be with him.

MOM DIDN'T TALK TO ME DURING DINNER. I tried not to let it bother me. Occasionally, when I was focused on my plate, I felt her eyes crawling over me like spiders on the hunt, but whenever I looked up her focus was elsewhere.

Once dinner was finished, she herded Chief Terry into the family living quarters. He was morose throughout the meal as the loss weighed on him. I couldn't do anything for my husband, so helping Chief Terry was out of the question. I could only hope Mom had an ability I lacked.

We left the *Haunted Traditions* crew in the dining room with the drink cart to talk about their episode plans and took refuge in the library.

"Are you sure this is the smart thing to do?" Thistle asked. Her boyfriend, Marcus, was with her, which meant Maya had been torn between drooling over Landon and him during the meal. She looked as if she was about to pass out from the effort to not drool more than once. "What if Mrs. Little only told that story to draw us in? I wouldn't put it past her to set us up. What if we get out there and the television crew shows up?"

She had a point. "What if that is her plan?" I used my most reasonable tone. "I've thought about it. My problem is, how would she know to glom on to the shadows as an enemy if it's not the truth?"

"Maybe she lucked out."

I planted my hands on my hips and turned to stare out the window. I was quiet for a long time and then exhaled most of the tension I was carrying. "I don't see that we have a choice. If the shadows attack and something happens to her, we'll never forgive ourselves."

"Speak for yourself," Thistle muttered.

"You can act brave and bold to your heart's content, but we both know you would feel guilty. If we go out there and it turns out to be a setup, we can always lie and say Aunt Tillie was trying to play a prank on her. Anybody who has ever watched Mrs. Little and Aunt Tillie interact will believe that."

Thistle looked momentarily torn and then nodded. "Fine. If I get killed by a shadow monster while protecting Mrs. Little, I'm going to be mad forever."

"You already warned me about that."

"I'm just repeating it in case you forgot."

With Thistle's support nailed down, I turned to Landon. "Maybe you should stay here."

Landon snapped his eyes to me, annoyance kindling and pushing back the misery he'd been hoarding like gold. "You're my wife. I'm going with you."

"It's just that your upset."

"I'll be way more upset if something happens to you." He adjusted his tone. "Bay, it's okay. I'm upset about Kevin, but that doesn't change the fact that you and I are a team. We'll go together."

He fell silent for a beat and then continued. "Besides, you might need an official presence if this is a trap."

I grabbed his hand and squeezed. "Thank you."

"No thanks are necessary." He kissed my forehead. "This is what we do."

"Maybe we should sneak out while the film crew is otherwise engaged," Thistle suggested. "We can park on the road across from Mrs. Little's house and watch for signs of movement. We might be stuck there for hours."

"Do you want snacks?" I asked Landon. "I might be able to talk my mother or Marnie into casting a spell on some leftovers for you."

"I'm fine. I don't have much of an appetite."

That was troublesome in and of itself. He *always* had an appetite.

"Then let's track down Aunt Tillie and get out of here." We were barely out of the library when we found her. Aunt Tillie had excused herself after dinner to change for our adventure. That change included a combat helmet, camouflage leggings, and combat boots. She'd managed to retrieve the stick she so often had at the ready, and she'd even managed to procure brown lipstick from somewhere.

"Oh, man." I couldn't stop myself from making a face when I saw her. "Seriously?"

Aunt Tillie, used to me reacting negatively to her outfits, shrugged. "I'm prepared for battle and reporting for duty."

"Awesome." I darted a look to Thistle and found her grinning. "You can't be okay with this outfit."

"Actually, I am," Thistle replied. "If this is a trap and Mrs. Little is setting us up, we can use this outfit to claim Aunt Tillie had a mental breakdown and we were following her to make sure she didn't get into trouble. It's a ready-made alibi."

She had a point. "Fine. Let's get this over with."

"Hold up." Aunt Tillie raised her hand. "Why am I always the one who has to explain my outfit? Maybe I don't want to be seen in public with you guys in those outfits. Have you ever considered that?"

I glanced down at my blue pullover and jeans. "What's wrong with my outfit?"

"It's embarrassing. I'm a colorful person, and you're as vanilla as they come. I can't be seen in public with you looking like that. You don't even have a stick."

"You'll survive." I ushered our group to the front door. There was no sense exiting through the back because we'd run the risk of the film crew seeing us. Unfortunately, escaping without notice wasn't in the cards because Reid was in the lobby looking through the front window when we appeared.

"I was just wondering where you went," he said. His eyes immediately flew to Aunt Tillie. His lips curved and straightened several times as he struggled to keep from laughing. "Going somewhere?" he asked.

I made up a lie on the spot. "They're having a costume contest at the senior center this evening. Aunt Tillie is entering, and we're going along for moral support."

Reid eyed the stick dubiously. "Who is she supposed to be?"

"John Wayne," Thistle replied.

"Interesting. Maybe I should go with you." Reid had a smile at the ready. "That might make for some interesting B-roll for the episode."

"I don't think you were invited," Landon replied. "It's a private affair. It's for family ... and some of the participants can't consent to being filmed, if you know what I mean."

"I don't think I know what he means," Aunt Tillie complained.

"He's means you're senile, you old bat," Thistle said. "Now shut your hole."

"Guess who's on my list," Aunt Tillie growled. "You're all ten slots. You should be proud."

Thistle ignored her. "It's not a big deal. They have a costume contest once a month, and we take turns babysitting Aunt Tillie for the show. Tonight just happens to be our turn."

"Okay." Reid's eyes were troubled, but he moved out of the way.

"I'm going to make you cry before the night is done, Thistle," Aunt Tillie grumbled as she strode through the door. "I'm going to kick you where it hurts just to be mean on top of that."

"What else is new?" Thistle met my gaze as we crossed the parking lot. "There's no way he bought that," she said.

"No, but by the time he asks Mom about it, we'll be long gone."

It was a possibility, but not one I was ready to entertain. "Good luck keeping up. We can let Aunt Tillie drive."

"That's not going to happen," Landon said. "I'm driving. If anybody is following, I'll know."

I would have to take his word for it. For better or worse, we were committed to a plan.

"R emember when our mothers decided to put Aunt Tillie in charge of teaching us about sex?" Thistle asked about an hour into our surveillance mission outside Mrs. Little's house. We were jammed into the backseat together—her, me, and Aunt Tillie—and we'd passed "bored" five minutes into the evening.

I smiled at the memory. "That was funny. We were convinced she didn't know what she was talking about."

"I'm right here," Aunt Tillie snapped. We'd forced her to take the middle seat out of fear she would jump out of the Explorer and do something crazy. "Also, I'm an expert when it comes to sex. I could do it professionally."

Thistle arched an eyebrow. "Do you want to rephrase that? Because try as I might, picturing you as a prostitute freaks me out."

"Not that part, you ninny." Aunt Tillie flicked Thistle's ear, a self-satisfied smirk appearing on her face when Thistle yelped. "I could've taught sex education for a living. I know everything there is to know about sex."

"I don't think we should have this discussion," Landon said from the driver's seat. "It will go to a very bad place."

"I agree with Landon." Marcus looked mortified. "Let's talk about movies or something. I hear they're making another *Ghostbusters*."

"I know about the Dirty Sanchez and the Angry Dragon," Aunt Tillie said, ignoring the men in front of us. "I know about the Camel Clutch, the Coyote, the Donkey Punch, and the Flaming Amazon."

"What's the Camel Clutch?" Thistle asked.

"Don't answer that!" Landon barked.

Aunt Tillie had apparently developed selective hearing, because she ignored Landon. "It's when she's on her stomach, and the man is behind her, and he pulls an Iron Sheik."

Landon swiveled in his seat. "Like the wrestler?"

Aunt Tillie's smile was serene. "You're picturing it now, aren't you?"

"I can't be part of this conversation," Marcus complained, burying his face in the window so he wouldn't have to look at any of us. "This is not happening."

"What other ones are there?" I asked. Hey, I was bored. This conversation was better than some of the others we'd shared over the years.

"Bay, you'll be the one sleeping on the couch tonight if this conversation doesn't cease right now," Landon warned.

It was an empty threat, and we both knew it, so I studied Aunt Tillie's profile in the limited light afforded by the radio.

"There's the Hot Lunch, the Oven Stuffed Rooster, and the New York Style Taco."

"I will gag all three of you," Landon snapped.

It felt good to laugh. Even though Landon wasn't smiling, he was animated.

"I only bring up Aunt Tillie's sex education class because I remember her teaching us to put condoms on bananas," Thistle said. "She wouldn't let us leave the house until we'd mastered it. And then, because we had so many stretched condoms sitting around, she had us fill them with yellow water and throw them at Mrs. Little's house in the middle of the night."

"Ah, good times," I said, smiling at the memory.

"How many condoms are we talking about?" Landon asked. He looked interested despite himself.

193

"Four or five boxes' worth," I replied.

"How old were you?"

"Thirteen."

"I was younger, but since Aunt Tillie was teaching Bay, she decided it was best to include me and Clove," Thistle explained. "Turns out our mothers didn't know how in-depth her lesson was going to be. They thought she was just going to tell us where babies came from ... like we didn't already know."

Landon managed a lazy smile as he rested his head against the seat pillow.

"I'm an excellent teacher." Aunt Tillie tapped the side of her nose. "And, if I'm not mistaken, none of you accidentally got pregnant. You waited until you were with your forever mates to procreate."

"Only one of us has procreated," Thistle pointed out.

"You will when it's time." Aunt Tillie smirked. "I hope you get a kid just like you."

"That's the meanest thing you've ever said to me," Thistle complained.

We lapsed into bored silence again. It lasted only a few minutes.

"We should look inside the house," Aunt Tillie announced.

"We're supposed to be waiting for the shadows," I reminded her.

"Yes, but we still don't know if she was telling the truth. For all we know she could be sitting in her living room laughing at us for falling for her lies."

"She doesn't even know we're out here," I argued.

"She might. She installed cameras last winter to catch me plowing her in. It's entirely possible she's already caught sight of us."

Oh, well, that just tore it. "Did you think to tell us about the cameras?" I demanded.

"No. I usually blind them when I'm playing my games. I didn't think about them this evening."

I pursed my lips and then leaned forward to touch Landon's shoulder. "What do you think?"

"I would prefer not getting caught on camera spying on Mrs. Little. If we stop now, we can say we stopped because Aunt Tillie was sick or something."

He had a point. I slid my eyes to Thistle, debating, and then popped open my door. "You guys should head back to the inn. We'll handle this."

"Excuse me?" Landon made a grab for my arm, but I was already out of the Explorer. "Don't even think about it, Bay." He killed the running engine and hurried outside to head me off. "Where do you think you're going?"

"Thataway." I pointed to the house. Mrs. Little had an unusually long driveway.

"What do you expect to find down there?" Landon asked. "If you give me a solid answer, I might agree to accompany you."

"We don't know if she's telling the truth."

"We don't," he agreed, "but what if she is? What if you cross some invisible line and trigger those ... things?"

"Then at least we'll know. We can fight them off." I hoped I sounded more certain than I felt. "We'll be fine."

"Bay." Landon sounded exasperated. He flicked his eyes to Marcus over the hood of the vehicle. "What do you want to do?"

"I'm not leaving Thistle," Marcus said. "I don't want to get caught spying on Mrs. Little, but I can't just walk away. If they're going, I'm going."

Landon nodded. "That's where I'm at." He pocketed his keys and fixed me with an expectant look. "Lead the way."

I wanted to argue with him. I wanted to tell him he could head back and there would be no hard feelings. Instead, I smirked and held out my hand. "Come on. It might be fun."

"The word 'fun' has never been used in reference to Margaret Little." He was deadly serious. "You, however, are fun, so you're stuck with me for the rest of your life."

"That's hardly a hardship."

Aunt Tillie, a smug smile on her lips, started up the driveway. Other than one window on the second floor, the house was dark. I assumed Mrs. Little was already in bed as we crept closer. Then I realized she was sitting in the dark on her front porch. I came to a stop and froze in place when we were still fifty feet away

"Don't stop now," Mrs. Little called out. "I've been waiting for almost two hours. I saw you park on the road and figured you'd head this way sooner or later. It took you a lot longer than I thought."

"It's a trap," Aunt Tillie hissed. "She's about to drop an anvil on us."

"An anvil?" Thistle made a face. "You've been watching too many cartoons. Where is she going to get an anvil?"

"It's a metaphorical anvil."

"Well, you're legitimately insane." Thistle planted her hands on her hips and gave Mrs. Little the sternest glare in her repertoire. "We're here for the truth. If you're going to lie to us, we'll leave you to your fate."

"Maybe I want to be left to my fate."

"Do you?" I asked.

Mrs. Little cocked her head, considering, and then shrugged. "I believe things may have gotten out of control. That wasn't my intention. You have to know that."

My heart rate picked up a notch. "What did you do?"

"Oh, don't use that tone with me, Bay." Mrs. Little looked caught between guilty and furious. "You're the ones who cast a curse on me, and I almost died. Yes, I know about that. I know how close I was to succumbing to that bad luck curse. No matter what you think, I'm not stupid."

"She's stupid," Aunt Tillie stage whispered. "Don't let her fool you. If they had a list of stupid people, she'd be at the top."

"Shut up, Tillie!" Mrs. Little barked. "Why are you even here? I didn't invite you."

I placed my hands in my pockets, ostensibly to keep my fingers warm on a brisk night, but also because they were itching to throw a spell at her. "You didn't invite any of us," I pointed out.

"Sure I did." Mrs. Little was blasé. "That's what that entire conversation was about in my store earlier. That's why I sent Connie to get your attention outside the police station. I knew mentioning the shadows would prompt you to approach me."

"You know what the shadows are." Anger grabbed me by the throat. "You know, and you didn't tell us."

"I don't *know* anything," she fired back. "I just think I know how the shadows got here."

"Did she just explain something?" Thistle asked me. "I'm confused."

She wasn't the only one. "I think you'd better tell us exactly what's going on." I was determined as I strode to the porch. Mrs. Little was tucked under a blanket, no makeup, and she looked as if she'd seen better days.

"I'm not quite sure what's going on," Mrs. Little replied. "I was … confused … after what happened with that curse. I couldn't believe Tillie would take things that far."

"Aunt Tillie didn't cast that curse," I snapped. "You were infected when you touched Bill Blake. He passed the curse on to you. We saved you, and then you passed the curse on to Aunt Tillie. We weren't the cause."

Mrs. Little looked genuinely shocked. "I did not realize that."

I threw my hands in the air and turned my back to her.

"Why don't you just tell us what happened," Landon prodded in his best cop voice. There was a reason he managed to forge such a good rapport on the job. He had one of those faces people naturally trusted. "We can't figure out a way to solve this problem if we don't know exactly what we're dealing with."

"I already told you that I'm not quite certain how it happened," Mrs. Little snapped. "It was an accident. One minute I was cleaning the lamp, and the next he was standing in my living room asking me what I wanted."

I was stunned. "Who was standing in your living room?"

"I think she's talking about a genie," Thistle offered.

"Genies aren't real," I growled.

"Oh, it was a genie." Mrs. Little said. "It exploded right out of the lamp, colored smoke and everything. I didn't know what to think when it occurred, and I just started blurting wishes."

Landon shot me an incredulous look. "Genies are real?"

"Not like you're picturing … and nobody is going to be wearing the *I Dream of Jeannie* outfit, so you can drop that idea right now." I rolled my neck. "Genies aren't a thing. Djinns are real, but I've never heard of one being trapped in a lamp."

"It might not have been a lamp," Aunt Tillie offered. "It could've been a cursed container. Throughout history, if a witch couldn't beat a djinn, she would entrap it and hope she would stumble across a creature strong enough to kill it down the line."

"So how did Mrs. Little end up with a djinn?" Thistle asked.

"I bought it at the flea market," Mrs. Little replied. "You know that one they had at the high school two weeks ago to raise money for new band uniforms? It was on one of the tables. I was still smarting from that curse and wanted to get in and out quickly, so I bought the first thing I found."

"And it just happened to be a lamp with a djinn in it?" I asked. Seriously, what were the odds?

"I guess." Mrs. Little held out her hands. "I was bored later that night, feeling sorry for myself, and under the influence. I decided to open the lamp."

"Gin?" Aunt Tillie asked.

"Schnapps."

"That's not a real drink. Get with the program, Margaret."

Mrs. Little shot Aunt Tillie a death glare and then sucked in a breath. "He was handsome when he popped out. I thought I might be seeing things. I assumed he was a genie and asked for my three wishes. He said he would gladly grant them if I gave him the lamp. I was in no position to argue—peach schnapps is the Devil's drink—so I gave him the lamp and then told him I wanted Tillie to die. He said he would handle it and left."

"Ha!" Thistle jabbed her finger in the air and yelled so loudly I almost jolted out of my skin. "I told you that shadow that attacked outside the greenhouse wasn't after Bay. It was looking for Aunt Tillie. Ha!"

"Put your finger away." Marcus covered her finger and then slid his arm around her back, anchoring her to his side so he could lend her some warmth. He looked worried.

"Let me get this straight." I folded my arms across my chest. "You stumbled across a djinn trapped in a lamp, managed to get it out of the lamp despite all the wards, and sent it on a mission to kill Aunt Tillie. Am I missing anything?"

"It wasn't hard to open the lamp. I just pulled on the top. It took a few tries, but it eventually came loose after I soaked it in some warm water."

"Oh, well, warm water. Who knew?" I rubbed my forehead. "Have you seen this djinn since you released it from the lamp?"

"No, and I'd almost completely forgotten about it until I saw the shadows last night. They were stalking the downtown area. I thought I was seeing things at first, but I hadn't had schnapps. After the third or fourth time, I realized I was seeing something ... and I figured I should probably find a way to tell you what I'd done."

"Why come to us?" Thistle asked. "I thought you hated us."

"Oh, I do. I planned to use the genie to expose your family in front of the television crew. I think the genie is doing something weird. He never mentioned calling shadows, and as much as I hate you guys, I don't want magical shadows wandering around. They could be dangerous."

"Oh, they're dangerous." My mind was working a mile a minute. "They're very, very dangerous."

"What does this mean?" Landon asked me. He looked hopeful for the first time in hours. "Can Kevin still be saved?"

"I don't know." I opted for the truth. Giving him false hope wouldn't help anybody. "It's possible, although I don't know how probable it is. I think the djinn gravitated toward the dealers on Sand Lake for a reason. At least one of them had a dark soul, and he knew he could use that to his advantage. Somehow things got out of hand though."

"What do we do?" Thistle asked.

"For starters, I need to know who sold you that lamp," I told Mrs. Little. "Then we need to conduct some research on djinn. I don't know enough about them to consider myself an expert."

"What did this genie look like?" Landon asked Mrs. Little.

"He wasn't wearing a turban, if that's what you're thinking," Mrs. Little replied. "He wasn't bare-chested or dark-skinned either. It was quite disappointing."

I sent her a sarcastic thumbs-up. "Thanks for embracing the racist stereotype."

She ignored me. "He was white. Brown hair. His eyes glowed red. He had a very bad attitude."

"Would you recognize him again if you saw him?" I asked. "I mean ... you were drunk, right?"

Mrs. Little hesitated. "I don't know."

I cracked my neck. "We're in trouble," I said. "If this djinn was powerful enough to be locked away instead of eradicated, he's powerful enough to take us on. We need to get it together and come up with a plan."

Landon nodded. "How do we do that?"

"All I know is that we don't have much time. He's going to make a move soon. He's building an army for a reason. When it comes time to make that move, we're all going to be in big trouble."

"And we can all blame Margaret," Aunt Tillie noted. "That sounds about right."

"It's not my fault," Mrs. Little whined. "It's your fault I was confused in the first place."

"It's your fault," Aunt Tillie fired back.

"Yours."

"Yours."

"Yours."

I shook my head and closed my eyes. We were in over our heads again, and this time I didn't know if we could save ourselves.

Twenty-Three

A djinn? How could she be so stupid? It was the sort of thing I would've expected from a teenager, or someone determined to use nefarious means to get ahead in life. Mrs. Little was an opportunist, but not when it came to magic. She shunned magic at all costs ... until now.

"I think we broke her," I said when we got to the road. "How else do you explain her getting drunk and letting a djinn loose?"

"She's horrible. What other explanation do you need?" Landon asked.

"Margaret has always been a wild card," Aunt Tillie said as I helped her into Landon's Explorer. "When we were younger, even when she was talking badly about me, you could tell she wanted to be just like me, including the magic."

Thistle's face was awash with doubt. "Are you sure that was really a thing, or did you just think it was a thing?"

"It was really a thing." Aunt Tillie was adamant. "I'm telling you, she's more interested in the magic than she lets on."

I remained lost in my head as Landon started the Explorer, but my eyes moved to the road ahead of us when a vehicle's brake lights flared to life and pulled away from our remote location.

"Who is that?" I asked.

Landon shrugged as he put the vehicle in drive. "Does it matter?"

"Maybe."

"Why?"

"There's nothing out here but Mrs. Little's house. Why were they parked in the middle of nowhere?"

"Why were we parked in the middle of nowhere?"

"You're proving my point."

Landon's lips curved down. "It's probably nothing." He didn't sound any more convinced than I felt.

When the vehicle turned down the road that led to The Overlook, my suspicions kicked into high gear. "Landon."

"I see it." He was grim as we followed, and sure enough, the vehicle pulled into the lot ahead of us.

"It's one of the film crew guys," Thistle said when a man hopped out of the Jeep. "One of the cameramen."

It was indeed one of the cameramen. I recognized Reid even though he had his head bent as he walked to the inn. He made a big show of not looking at us. Landon hadn't even pulled to a full stop when I hopped out of his Explorer and raced to catch up with the *Haunted Traditions* employee.

"What were you doing?" I demanded when he reached the front door.

Reid was the picture of innocence when he turned. "I just went out for a drive."

"To Mrs. Little's house?"

"Is that where you were coming from?" Reid lifted one shoulder in a shrug. "I was just driving to clear my head. This town can do a real number on you if you're not careful."

He was lying. I licked my lips as the rest of my group caught up with us. "Did you have fun?"

"It was very enlightening," Reid replied. "I think the question is, did you have fun on your outing?" The comment made me queasy. He didn't have a camera, but he'd obviously been watching us.

"I don't want to be part of your television program." I refused to break eye contact. "Steer clear of me when I'm out and about."

"Has it occurred to you that I didn't even know you were there? I was just taking a break, thinking. We're putting together an episode, and not just any episode, the premiere episode. Believe it or not, that requires a lot of brainstorming."

"Which I believe your group was doing here, in the dining room, when we left."

"When you left for a costume contest at the senior center. That's what you said."

I knew that lie would come back to bite us. "Don't worry about what we were doing." My temper flared as my mother appeared in the doorway, looking confused. "What we do is our business. You worry about your television show, which we aren't a part of."

"I'm totally going to be a part of it," Aunt Tillie countered. "I'm going to be the star."

Reid's smile was a little too "cat that ate the canary" as he regarded her. "Did you hear that? She's going to be the star. She's part of the show."

"Well, Bay isn't," Landon interjected, drawing Reid's eyes to him. "She's made her feelings on the subject very clear. She's not part of this."

"I didn't say she was." Reid held out his hands. "Look, I was just taking a drive. I don't know why you're so worked up. It's not as if a clandestine meeting in the middle of the night makes for good television ... unless you'd like to tell me what you were talking about."

"Not so much," I snapped.

"Well then..." Reid's smile never wavered. "I think I'll call it a night. You guys have a good evening." He flashed his charming grin at Mom and then edged around her before disappearing inside.

"What was that?" Mom demanded.

"He followed us," Landon replied. "Actually, he didn't follow us. We would've seen him. Somehow, he ended up on the road across from Mrs. Little's house. He was there when we were."

"What were you doing at Margaret's house?" Mom was clearly spoiling for a fight as she gripped her hands together in front of her. "Please tell me you didn't let Aunt Tillie torture her. We have enough going on."

"There's always time for torture," Aunt Tillie offered.

"Nobody was torturing anybody," I added. "Mrs. Little was waiting for us. She knew we would come. Turns out she's the reason we have shadow monsters and missing meth dealers."

"Margaret is the reason?" Mom was understandably dubious. "How does that even work?"

"It's a long story."

"She found a lamp at the high school flea market, tried to clean it, and freed a djinn," Thistle volunteered. "She then asked the djinn to make Aunt Tillie pay for the bad luck curse ... which she thought we cast on her. She's now second-guessing her wish."

"Apparently, the story wasn't that long after all," I mused.

"Margaret freed a djinn?" Mom's forehead lined with confusion. "I don't understand."

"We don't either, but tomorrow we need to start tracking it down," I said. "It already has a foothold in town. We have to make sure that it doesn't take over and do whatever djinn do these days."

"Can you beat it?" Mom looked genuinely worried.

"We don't have a choice. People are likely dying. At the very least, they're being transformed into monsters. We have a missing undercover agent ... and now that all the dealers are gone, do you really think the djinn is going to stop with the bad guys?"

Mom lowered her head. "I don't think it will stop."

"We have to stop it, and we have to do it with a television crew breathing down our necks. It's going to be great fun. What do you think?"

"I don't like your attitude, Bay," Mom growled. "You're rude and obnoxious."

"Get used to that." I was officially at the end of my rope. "We're in big trouble. I know I said it before, but it's even worse now. We have to get this under control, and we're almost out of time."

"I can help," Mom offered. "I can do whatever you need."

"Just keep that film crew out of our business." They weren't my biggest worry, but they were big enough that I felt the walls closing in. "If they decide to follow us and catch the wrong thing on camera, our lives will change forever."

"I'm sure it was just a coincidence," Mom insisted. "They seem fine."

"Yeah, you keep telling yourself that."

I SLEPT FITFULLY AND WOKE IN A BAD mood the next morning. Landon seemed worried when I immediately climbed out of bed and skipped our normal morning cuddle. We had too much to do, and my head wasn't in the right place for romance.

"Just don't engage with your mother this morning," Landon suggested as we let ourselves into the inn through the family living quarters. "You two are like fighting cats right now. You should steer clear of one another."

"She started it," I groused.

"I'm sure she's telling Terry the same thing about you."

"He won't believe it. He knows I'm an angel."

"Don't put him in a position where he has to choose between you," Landon warned. "It will make him sick to even think about it ... and with Kevin missing, he's dealing with enough."

He was right, so I decided to let it go ... for now. "Let's just have breakfast and then get to town. Mrs. Little said she bought the lamp from Kelly Silverman. That's Joni Silverman's daughter. That's where we have to start our search."

"Do you know her?" Landon asked.

"Joni was ahead of me in school by a good eight years or so, but her little sister Carrie was in our grade. She drowned in an incident out at the lake. Joni was supposed to be watching her, but she got distracted."

"How old was Carrie when she died?"

"I think she was about nine. Joni was in high school. I'm pretty sure she was a senior. She would've been seventeen or eighteen at the time. People say she was distracted by her boyfriend."

"I'm sure she felt guilty."

I bobbed my head. "She always seemed scarred. She moved to Traverse City for a bit after graduation—maybe because she wanted to get away from the memories—but returned when she was in her mid-twenties. She was divorced by then and had Kelly in tow."

"She has just the one girl?"

"Yeah. Kelly seems like a good kid. I've never known her to get in trouble. I think she's sixteen or so now. I'm guessing she just grabbed things from the attic for the sale. She probably didn't even know what she had. I want to talk to Joni. If anyone in that house knows what was in the lamp, she does."

We cut through the kitchen, which was bustling with activity, and I steadfastly avoided eye contact with my mother.

"We weren't sure you were coming this morning," Marnie said when she caught sight of me. "We made more than enough food. We went with eggs."

I shot her a reassuring smile—she was obviously trying to smooth things over—and kept walking toward the swinging doors that led to the dining room. "That sounds great."

"Are you going to be busy all day?" Twila asked. "If you need help and you don't want your mother along, I can be your sidekick for the day."

That was the worst offer I'd had in ... well, I didn't know how long. "I'm going to keep Landon as my sidekick today," I replied.

"Yes, I'm going to borrow Aunt Tillie's cape and scooter and do it up right," Landon drawled.

"I could do that." Twila was deadly serious. "I bet I would look fabulous on camera in that cape. Maybe I should consider an outfit change."

I didn't care what she was going to wear. It was the camera part that caught my attention. "Have you sat for an interview with them?"

"Several." Twila's smile was wide. "They say I have great presence. They're going to be downtown for most of the day. They mentioned something about wanting to catch whatever show Mrs. Little is putting on later. I'm not sure what they mean though. Margaret doesn't put on shows."

I knew exactly what they meant. "Speaking of that, you should skip today's show," I instructed Aunt Tillie, who was stretched out in her easy chair in the corner. "They'll be expecting it. You should defy expectations and do nothing."

"I've got it covered." Aunt Tillie made a face. "I know what to do."

That didn't fill me with warm and fuzzy feelings. "You're going to do nothing."

"I said I've got it. Geez." She rolled her eyes. "Why did you raise such a nag, Winnie? She's turning into a mini you."

I extended a warning finger in her direction. "That is the meanest thing you've ever said to me, and I'm going to make you eat dirt if you're not careful."

Aunt Tillie didn't look worried in the least. "Yeah, yeah, yeah." She waved off my threat. "You worry about you; I'll worry about me."

She wasn't going to skip a day. That much was obvious. "Just don't be weird when you do whatever it is you're going to do."

I was grumpy when we made our way into the dining room. The film crew was already seated at the table. Chief Terry was there too, and he looked tired and sad. It hurt my heart to see the lines around his eyes.

"Hey." I sat in the chair next to him and leaned in to give him a side hug. "How are you?"

To my surprise, Chief Terry had a smile at the ready. "I'm okay. How are you?"

"I've got a lot on my mind."

Chief Terry looked to Landon, something unsaid passing between them. "Have you and your mother made up?" He looked so hopeful it almost crushed me.

"No, and it's not happening today."

Chief Terry didn't look happy with my answer, and I sensed a lecture in my future. To head it off, Landon rested his hand on my back.

"They'll work things out on their own," he said. "Us getting involved won't help, so it's best we just stay out of it."

Chief Terry nodded. "Fair enough. Do you have special plans for today?" he asked me.

"I do, but it's best we not talk about those either." Because I felt multiple sets of eyes on me from the other end of the table, I decided to tackle another problem head-on. "I have a lot of work to get done today, Debbie." I called out the producer specifically. "I need to be able to focus. I can't do that when your cameramen are skulking around following me."

Shock—was it genuine? I couldn't say—reverberated across Debbie's face. "I would never send my people to follow you against your will."

"That's good, because if I see your people following me, I'm going to be really mad. I've been as nice as I can possibly be, polite even, when explaining that I'm not comfortable in front of the camera. No matter how you try to trick me into agreeing to be filmed, it's not going to happen."

Debbie worked her jaw, glanced between her co-workers, and then focused on me again. "I think there's been some sort of mistake. I don't want to trick you into being on camera. If you're against it, you're against it. I would be lying if I said I wasn't disappointed, but that's not how we operate. You don't want to be involved, and I accept that."

"Good." I flicked my eyes to Reid and found him watching the exchange with unreadable eyes. "That goes for everybody in your group, correct?"

"Of course."

"Great. Then there will be no miscommunication today." I accepted the juice Landon slid in front of me and cast him what I hoped was a relaxed smile. "Everything is going to work out. It's going to be a great day."

He returned my smile, but there was doubt in his eyes.

Twenty-Four

J oni Silverman lived on the west side of town. Nothing in Hemlock Cove was rundown—Mrs. Little made sure of that— but the homes in Joni's subdivision were modest. Landon parked in the driveway and then pinned me with a serious look.

"Let me do the talking."

"You don't know her," I reminded him.

"I'm the official presence."

"Right." I debated how I wanted to phrase the next part. "How are you going to explain that you're looking for information on a genie lamp?"

His scowl was pronounced. "I'm not going to explain it like that, smartass. I'm simply going to say that it has come to our attention that the lamp might've been missing from a traveling collection. I want to hear what she has to say."

I had to give it to him, it was a fairly good cover story. "Okay. I'll agree to your story."

Landon's lips quirked. "Thanks so much for your permission, wife of mine."

"I was just going to say that Mrs. Little was complaining about being ripped off at the flea market and play it off as Mrs. Little being Mrs. Little, but your story is good too."

He stilled. "Huh. Now I kind of like your story."

"We're such a good team. We both come up with great stories." I gave his cheek a jiggle and then giggled when he lightly pinched my flank.

"Let's play it by ear," he said as he hopped out. "The important thing is that we don't make her suspicious."

I didn't see a way around Joni being suspicious. We were coming to her door to ask about what she likely considered a junk lamp. There was no way she wouldn't ask questions.

Landon had to knock twice before Joni appeared. She was dressed in slacks and a nice shirt as though she'd been preparing to go somewhere. She smiled when she saw us.

"I'm guessing you're not here to sell something," she said. "I hate salesmen. Though I guess you could be selling newspaper subscriptions, Bay."

"We're not here to sell anything," I reassured her. "We're here on another matter."

Joni went stiff. "Kelly?"

I shook my head quickly. "No. I'm sorry if we frightened you, but that's not why we're here."

"Okay." Joni's expression was hard to read. "Would you like to come in?" she asked when we hadn't said anything for several seconds. She didn't look keen to invite us into her home, but we were making things awkward enough that she didn't have a choice.

"That would be great." Landon prodded me to enter in front of him, and we followed Joni to a homey living room. The furniture looked well-worn and loved, and while there was nothing fancy on display, the house was clean and comfortable.

"I'm going to get straight to the point," Landon said as he sat next to me. "Mrs. Little has been talking about a lamp she bought from your daughter at the high school flea market."

Joni snorted. "Are you kidding me? Does she want her three bucks back?"

"She's just being difficult," Landon replied. "She seems to think the lamp might've come from a museum or collection. You know how she is. Since she made a complaint, I thought I'd put an end to it right away."

Joni looked as if she wanted to strangle someone. It didn't take a huge leap to figure out that Mrs. Little was the likely target. "That lamp has been in my family for forty or fifty years. It was in a box of stuff I got when my grandmother died. I didn't even look in the box. Kelly found it while she was looking for stuff for the flea market. I said it was fine if she sold it."

"Your grandmother?" I searched my memory. "Doris Stinson? She was your grandmother."

"Yeah." Joni's forehead creased. "Did you know her? She's been dead a long time."

"She was friends with Aunt Tillie."

"I didn't think Aunt Tillie had any friends," Landon countered.

"She did when she was younger. Your grandmother hung around with her and Mrs. Gunderson. I've heard stories from my mother."

Joni looked as if she was trying to remember as she sat across from us. "I didn't know my grandmother all that well. She was a good woman as far as I can tell, but she died when I was about thirteen. My mother dropped off the box of stuff. She thought I should have something to remember my grandmother by."

There are a lot of stories from back then, when Aunt Tillie was hanging around with Mrs. Gunderson and Doris. A few of them stood out. "Did your grandmother practice witchcraft?" The question was out of my mouth before I could think better of it. I didn't look at Landon to gauge his reaction, but the way he stiffened told me all I needed to know. He was ticked off.

"How did you know about the witch thing?" Joni's smile was soft and wide.

"Aunt Tillie is still around. She likes to tell stories."

Joni shook her head. "That was a stupid question. As for the witch-craft, yeah. The family legend says that Grandma was a witch, and she cast a spell on Grandpa Joe before she died. She made it so he couldn't get it up, karmic retribution because he cheated on her throughout their marriage."

"Didn't he die a couple years ago?"

"Yeah. He lived at that Sand Lake house on his own for a really long time, but when he got into his eighties, he couldn't keep the house up, so he had to sell it. Then he moved into an assisted living center in Shadow Hills."

Realization dawned on me. "He owned Bob Johnson's house."

Landon jerked his eyes in my direction but didn't speak.

"Right." Joni didn't understand why that was of importance. "Bob fixed up the house. At least that's what I heard. I think it was basically stripped down to the studs and rebuilt."

"Your grandmother stayed with your grandfather until her death?" I was organizing the story in my head. "Even though he cheated, she never divorced him."

"No. They stayed together, but they had separate bedrooms for as long as I can remember. They were basically roommates sharing a home when I was a kid. I don't ever remember them being affectionate, but I do remember my grandfather crying at her funeral. He seemed to have regrets."

"What did your grandfather say about the witchcraft?"

Joni focused her full attention on me now. "What's this about, Bay? You might as well tell me. It will save you time, and you won't have to beat around the bush. If it's something weird, I don't care. This whole town is full of weird. I heard there were talking rats running around last night."

"Someone actually heard the rats talk?" I asked.

"People are freaking out and blaming Mrs. Little. Maybe she's trying to distract everybody from the rats by calling attention to the lamp, which was nothing but an old hunk of metal. It didn't even open."

"Did you try to open it?"

"Of course. My grandmother was notorious for shoving money in little boxes and containers. She didn't trust banks."

"Or maybe she didn't trust your grandfather to not spend her money on his girlfriends," I suggested.

Joni laughed. "That's also a possibility. Kelly and I both tried to open the lamp. It was stuck tight. I told her she could sell it, and I assumed that was the last we'd see of it."

I felt as if I was on the verge of an important breakthrough, but I didn't know where to push. Landon took over the conversation, asking what I'm certain he believed to be pertinent questions. After about ten minutes, Joni told us she had an appointment for a haircut, and we started for the door. That's when photos on a shelf caught my attention. They were in one of those frames connected with a hinge. One photo showed Joni as a teenager, flanked on either side by two boys. One looked to be a year or two older. One was significantly younger, essentially a toddler. The photo next to it showed Joni again in the center flanked by two men.

"Who are they?" I went ramrod straight as I pointed at the photo.

Joni followed my finger. "They're my cousins."

I slowly turned to look at Landon.

"These are your cousins?" Landon pointed at the photo with the older faces. "These men right here? Both of them?"

"Yeah." Joni looked confused. "Why?"

"Because both of these men are in town right now," Landon replied. "I work with this one." He pointed at Kevin in the photo. "When was the last time you saw him?"

"Not for two weeks. He said he was going on an undercover assignment and was really excited." Joni's face was blank. "I guess I didn't think about it. Of course you know Kevin."

"He's a good guy," Landon said. "And Reid here?" He pointed to the image of the cameraman who had followed us the previous evening. "Is he Kevin's brother?"

"No, he's a cousin too." Joni planted her hands on her hips. "We were all tight growing up because we didn't have siblings." Joni's face clouded. "Well, we didn't have siblings after a certain point." She didn't mention her sister, and I didn't push. "What's going on here?"

"I'm not sure." Landon pulled his phone from his pocket and snapped a copy of the photograph without asking permission. "Have you seen Reid since he's been in town?"

"I didn't even know he was in town. He only visits once a year."

"He's here with the television show," I volunteered. "He's one of the cameramen."

Joni let loose a snort. "He's a mechanic. Why would he be with the television show? I think you're mistaking him for somebody else."

I wasn't, but something was definitely going on. "I guess that's possible," I lied. "Thank you so much for your time."

"Don't worry about the lamp," Landon said. "I don't think Mrs. Little will pursue her complaint. Sometimes she talks just to hear herself."

"She's a total menace," Joni agreed. She paused, her hand on the door as she held it open to usher us out. "Are you sure there's nothing I should know about?"

"We're still figuring things out," Landon replied. "When we do wrap our heads around what's going on, you'll be the first to know."

Joni nodded, but she still looked dubious. "Okay. Thank you."

"No, thank you," I offered. "You've been more help than you can imagine."

LANDON DROVE STRAIGHT DOWNTOWN. There was no question about who we were looking for. The SUV from the previous evening was parked in front of Hypnotic, so Landon took the space next to it, and we headed inside. There was only one problem: Reid wasn't present. Debbie and Greg were.

"Where's Reid?" Landon demanded.

Thistle was behind the counter with Clove, and her eyes were alert when they found mine. "What's going on?"

"We learned some interesting information," I replied. "I'll tell you about it in a few minutes. We need to find Reid."

"I don't know where he is," Debbie replied. "He was supposed to film the store with me but said he wasn't feeling well and took off. It's possible he got a ride back to the inn. Why do you care?"

"We'd like to talk to him," Landon replied. "It seems he has ties to this area that run deeper than we realized."

Debbie looked confused. "That's why he got the job when Richard stopped showing up for work."

If I'd been walking when she said it, I would've tripped. "What's that?"

"We needed a cameraman on the fly," Debbie replied. "We advertised on a Michigan website and Reid applied. It was his ties to Hemlock Cove—well, Shadow Hills, but close enough—that gave him the edge."

"He's not your normal cameraman?" Landon asked.

"No. Richard Silver is our normal cameraman. He didn't show up when the new season started. He ghosted us."

"Was that out of the ordinary?"

"Richard has always been diligent. You can't always tell what people are going to do, though, so after he didn't respond, we moved on."

"Did anybody report him missing?" Landon demanded

"Missing? Why would we report him missing? He just didn't show up for work."

"How long did he have the job before he stopped showing up?" Landon growled.

"This is our second season. He worked the entire first season."

"And before that?"

"He worked on a Discovery show about sharks. I believe he was there for the entire seventy-five episodes."

"So, it didn't strike you as odd when he didn't show up despite his previously stellar work ethic?"

"I ... guess not." Debbie was crestfallen. "I need to know what's going on here. You're all acting very strange."

"Yes, well, there's a reason for that." Landon sucked in a breath and then looked at me. "We need to find Reid. I'm not sure how he ties into this, but it's too much of a coincidence. He's related to Joni and Kevin. He shared a grandmother with them, and the item Mrs. Little bought at the flea market is a source of strife. When you factor in Bob Johnson's house ... there are just too many coincidences."

He was right. There were far too many coincidences, but that didn't explain what we were up against. "We still don't know exactly what this is," I reminded him.

"But we know we have to find Reid. He's our priority. I'm going to have Terry issue a BOLO. If he's running, he won't make it far."

"Why would he be running?" Debbie demanded. She scampered

after Landon, through the door and onto the street. "And what's a BOLO?"

I left Landon to explain a "Be on the Lookout" to her and remained rooted to my spot.

Greg remained behind as well. He looked torn but not as upset as the producer. "I knew there was something weird about that guy," he said. "Is he an international arms dealer or something?"

"He's something," I replied. "How well do you know him? Where would he go?"

"I have no idea. I just met him about a week ago. He seemed okay. I don't know Reid well enough to say whether I like him or not."

"Did he say anything to you about the town? Did he mention he had relatives here?"

"No, but that might explain where he was going at night."

"Where was he going at night?"

"I don't know. He left every night. He waited until we were three drinks in—he never drinks—and then took off. I have no idea where he was going or what he was doing."

I didn't know either, but I had my suspicions. "He took a job that was open because another man disappeared. He has ties to another missing man. All of that is way too convenient."

"Is he in trouble?" Greg asked. "Do you think someone is going to hurt him?"

"I think he's been involved in hurting others. I just need to figure out where he's going. We have to get ahead of him."

"What's he going to do?"

"That's what I'm going to find out." I moved to follow Landon and then paused by the door and turned back to meet Clove's and Thistle's questioning gazes. "Meet us at the inn. We need to come up with a plan. Reid is out there ... and he's not alone. We need to find him."

"And then what?" Greg demanded. He wasn't happy with my answer to his previous question. "What are you going to do?"

"All I know is we're going to stop him and end this ... one way or another." With that, I strode out of Hypnotic and headed toward the police station. Things were finally coming together.

Evan was in the kitchen with my mother and aunts when we arrived at the inn. Chief Terry sent out the BOLO notice the second Landon caught him up on what we'd discovered. Chief Terry warned law enforcement not to approach the man and to call him immediately if he was sighted.

"What are you doing here?" I asked Evan.

"Tillie called. She said a rat told her that trouble was coming. I have no idea what she was talking about, but I figured it was better to be present and not needed than the alternative."

"We called Scout too," Mom said. She looked grave. "What are we dealing with?"

"We're not quite sure," Landon replied. "We know that Mrs. Little bought a lamp—one of those tacky items you might see in a bad television show—and opened it while drunk. She released a genie."

I made a face. "Let's not call it a genie. That sparks images of cartoons and Barbara Eden. It's a djinn."

Evan looked horrified at the thought. "That's a stereotype nobody needs to see."

"Yeah, well, we'll figure that out later." I had a million questions and no idea how to organize them. "Mrs. Little wished for the djinn to go after Aunt Tillie. We all know djinn are tricksters. Instead of going after Aunt Tillie himself, the djinn sent a shadow."

"Do we think that's the shadow that attacked you?" Marnie asked as Thistle strolled into the room.

"That's my guess," I replied. "It happened outside the greenhouse, which is Aunt Tillie's domain."

"Okay." Mom nodded. "Remind me to have a conversation with Margaret about being the world's worst person. Who makes a wish of a random guy?"

"She thought we cursed her with the bad luck thing," I replied. "I'm not making excuses for her, but I kind of get it."

"Except Aunt Tillie's curses have never been of the life-endangering variety," Mom argued. "Farting unicorns and belching buildings are very different from trying to kill someone."

"You and I get that, but Mrs. Little doesn't understand the magical world," I said. "But the problem we have is Reid and Kevin."

"Who is Kevin?" Twila asked.

"My undercover agent," Landon replied. "He's missing, along with the other meth dealers who were at Sand Lake."

"He'd only been with them for twenty-four hours, right?" Mom asked.

Landon shook his head. "He was with them two weeks. It was a test run of sorts. He was free to come and go. He had to establish residency. We did that in Hawthorne Hollow because they've got that rundown motel out on the highway. It's cheap if you pay by the week, and nobody on the right side of the law stays there.

"We had a story in place," he continued. "We said he was waiting to get the motorcycle his uncle left him following his death. That allowed Kevin to get a foothold, but he wasn't expected to stay out there every night. It was a way to gauge the situation."

"I saw Kevin the day I was out there with Aunt Tillie," I volunteered. "I thought his eyes were going to pop out of his head when he saw me. I covered, and nobody even looked at Kevin, so I figured it was fine."

Chief Terry stirred. "At this point, we have no reason to believe that Kevin's identity was discovered," he said. "He went missing with the rest of the dealers."

"I'm still not sure what's happening," Mom admitted. "I understand that Margaret Little made a wish to a djinn and that an undercover agent is missing, but how does the cameraman play into this?"

"Joni Silverman," I replied. "She's at the center of it, though I think she's completely innocent in this. She had the lamp in her attic. She said her mother boxed up things after her grandmother's death, and the lamp was in one of the boxes."

Mom looked momentarily thoughtful. "I guess that makes sense. Her grandmother, Doris, was a witch."

I nodded. "She used to hang out with Aunt Tillie back in the day."

"Speaking of Aunt Tillie, where is she?" Landon glanced around. "I have a feeling we're going to need her."

"She's getting dressed," Mom replied. "She'll be down in a few minutes. I still don't understand exactly what we're dealing with."

I tugged on my limited patience and reminded myself that she wasn't being difficult simply to be difficult. "Joni said there were family legends about her grandmother. She wasn't surprised when I mentioned witchcraft. I'm almost positive she knew nothing about the djinn.

"Her grandfather used to own the Bob Johnson house," I continued. "The meth dealers were using that house. This is just a hunch, but I think the djinn was looking for something. His touchstone in Hemlock Cove—it would've been Walkerville back then—might've been Doris Stinson's house. She died, but her husband lived there until he was forced into a home."

"And a djinn might not have understood the passage of time while trapped in a lamp," Mom surmised. "So, you think the djinn targeted the meth dealers because they were by the lake."

"It's just one idea," I confirmed. "The problem is that Kevin was Joni's cousin. He was familiar with the Johnson house too."

"He never mentioned that," Chief Terry noted.

"He was young," Landon pointed out. "He might not have ever been in that house. He's much younger than Joni and Reid."

"How does Reid play into this again?" Mom prodded.

"He's another cousin," I replied. "He's not a regular member of the *Haunted Traditions* team. They had a cameraman named Richard Silver. He didn't show up for work at the last minute when they were leaving, so they advertised for Michigan talent, and Reid applied."

"Do we think Reid did something to this other cameraman?" Marnie asked.

"It's a little too coincidental to believe otherwise," I hedged. "*Haunted Traditions* is based in New York. I'm not sure I buy that Reid, a mechanic, managed to get to New York, kill the cameraman, get back to Michigan, and arrange to get the man's job. That feels like too much."

"Maybe he just took advantage of the opening," Mom suggested. "Maybe the cameraman really didn't show up for work."

"That's another thing we'll have to chase when this is over," Chief Terry said. "We can't be sure of anything right now."

"So, what do we know?" Ever calm, Evan sat on one of the stools and kept his focus on me, taking it all in.

"We know that there's a djinn who looks like a man in town," I replied. "We know that the meth dealers are missing. We know there are shadow monsters hanging around town. Mrs. Little mentioned seeing them, and that's why she finally decided to engage us to help. We know that Kevin had ties to the area and is also missing. Reid figured out that we were about to catch on to his identity. We have a lot of things that are too coincidental not to be connected, and yet we still don't know how this all happened."

Landon rubbed his hand over my back as the room absorbed the news. He seemed lost in thought, and I couldn't decide if it would be worse for him if Kevin turned out to be innocent and dead or guilty and still alive.

"I think that Kevin and Reid wanted the djinn," Mom blurted. "I think that they knew the djinn was real. Joni might not have known, but they did ... and somehow, they figured out the lamp was in the wind. That's why they descended on the area."

"That might be true for Reid," Landon argued. "The decision to send Kevin undercover was made weeks ago."

"Maybe he called Reid," Mom suggested. "He could've figured out that the motor inn is near his grandmother's house and wanted backup to get inside."

"Heck, he could've suggested the house to Mickey," I offered.

Landon pressed his lips together. "I can see it going that way. What I don't understand is where the djinn is. Is he still in the area? What does he want?"

"He might be looking for retribution," I said. "He was locked away in that lamp for a long time. He might've decided to make those involved pay."

"Including Aunt Tillie," Mom replied grimly.

"What?" Chief Terry straightened. "Obviously I'm missing something."

"Aunt Tillie was friends with Doris," Mom replied. "It's entirely possible they trapped a djinn together. I mean ... a lamp? That's something Aunt Tillie would do just for fun."

"It also might explain why she's not here now," I said. "She knows we're going to figure it out."

Mom rubbed the back of her neck. "Well, come on," she said wearily and started for the family living quarters. "She's going to have to tell us the truth whether she likes it or not."

I was resigned to things turning ugly. I flicked my eyes to Landon. "We have to head out as a group once we get Aunt Tillie on board. We have to keep law enforcement away. You might want to get ahead of that."

Landon nodded. "Just one thing: where are we going to look?"

There was only one place I could think of. "Sand Lake. That's where the djinn is comfortable."

Landon lightly grabbed my wrist before I could walk away from him. "Do you think Aunt Tillie has been involved in this from the beginning?" He looked horrified at the thought.

"No. I think she figured out at least some of what was going on before us," I replied. "She could've filled in the gaps twenty-four hours ago but didn't. Now she's probably in her greenhouse fretting about how she can end this without getting in trouble. We need to get her in line."

"Do you want me to come with you?"

I shook my head. "This is something we need to do on our own. But get ready. Once we get Aunt Tillie back on track, we need to head out. We need to put an end to this ... today."

AUNT TILLIE WAS IN HER GREENHOUSE. She was dressed for war—including body armor—her shotgun gripped in her hand. She also had a huge duffle bag on the floor next to her. She didn't look up when we entered.

"Well, I guess that answers that question," I drawled.

"Oh, Aunt Tillie." Mom planted her hands on her hips and glared. "You knew!"

"I didn't *know*," Aunt Tillie shot back, guilt creasing her features. "Last night I realized that I could've—maybe might have—played a part in some of this."

"You knew about the djinn," I insisted.

"I helped Doris trap a djinn a very long time ago," Aunt Tillie countered. "It was long before you were even born, Bay. It was before Doris had any grandchildren at all. The thing just showed up here one day and started wreaking havoc."

"I don't remember this story." Mom cocked her head.

"You were a teenager. You were running around with your friends. Your mother was still alive. She helped us trap the djinn. We needed three witches. If we'd had seven, we probably would've been able to kill it."

"Why seven?" I asked, doing the math.

"Seven is a magical number for a reason, Bay. Three is good. Seven is much better."

"Well, if we include Scout and Stormy, we can have seven witches today. We won't even have to tap Clove, who can stay at the inn with Calvin. We'll be able to end this."

"Oh, I'm going to end it." Aunt Tillie rubbed her hand up and down the barrel of her shotgun. "I'm going to make that thing pay like you wouldn't believe."

"Not with a gun you're not." Mom strode forward and snagged the weapon. "If we're going to do this, we're going to do it right. We use magic, not guns. Scout is unbelievably strong. She should be able to anchor any spell we cast."

"Bay will have to do it." Aunt Tillie shot me a rueful look. "You're the necromancer."

"What does that have to do with anything?"

"Those shadows are shades. I figured it out last night. I was up pacing for a long time, and now I get it. The djinn killed the dealers and turned them into shades. He's making minions."

"Do we know the djinn?" Mom looked frustrated. "Is it Reid?"

"I don't think so." I shook my head. "I think Reid wants to control the djinn. He likely heard stories growing up. He probably shared those stories with Kevin."

"Kevin is still alive?" Mom looked hopeful. "That would be better for Terry."

"Unless Kevin is working with Reid to gain control of the djinn," I pointed out. "Then we're going to have a different sort of problem on our hands." *And one that might result in Kevin's death after all*, I added to myself.

"Do you know what sort of spell we need to kill the djinn?" Mom asked Aunt Tillie.

"I think I know what to do." I'd never seen Aunt Tillie this uncomfortable. It was a sight to behold. "We need to draw a trap and entice the djinn in. Then Bay can command the shadows to kill him. He created them, so they can destroy him."

"Until he's trapped, the shadows will do his bidding?" I asked.

Aunt Tillie held out her hands. "I'm not sure. It's possible you can overrule his magic. You're extremely powerful."

"So, we have to set a trap for the djinn, evade the shadows, figure out if Reid is evil, and also deal with the Kevin situation," I surmised. "Lovely."

"This isn't my fault," Aunt Tillie groused. "We locked that djinn away. He should've stayed locked away. This is Margaret's fault."

"No, it's your fault," Mom snapped. "You don't trap a djinn in a lamp and ignore it. Why not bury it somewhere? Why not lock it in a safe? Anything would've been better than what you did."

Aunt Tillie's shoulders slumped. "We forgot."

"You're in so much trouble when this is over." Mom shook her head and focused on me. "Can you get Stormy here? Scout is on her way, but we need one more. We'll need the full seven witches. And you're right about not including Clove. She shouldn't be separated from Calvin this early."

"I'm sure I can get her," I said. "I'll call and have anyone not currently present meet us at Sand Lake."

"And I'll get everybody else ready to go." Mom grabbed Aunt Tillie's duffle. "Are you going to be a problem for this operation? If so, I'm going to sell your plow truck and ground you for the entire winter."

Aunt Tillie balked. "You can't ground me. I'm an adult."

"Try me." Mom paused at the door. "Bay, about the argument we've been having..." She looked as uncomfortable as Aunt Tillie had moments before.

"It doesn't matter," I replied. "We're family. We fight and we get over it. That's what we do."

"Yes, but you were right. The film crew is a danger to us ... in more ways than one, it turns out. I'm sorry for the added weight I placed on your shoulders. That wasn't my intention."

Did she just say I was right? That felt like a magical occurrence. "It's done now. We have to sort through this mess today. We can't risk it continuing. The djinn is dangerous. He's going down."

"And after that?"

"We have to prioritize. You taught me that." I shot her a cheeky grin, which she returned.

"I'll make whatever you want for dinner tonight if we can finish this," Mom offered. "I'll even make an entire cake for Landon and let you pretend you baked it."

"Let's just get through this. We'll worry about the food later ... though I like the idea of letting Landon believe I baked an edible cake."

"You're strong, Bay," Mom said. "However this goes, you'll handle it. We'll be there to help."

"You always are," I said, my eyes drifting to Aunt Tillie. "Are you ready to do this?"

"I could do this professionally," Aunt Tillie shot back.

That was both true and sobering. "Then let's finish it. A djinn awaits."

Twenty-Six

W e parked in front of the motor inn. We weren't hiding our approach, so there was no reason to sneak around. Scout and Gunner were already prowling through the ravaged field, and Scout motioned to a central spot without looking in our direction as we piled out of the vehicles.

"Let's set the trap here," she said. "It's flat. We can see anyone incoming from all sides. It's a good spot."

I didn't disagree, but there was one problem. "What if the shades come through the ground like they did that first night we were here?"

Her mouth curved into a smile, and she pulled out a huge canister of Morton's salt. "I've got it." She started shaking it over the ground without further prodding, a low hissing causing me to jump as the ground rippled beneath Gunner's feet.

"They're already here," he noted, extending a hand and allowing it to shift as he bent over and started rooting around amid the charred foliage. "They're watching us."

"I'm sure they're watching the entire area," I agreed. "The djinn has full control of them."

"But you're taking control?" Scout asked. "You are a necromancer. They're shades. You should be able to control them."

I swallowed hard. "That's the plan." I directed my attention to the woods behind the cabins. "It's not just the djinn we're here for. We need to find Reid ... and hopefully Kevin."

"So, how do you want to do this?"

"You're going to stay here with Aunt Tillie, my mom, and the aunts," I replied. "In fact, all of you can stay here. I'll head into the woods myself and serve as bait."

Landon shook his head. "That is not going to happen, Bay. We're not letting you go out there alone."

"Definitely not," Mom agreed. "You need backup."

I didn't disagree, but I didn't know how to decide who would go with me. Thankfully, Scout did it for me.

"Gunner and I are going," Scout announced. "Evan too. We're all paranormal. We can fight. Stormy is on her way with Hunter. Keep her here when she arrives. We might need that neat fire thing she does when it's time to spring the trap."

"I've got an idea about that," Aunt Tillie said. "I'm going to use her to feed my trap. She should definitely stay here."

"I want to go with you, Bay." Thistle moved closer. "One of us should be with you. It's just ... right." She was earnest as she appeared to be digging in for a fight. "Take me with you."

I hesitated, unsure. Scout swooped in again.

"You can come," she said. "We might have need for maximum sarcasm."

"I'm going too," Landon said, immediately extending a finger as a warning when I opened my mouth to argue. "Don't, Bay. You need me. If Kevin is out there, somebody in a position of authority has to be ready to argue with him."

I hadn't considered that. "You have to do what I say." I wouldn't back down from that. "If I tell you to run, you need to run."

He didn't look happy with the edict, but he nodded. "You're in charge," he said. "This is your show."

"Definitely," Scout agreed. "We're the sidekicks here. Bay is definitely the queen."

"I'm the queen," Aunt Tillie countered. "I will cede my crown for today, however, if that's necessary." She shrank in the face of Mom's fury. "Oh, don't look at me like that. I still maintain this isn't my fault."

"You're in so much trouble," Mom groused as she took the salt from Scout. "As soon as we're done here, the very second this is finished, you and I are going to have a very long talk about what is and is not acceptable behavior."

"I can't wait for that."

Scout's smile was impossible to ignore as our group started toward the woods. She was excitable by nature when it came to a fight. She enjoyed using her mouth as a weapon. The way she carried herself today told me she was going to be full of herself.

"Did she really shove a djinn in a lamp?" she asked as we crossed into the trees. "That is such a *Charmed* thing to do."

I frowned. "*Charmed*?"

"The television show," Gunner replied. "Scout likes watching it and making fun of the stupid decisions they make."

"You still do that?" Evan looked incredulous. "Can't you find a different show to make fun of?"

"There's always the Kardashians," Scout drawled. "But they're real people, and I get irrationally angry if I watch too many episodes in a row. I have to break it up with other shows, and who doesn't like a show where magic actually causes them to be half-naked most of the time?"

"I don't know what they were thinking with the djinn," I admitted. "Aunt Tillie knows better. She claims she forgot, but who forgets a djinn?"

"She's embarrassed," Thistle volunteered. "She purposely let the djinn slip her mind, and now it's come back to bite her. She's supposed to be an all-powerful witch who never makes mistakes. This reflects poorly on her."

"And then some," I agreed. "We'll have to deal with her spotty memory later."

"And Mrs. Little," Thistle said. "She needs a firm talking to also."

I didn't want to think about Mrs. Little. It bothered me that she'd been responsible—at least in part—for creating this mess.

"Keep your eyes open," I ordered. "The djinn isn't the only one out here. There's Reid, and maybe Kevin."

"Where would Reid go?" Thistle asked.

I could only think of one place. "Let's head to the house."

IT TOOK US ALMOST TEN MINUTES TO REACH our destination, carefully picking our way through the woods. Every sound had me jumping. Every rustling branch had me searching the foliage for a source. A few times I was convinced that I saw moving shadows. When we finally reached the house, a feeling of dread washed over me.

"He's here," I whispered.

"The djinn?" Landon moved closer to my side, his hand automatically reaching for his weapon.

I shook my head and pointed to the porch. The screen door had opened, a familiar figure emerging.

Reid, a smug look on his face, rested his hands on the railing and grinned. "Well, it took you long enough to figure it out."

"To be fair, we had no reason to think you were even partly behind this," I replied.

"I guess that makes me smarter than you."

"That's an interesting conclusion to jump to." I slid to my right, Evan and Landon moving with me. Scout moved to the left with Gunner and Thistle. "What are you looking for?" I was honestly curious. "I haven't figured that out yet."

"I'm guessing you haven't figured out most of it," Reid replied. "Why should I fill in any of the holes for you?"

"Because we're here ... and it's always best to embrace the *Scooby-Doo* moment," I replied.

"Should I start swearing about rascally kids?"

"You should start sharing information." I folded my arms over my chest. I had to trust that Evan would react if the djinn moved on us. "I talked to your cousin Joni this morning. My gut tells me she doesn't have anything to do with this. I hope I'm right."

"Joni has always been too bland to get involved in the interesting stuff," Reid supplied. "She's a good person, but she's dull. She's more interested in raising her kid than claiming our birthright. I tried talking to her last year about what we were owed and how we could get it. She just kept saying the past was in the past and we should let it go."

"But you knew about your grandmother," I pressed.

"Of course I knew. Everybody knew the stories. Some didn't believe them, but I knew better. My grandfather told me she was the real deal. I was with him on his deathbed. Even then, despite all the mistakes, he hoped she would somehow swoop in from the great beyond and save him."

"You still haven't told me what you're looking for."

"My grandmother took her magic with her when she died. She didn't pass it on to anybody. Apparently, the magic jumps from female to female, but as far as I can tell, it didn't jump to Joni. That means it's out there somewhere, waiting. I'm here to claim it ... and everything else that was lost."

"I don't understand." I flicked my eyes to Landon. "You ran the family through official search engines while everybody was getting ready. What is it he thinks they're owed?"

"I think it's money," Landon replied. "Doris and Joe were supposed to have some, but by the time Joe was forced into the home, there was nothing to distribute among the heirs."

"They had a ton of money hidden," Reid insisted. "Our parents sold this house without even looking for it. My grandmother shoved things everywhere, in little boxes and cans. I'm sure some of it is still here."

"Buried in tins under the porch?" I asked.

"Maybe. You don't know."

"I have an idea," I countered. "I'm still in the dark about a lot of this, but did you kill Richard Silver?"

Genuine bafflement washed over Reid's face. "I don't know who that is."

"He was the man who had your job before you."

Realization dawned, and Reid let loose a hoarse chuckle. "Sorry to disappoint you, but I'm not a murderer. I just happened to be looking for a way back to this area that wouldn't draw attention ... especially from Joni. It fell into my lap. I didn't kill anyone to get the job."

"And the djinn? Did he just fall into your lap?"

Reid shrugged. "I'm not here for him. His appearance was a happy coincidence. He's looking for something too. We have common interests right now."

"You know where he is. Tell us."

"What do I get out of that?"

"You get to leave," Landon replied before I could. "You say you didn't kill Richard Silver. You're not part of the massacre the djinn perpetrated. You technically haven't broken the law."

"I'm a law-abiding citizen," Reid readily agreed.

"The djinn is dangerous," I insisted. "He's got to go. If you're here when he shows himself, we won't be able to protect you."

"That sounds like a real bummer." Reid's voice was bright. "I have to hand it to you guys." He let loose an annoying wink. "Real witches hiding in a town that's famous for having fake witches is just plain diabolical. Who thought of that?"

"It doesn't matter," I replied. "Your grandmother was a real witch. You were familiar with the town before you even arrived."

"I was here a full week before the television crew. I acted like a tourist and hung around town. I watched all the players. I watched you interact with almost everybody you love." He grinned at me. "You and your husband are so sugary sweet you make me want to puke."

"Nobody asked your opinion," Landon shot back.

Reid ignored him. "You and your cousins are funny. You sit around and gossip constantly. I was much more interested in watching you and the biker chick interact. She's obviously a badass. Everybody thinks so."

"Who is everybody?" Scout demanded.

"Everybody." Reid extended his hands and gestured to the trees. When I risked a glance, we were being surrounded by shadows. They'd been called to do their master's bidding, which meant the djinn was close.

"What do you want out of this situation, Reid?" I asked. "You said it was money, but it must be more than that, because we can't help you with the money. Neither can the djinn."

"That's where you're wrong." Reid made a tsking sound with his tongue. "The djinn and I have struck a deal. He's going to help me find the money—he has plenty of people to do the manual labor—and I'm going to help him with a little something he's working on."

"What's that?" Landon demanded.

"Why, it's you." Reid pushed himself away from the railing. "Thanks for making it so easy." He turned to enter the house. "They're all yours. Remember he wants the blonde alive ... not the one with the endless mouth. Her you can kill."

Reid was already gone when the shades started detaching from the trees, growling as they moved toward us.

"Well, we walked right into that one," Gunner muttered as he flexed his hands. They'd transformed into claws, and he appeared to be readying to finish the transformation. "I guess we should've expected it."

"Definitely," I agreed. "Well, crap." I lashed out without putting much thought into it, catching the nearest shade in a dampening field as he tried to advance. Once he was frozen in place, I shredded him ... and then watched with annoyance as he put himself back together.

"That didn't work," Thistle said.

"Thanks for the news bulletin, Thistle," I growled.

"Any other bright ideas?" Scout asked.

"Just one." I closed my eyes and raised my hands, tapping into my necromancer powers. A whisper rippled through me. *Call them.* And when my hands caught fire, so did my temper.

The ghosts I summoned arrived in a flurry, Viola in the lead. They immediately started fighting with the incoming shades, causing them to retreat in the opposite direction. Some showed interest in returning to their previous plan of action, but the others looked as if they wanted to be anywhere else.

"*Purgo,*" I intoned, scattering the ghosts that had appeared to do my bidding and sending them on a mission with a single order. I started in the direction of the house when a path had been cleared.

"What are you doing?" Thistle asked as she scampered after me. "Are you going to kill him?"

"I'm going to end this." I slowed my pace when a shade appeared at the door. There was something familiar about the creature. When he opened the door for me to enter, I knew.

"Kevin," I said, my heart twisting.

The shade nodded. "I didn't know until it was too late." He sounded sad. "I'm sorry." The apology was directed at Landon. "I should've known Reid was up to something. I should've known after the djinn showed up. I was too focused on the case. I didn't realize until it was too late that the case was actually secondary."

"Is the djinn inside?" I asked.

Kevin nodded. "He's powerful. He holds us all in his sway. We have to do his bidding."

"Not for long," I replied. "I'll free you. I promise."

"And then what? Do we go back?" Kevin sounded hopeful.

"You move on." I started through the door and then stopped. "Did you abandon your bike in Hawthorne Hollow?"

"I was hoping it would serve as a message."

"It was a red flag," I said. "We knew something was wrong. Where are the other bikes?"

"In the lake."

"Are they all gone?"

"All but one." Kevin's voice was barely a whisper. "He's inside, and he wants you."

A chill ran through me, but I nodded. "I've got this. You'll be free before you know it."

"But this life is gone?" he said.

"It is. I'm sorry."

His shoulders slumped. "Well, hopefully I did a little good before the end."

"More than you know," I promised. "You did great. You just have to trust me a little longer."

Twenty-Seven

I was done messing around, and the air sparked around me as I stormed into the house. Reid, who was in the living room with another man, looked up in surprise.

"W-what..." He trailed off, no longer looking smug.

"Who's your friend?" I demanded.

Slowly, the individual in the chair turned. Mickey, or rather the djinn who'd fashioned himself to look like Mickey, beamed at me. "Hello, again."

I could feel the strength of my friends as they moved in behind me. "I guess I should've known," I said when he didn't stand up to greet me. "I knew there was something off about you that day."

"Yes, and I recognized you as well." Mickey's smile was a little too wide, his eyes a little too bright. He reminded me of a cartoon character, but not the sort that would elicit warm feelings. "I worried you'd recognize me for what I am that day, but you didn't. I, of course, recognized you." His eyes flicked to the individuals standing behind me. "Where is the old one? I'd really like to have a discussion with her."

"Is he talking about Aunt Tillie?" Thistle asked. "Dude, she's not going to like you calling her old to her face. I want to be there when you do."

"Perhaps that can be arranged." Mickey remained sitting and flicked his eyes back to me. "Would you like to discuss how this is going to go?"

"I'm pretty sure your minion just gave me a hint." I inclined my head to Reid. "He just ordered those shadows to kill us."

"Not you," Reid shot back. "I didn't want you dead, just incapacitated."

"No, he knows better than to kill you," Mickey said. "I have plans for you."

"Should I thank you for that?"

Mickey lifted one shoulder in a lazy shrug. "I don't really care if you're grateful. I just need you to fall into line."

I still had questions, so I opted to launch into them to buy myself time. "Where are the bodies?"

"What an odd question," Mickey mused, his brow furrowing. "I thought you were going to ask me how I got here."

"I know how you got here. Aunt Tillie and Doris Stinson cursed you into a lamp. I mean ... a freaking lamp. Then, instead of disposing of you in proper fashion, they shoved you in a box and let the next generation discover you. It was lazy witch work, so here we are.

"Mrs. Little got drunk, somehow opened the lamp, and freed you," I continued. "Then she asked you to go after Aunt Tillie. You wanted retribution and were happy to oblige. Only I'm guessing you weren't quite full strength when you were released, so you had to take things slow. That's why you took out the initial gang members one at a time. It's also why you made the mistake of sending one of those first shades after Aunt Tillie, but it attacked me instead."

Mickey looked delighted. "Well, that's entertaining," he said. "You're much smarter than I thought. In fact, I was debating if you were an idiot during that first meeting, especially after you sat there and did nothing while your aunt burned my field."

"Don't let this blond hair fool you." I pointed to my head. "I have questions."

"What makes you think I have any interest in answering them?"

"It's only fair. You must have some questions."

Mickey hesitated and then nodded. "Fine. Ask your questions."

"Did you come back to Sand Lake because that was the area you remembered? You were looking for Doris?"

"Pretty much. She had something I wanted."

"What?"

"A talisman. It was mine, passed down through my people, and she stripped it away from me when she trapped me in that ridiculous lamp. It was pink inside ... and fluffy. The lamp, I mean. It was awful."

I had to press my lips together to keep from laughing. It was just like Aunt Tillie to fully embrace the *I Dream of Jeannie* model. She would've known it was a special punishment for the djinn. "Did you find your talisman?"

"I did not. This house isn't the same. I'm not even sure it's here." His eyes narrowed. "I will find it. I have my minions looking right now."

"I think I know where your talisman is," I offered. It was a lie. Well, mostly. But I was ready to embrace the lie because I knew it would ultimately get me what I wanted. "I still have questions. I won't tell you where it is until I get answers."

Mickey looked as if he was considering ripping my head from my neck to propel me to volunteer the information, but ultimately, he nodded, letting loose a weary sigh as he sank back in the chair. "Ask your question. You're wearing my patience thin."

"Okay." I rubbed my hands on my jeans. "How long have you been masquerading as Mickey?"

"Two weeks. I came to the lake, found the house empty, and started looking around. The only action was in the cabins. I hung back for a day, got the lay of the land, lured Mickey out, killed him, and took his place." He recited it as if reading from a to-do list.

"Where is his body?"

"The woods. They're *all* in the woods."

"Except for the body that was found downtown," I argued. "Why did you leave that one out in the open like that? It's the only reason we knew to start looking for you."

"I didn't do that." Mickey looked momentarily disgusted. "That was one of the originals. The first two I took out didn't go down easy. It was ... more difficult ... than I remembered."

"You were weak."

"Don't kid yourself." Mickey's voice was laced with warning. "Even at my weakest, I'm stronger than your kind."

"Says the guy who got locked in a freaking lamp for decades," Scout muttered.

"You might want to be careful, pixie," Mickey growled. "My kind has been eating your kind for lunch for a millennium."

Scout didn't look bothered in the least. "I'm more than one thing."

"I'll still kill you."

"You might want to watch your mouth," Gunner threatened. All traces of his trademark charm were absent. "I'll shut it for you if you don't."

The snort Mickey let loose was disdainful. "I'm not afraid of you either, mongrel. I don't even understand why you're all together. In my day, shifters weren't chummy with witches. The pixies weren't mating with the witches. Nobody had dominion over the dead. Oh, and what's with the vampire who can walk in the sun?"

"You were chasing me that day," Evan surmised. He didn't look upset as much as intrigued. "I wondered. Simple meth dealers shouldn't have been able to track me the way they did. They kept finding me when it shouldn't have been possible."

"I sensed you," Mickey replied. "I sensed you the minute you crossed onto the property. Then I saw you with the old witch. I knew there was something wrong with your union."

"And that's why you decided to pick up in the middle of the afternoon and run," I deduced. "It was seeing Evan and Aunt Tillie together that frightened you."

"Nothing frightens me." He said it too fast, and I didn't believe him.

"You're terrified," I shot back. "There are more of us than you. Reid was supposed to serve as your shield on the porch. He did what he was told, but your shades can't touch us."

"I think you're reading more into the situation than is there, but I am curious," Mickey said. "What do you think you're going to accomplish today?"

"I'm going to end you. But I haven't gotten my answers yet."

"Oh, by all means, continue." He let loose a grand wave full of sarcasm.

"You killed Mickey, dumped his body in the woods, and took his place," I prodded. "Didn't anybody question you? How did you know the right things to say?"

"He was hardly one of the great thinkers of our time," the djinn said. "Nobody questioned me. Nobody dared. By the time Dane realized something was going wrong, it was too late. I ordered them to retreat to this very house. By then, my full strength returned, and I took out the whole lot of them. It was over in minutes."

I darted my eyes to Landon. He was stoic, his mouth glued shut.

"Oh, look at that," Mickey said with a gleeful laugh. "He's upset about the cop. Did you think I didn't know what he was?" he asked when Landon's shoulders jolted. "I knew the minute I met him. I didn't care about the nonsense taking place here, so I didn't care about him joining the operation. When it came time for them to die, I didn't care about saving him. The decision was quite easy."

"Even though he was Doris's grandson?" I asked.

"That meant nothing to me. As much as I wanted revenge, I wasn't ready to swear a blood oath to take them all out. I didn't care."

"Even when you somehow found Reid?" I gestured to the man in question, who had remained mostly silent since our arrival. He'd made a few odd faces, but he hadn't said anything. "Did you know he killed your cousin, Reid?"

"Not until it was done." Reid's voice was low. "He's going to bring him back. That's part of our agreement."

"Is that what you told him?" I asked Mickey. "Interesting."

"Keep your mouth shut," Mickey warned.

"Oh, no," I sang out. "I want to hear how you're going to reverse death."

"What does she mean?" Reid demanded, his full focus on Mickey. "What is she talking about?"

"Don't worry about it," Mickey growled. "She's trying to turn you against me. Don't listen to her."

"He can't bring Kevin back," I said in a measured voice. "Dead is dead. He's still here in spirit, but when it's over, when we kill the djinn, Kevin will move on."

"If he can move on, why can't he return?"

"Because his body is dead," I replied. "I'm guessing it glowed like the other one and is in the woods with the real Mickey. We'll find it. We'll make sure he has a proper burial."

I turned back to Mickey, my temper ratcheting up a notch. "It was smart for the shades to take advantage of your weakness and move the body downtown. That's what tipped us off. I'm guessing they knew that's how it would play out."

"Probably," Mickey agreed. "But I'm still here. I'm still going to find my talisman. You're going to help. You're a necromancer. You can further control the shades and force them to do my bidding."

"Are you having trouble with your minions?" I shot back. "I'm not surprised. You can't control souls for the long haul. It doesn't work like that."

"I might not be able to, but you can," Mickey sneered. "You have dominion over the dead. Why else do you think I wanted you so badly?"

I had all the answers I needed. "You're not going to get me."

"Oh, but I am." Mickey finally climbed to his feet. He was far from imposing, but he was ready to make his move. "You're going to help me. You're going to do my bidding. In exchange, I won't kill your husband. But I make no promises about the pixie."

Threatening Landon riled my stomach, but I held it together. "No. You're done."

"You're not strong enough to stop me," Mickey seethed. "Besides, I have the lamp."

"But don't you remember?" I taunted him. "I have the talisman."

Mickey jerked toward me, his hands outstretched. I was expecting the move, and yet I was still caught off guard. Scout was another story. She threw up a shield spell with a split second to spare, and the djinn slammed against it with enough force to rock the magical wall we hid behind.

"Now would be the time to start back," Scout demanded.

I nodded without hesitation and gave Landon a shove toward the door. "Back to the cabins," I ordered.

Scout threw out a blast of magic that had the djinn flying into the wall and Reid sailing over the couch to hit the floor with enough force the collision echoed. "Nobody stops until we get there," she roared as we moved outside.

The shades, which had been fighting furiously with the ghosts I'd called for backup, were gone, as were the ghosts.

"We can't worry about them now." Scout grabbed my arm and tugged me forward. "We'll deal with them after. The djinn is our concern. We need to get him back to the cabins."

The roaring inside the house told me she was right. "Let's go."

WE RACED THROUGH THE WOODS. I kept my head down so I wouldn't trip. I was out of breath when we made it back to the cabins, but the fury following us through the woods forced me to keep a good pace. I practically skidded to a stop when we got to the trap. Stormy was there, flanked on either side by Mom and Aunt Tillie.

"Are we ready?" I asked as I pressed my hand into my side to stop the stitch pinching my side.

Aunt Tillie's expression was grave. "The question is: are you ready?"

"I'm ready." I stepped into the trap. I felt it undulating with power beneath my feet.

Scout shoved Landon and Thistle, so they were with the rest of our group, but she remained at the front with me. Gunner and Evan moved to the opposite side of the trap and waited.

And then Mickey appeared.

"I should've known," Aunt Tillie complained. "He was dressed like a moron right from the start. That outfit has 'tool' written all over it."

I ignored her and kept my eyes locked with Mickey's furious glare. "Are you sure you want to do this?" I asked. "There are easier ways."

"Nothing about this is going to be easy," Mickey snarled. "I want what I want ... and there's nothing you can do to stop me."

"Then I guess we have to play this out." I waited until Mickey was right next to the trap. We needed him to step over the threshold.

"I'm going to kill your family," Mickey warned as he raised one foot. "I'm going to make it hurt. I'm going to start with your husband. You'll wish you'd agreed to work with me from the start. That's how painful I'm going to make it when I rip him to shreds."

"If you say so."

Evan slipped in behind Mickey. Obviously, the djinn wasn't moving fast enough because the vampire gave him a terrific shove. At the same moment, Landon wrapped his arm around my waist and dragged me back.

When the trap flared to life, I was clear of the circle. Mickey went rigid, a thin scream escaping, and he desperately threw his shoulders left and right in an attempt to escape.

"What are you doing?" he demanded, his eyes fierce. "I won't go back into that lamp. You can't make me."

"There's no lamp this time," I said as my gaze drifted to the trees. The shades had followed us but showed no sign of attacking. They were here to watch the end of the creature that had made them. "We're not trapping you. We're ending you."

"You don't have the power," Mickey gritted out.

"That's where you're wrong." I slid my eyes to Stormy and extended my hand. She took it without a word. I could feel the magic rolling through her. The fire magic was strong. She was just now figuring out how to use it, but she had more than enough firepower for our needs.

Aunt Tillie took Stormy's other hand and uttered a curse. "*Ignis.*"

Stormy's magic raced out, guided by the two of us, and the trap caught fire in an instant. Mickey's panicked scream caused chills to rush up and down my spine, but I held his gaze until the end. I saw the moment the life went out of him, and still he continued to burn.

Slowly, I slid my eyes to the shades as they watched the scene play out. "You're free to go now," I said. "We'll find your bodies and return them to your families."

"Thank you." I recognized Kevin's voice as one of them stepped forward. "I'm sorry I failed you," he said to Landon. "I'm sorry I didn't do this right."

"You didn't fail me," Landon assured him. "This was out of our control. Find some peace wherever you go. You've earned it."

Kevin nodded and then started to disappear. Within seconds, all of the shades were gone.

"Well, that was fun," Mom said, breaking the silence that had descended. "Where is Reid?"

That was a good question. "I'm sure he fled," I replied. "He saw the writing on the wall. He won't hang around in case we have retribution in mind for him too."

"He didn't kill anyone," Landon noted.

"No, but he might've been able to save a few people if he hadn't been thinking about himself."

"That's not a crime."

I leaned against him and slipped my hand into his. "It's sad, but it's not a crime."

"Is it over?" Twila demanded. "I'm ready to go back to the inn for my final interview, but this needs to be over first. I can't think about two things at once. Everybody knows that."

"It's over," I said. "There's still some cleanup to deal with, but it's definitely over."

Twenty-Eight

TWO DAYS LATER

I t was sunny but the temperatures weren't getting out of the thirties today. Winter had officially arrived, even if the calendar promised it was still a few weeks off. I stood on the patio of The Overlook, coffee in hand, and greeted what was supposed to be another day of training.

There was just one little thing that needed to be finished before we tackled that.

"Your mother said I would find you out here." Debbie sounded nervous as she strode onto the patio. She remained near the door. "You wanted to talk to me?"

"Yeah." I sipped my coffee and swiveled to face her. I'd given it a great deal of thought the past few days, and I knew how I wanted this to play out. "I want you to cut Mrs. Little out of the episode."

Whatever Debbie was expecting, that wasn't it. Her eyes went wide. "What?"

"You heard me."

"She invited us here. We filmed footage of her store."

"You can keep the footage of the store belching," I offered with a half smile. "The rats are fair game too. But I don't want her in the episode."

"Why not?"

"It doesn't matter. She's a pain, and I don't want her getting even a hint of a win. I want her getting what I believe she deserves."

"Which is?"

"Let me handle that." I folded my arms across my chest. "Are we agreed?"

"I don't know," Debbie hedged. "It feels like I should get something out of this deal. You know, an interview or something."

I shook my head. "You've already interviewed everybody in my family for the most part. You don't need me."

"And yet something tells me you're the one I should've been after right from the start."

"Weren't you?"

"Not as diligently as I could have." Debbie sniffed, looked to the bluff, and then nodded. "I'll cut her out as much as possible. I can't make any guarantees regarding background footage. We need to use what we have."

"I can live with that. I heard you talking to my mother last night after dinner. They found Richard?"

"Turns out he decided to retire and took off for Florida. He apologized for not telling us, but he didn't think it would be a big deal. It's fine. We'll have a new cameraman within a week."

"That's good."

"We still don't know what happened to Reid," she said.

"I'm not sure. My guess is you don't have to worry about anything too bad. He was never going to be a solid employee."

"He was a bad cameraman. Greg's footage is thankfully usable, but Reid's wasn't. I'm guessing he didn't have any idea what he was doing and lied on his application."

I rolled my neck and sighed. "Don't worry about Reid. He didn't meet a terrible fate in the woods."

"I'm sure you can understand my worry given the fact that you guys brought back the rental car and then announced six hours later that you'd found thirty bodies in the woods."

I understood her fear. Unfortunately, I couldn't completely alleviate it. "Listen ... Reid didn't kill those people. He knew who did and stood back and did nothing, but he didn't kill them. And he wasn't killed during the takedown."

"But you were there?" Debbie seemed to be having trouble wrapping her head around how things had played out. "You saw how it all went down."

"We had a small group looking for the bodies," I lied. Landon had come up with a story before we called to request help from the Feds. "We knew something bad had happened when the FBI agent didn't check in as he was supposed to."

"And all this plays into the body that was glowing downtown the first day we arrived," Debbie pressed.

"It does," I confirmed. "They used some sort of compound to achieve the glow. They were trying to scare off any enemies who might be trying to move in on their turf and blame it on magic, while at the same time hoping to throw law enforcement off their trail. They're still trying to identify all the components of the compound."

"Well, that's something I guess." Debbie huffed out a sigh and then shook her head. "You're not going to tell me what happened, are you?"

"I've already told you."

"You haven't told me all of it."

"Most of it was tied to an undercover assignment, so it's fair to say I can't tell you the rest." That was also part of Landon's plan. "Just suffice it to say that the world is a better place now, safer."

"And Reid was somehow involved in it."

"Reid was up to some hinky crap, but he did not kill anybody. He's on the run, but he's not a fugitive. I'm sure someone will take him in for questioning at some point."

"Well, I guess that's okay."

I forced a smile as I turned. "You're leaving now?"

Debbie chuckled. "We'll be out of your hair in twenty minutes."

"That will be best for all."

"I can see why you'd think that." She reached for the door. "I'll never understand all of it, will I?"

"No, you won't." I sipped my coffee when she was gone, smiling when I heard the door open again. "Did you stick to your three slices of bacon?" I asked Landon without turning.

"Have I mentioned you're the love of my life?" he asked as he wrapped his arms around my waist and pressed himself against my back. "You're the sweetest person I know. Loving to a fault. You're ... my everything."

"Oh, so schmaltzy," I said as I leaned my head against his shoulder. "I take that to mean you ate more than three slices."

"It's been a long few days, Bay."

"Yeah, yeah, yeah."

He rubbed his cheek against mine. "How did things go with Debbie?"

"As well as can be expected. She knows something weird happened. She can't prove it. She has agreed to cut Mrs. Little from the episode."

"That will go over well." Landon snickered. "She'll melt down when she finds out."

"I don't care. She could've saved a lot of lives if she'd told us what was going on from the beginning."

"I think she was afraid."

"Since when do you take her side over mine?"

"Never. I'm just saying that she ultimately did the right thing."

"It was too late to save Kevin."

"Ah, Bay." Grief rippled off of him. "We might never have been able to save Kevin. I'm coming to grips with it. I wish you would too. Just ... let it go."

I didn't want to let it go. I was angry. Still, he was right. "The film crew will be gone in twenty minutes. I put the newspaper to bed last night. I'm supposed to be training with Stormy and Aunt Tillie this morning, but I have an idea." I was all smiles as I turned to face him.

"Am I going to like this idea?" he asked, gentle fingers brushing my hair from my face.

"How would you feel about locking ourselves in the guesthouse all day and pretending we don't have clothes?"

"Well." Intrigue lit his features. "That might be the best offer I've had all day."

"I thought you might like it. I'm sure you can take the day off after ... well, after." We'd cast a spell in the wake of the djinn's death and found the bodies within thirty minutes. They were thrown in a field like garbage. Landon had almost fallen apart that day. He was much better now.

"I would love nothing better than to spend the day with you." He rested his forehead against mine. "I'll call in to the office and tell the boss I'm sick."

"Or you could just tell him you need the day." I wrapped my fingers around his wrist. "He'll understand."

Landon swayed with me in his arms for several moments. "Will your mother send us back to the guesthouse with snacks so we don't have to worry about food?"

"I'm almost positive that can be arranged."

"Then that's exactly what I want to do with my day. You, me, and nobody else. We'll shut out the rest of the world."

"I'll go in and tell her." I kissed his cheek and then hurried for the door. "You'll be okay until I get back?" It wouldn't have been a worry before losing Kevin.

"I'm fine, Bay. I'm ... accepting it. I'll never be okay with it, but I won't melt down. Go finalize the menu with your mother. I'll be waiting for you here."

"It's going to be a fun day," I assured him.

"It's going to be an amazing life," he replied, his eyes soft. "Now, get me some cake or something. I want to make sure we have everything we need for the day. Once our clothes are off, they're not going back on."

"I'm on it. See you in ten minutes."

"I'll be waiting for you ... as always."

"Forever," I agreed.

"Forever."

Printed in Great Britain
by Amazon

42849707R10142